Unless

THE WORK OF CAROL SHIELDS

POETRY

Others

Intersect

Coming to Canada

NOVELS

Larry's Party

The Stone Diaries

The Republic of Love

A Celibate Season (with Blanche Howard)

Swann

A Fairly Conventional Woman

Happenstance

The Box Garden

Small Ceremonies

STORY COLLECTIONS

Various Miracles

The Orange Fish

Dressing Up for the Carnival

PLAYS

Departures and Arrivals

Thirteen Hands

Fashion, Power, Guilt and the Charity of Families
(with Catherine Shields)

Anniversary (with David Williamson)

CRITICISM

Susanna Moodie: Voice and Vision

Jane Austen

ANTHOLOGY

Dropped Threads: What We Aren't Told
(Edited with Marjorie Anderson)

Unless

Carol Shields

TED SMART

This edition produced for The Book People Ltd,
Hall Wood Avenue, Haydock, St Helens WA11 9UL

First published in Great Britain in 2002 by
Fourth Estate
A Division of HarperCollins*Publishers*
77–85 Fulham Palace Road
London W6 8JB
www.4thestate.com

1 3 5 7 9 10 8 6 4 2

A catalogue record for this book is available from the British Library.

ISBN 0 00 767389 2

Typeset by Rowland Phototypesetting Ltd,
Bury St Edmunds, Suffolk
Printed and bound in Great Britain by
William Clowes Limited, Beccles and London

To Ezra and Jay

If we had a keen vision and feeling of all ordinary human life, it would be like hearing the grass grow and the squirrel's heart beat, and we should die of that roar which lies on the other side of silence.

GEORGE ELIOT

Here's

It happens that I am going through a period of great unhappiness and loss just now. All my life I've heard people speak of finding themselves in acute pain, bankrupt in spirit and body, but I've never understood what they meant. To lose. To have lost. I believed these visitations of darkness lasted only a few minutes or hours and that these saddened people, in between bouts, were occupied, as we all were, with the useful monotony of happiness. But happiness is not what I thought. Happiness is the lucky pane of glass you carry in your head. It takes all your cunning just to hang on to it, and once it's smashed you have to move into a different sort of life.

In my new life—the summer of the year 2000—I am attempting to "count my blessings." Everyone I know advises me to take up this repellent strategy, as though they really believe a dramatic loss can be replaced by the renewed appreciation of all one has been given. I have a husband, Tom, who loves me and is faithful to me and is very decent looking as well, tallish, thin, and losing his hair nicely. We live in a house with a paid-up mortgage, and our house is set in the prosperous rolling hills of Ontario, only an hour's drive north of Toronto. Two of our three daughters, Natalie, fifteen, and Christine, sixteen, live at home. They are intelligent and lively and attractive and loving, though they too have shared in the loss, as has Tom.

And I have my writing.

"You have your writing!" friends say. A murmuring chorus: *But you have your writing, Reta.* No one is crude enough to suggest that my sorrow will eventually become material for my writing, but probably they think it.

And it's true. There *is* a curious and faintly distasteful comfort, at the age of forty-three, forty-four in September, in contemplating what I have managed to write and publish during those impossibly childish and sunlit days before I understood the meaning of grief. "My Writing": this is a very small poultice to hold up against my damaged self, but better, I have been persuaded, than no comfort at all.

It's June, the first year of the new century, and here's what I've written so far in my life. I'm not including my old schoolgirl sonnets from the seventies—Satin-slippered April, you glide through time / And lubricate spring days, de dum, de dum—and my dozen or so fawning book reviews from the early eighties. I am posting this list not on the screen but on my consciousness, a far safer computer tool and easier to access:

1. A translation and introduction to Danielle Westerman's book of poetry, *Isolation*, April 1981, one month before our daughter Norah was born, a home birth naturally; a midwife; you could almost hear the guitars plinking in the background, except we did not feast on the placenta as some of our friends were doing at the time. My French came from my Québécoise mother, and my acquaintance with Danielle from the University of Toronto, where she taught French civilization in my student days. She was a poor teacher, hesitant and in awe, I think, of the tanned, healthy students sitting in her classroom, taking notes worshipfully and stretching their small suburban notion of what the word *civilization* might mean. She was already a recognized writer of kinetic, tough-corded prose, both beguiling and dangerous. Her manner was to take the reader by surprise. In the middle of a flattened rambling paragraph, deceived by warm stretches of reflection, you came upon hard cartilage.

I am a little uneasy about claiming *Isolation* as my own writing, but Dr. Westerman, doing one of her hurrying, over-the-head gestures, insisted that translation, especially of poetry, is a creative

act. Writing and translating are convivial, she said, not opposi-
tional, and not at all hierarchical. Of course, she *would* say that.
My introduction to *Isolation* was certainly creative, though, since
I had no idea what I was talking about.

I hauled it out recently and, while I read it, experienced the
Burrowing of the Palpable Worm of Shame, as my friend Lynn
Kelly calls it. Pretension is what I see now. The part about art
transmuting the despair of life to the "merely frangible," and
poetry's attempt to "repair the gap between ought and naught"
—what on earth did I mean? Too much Derrida might be the
problem. I was into all that pretty heavily in the early eighties.

2. After that came "The Brightness of a Star," a short story that
appeared in *An Anthology of Young Ontario Voices* (Pink Onion Press,
1985). It's hard to believe that I qualified as "a young voice" in
1985, but, in fact, I was only twenty-nine, mother of Norah, aged
four, her sister Christine, aged two, and about to give birth to
Natalie—in a hospital this time. Three daughters, and not even
thirty. "How did you find the time?" people used to chorus, and in
that query I often registered a hint of blame: was I neglecting my
darling sprogs for my writing career? Well, no. I never thought in
terms of career. I dabbled in writing. It was my macramé, my knit-
ting. Not long after, however, I did start to get serious and joined
a local "writers' workshop" for women, which met every second
week, for two hours, where we drank coffee and had a good time
and deeply appreciated each other's company, and that led to:

3. "Icon," a short story, rather Jamesian, 1986. Gwen Reidman,
the only published author in the workshop group, was our leader.
The Glenmar Collective (an acronym of our first names—not very
original) was what we called ourselves. One day Gwen said, moving a muffin to her mouth, that she was touched by the "austerity" of my short story—which was based, but only roughly, on my
response to the Russian icon show at the Art Gallery of Ontario.
My fictional piece was a case of art "embracing/repudiating art,"
as Gwen put it, and then she reminded us of the famous "On First
Looking Into Chapman's Homer" and the whole aesthetic of art

begetting art, art worshipping art, which I no longer believe in, by the way. Either you do or you don't. The seven of us, Gwen, Lorna, Emma Allen, Nan, Marcella, Annette, and I (my name is Reta Winters—pronounced Ree-tah) self-published our pieces in a volume titled *Incursions and Interruptions,* throwing in fifty dollars each for the printing bill. The five hundred copies sold quickly in the local bookstores, mostly to our friends and families. Publishing was cheap, we discovered. What a surprise. We called ourselves the Stepping Stone Press, and in that name we expressed our mild embarrassment at the idea of self-publishing, but also the hope that we would "step" along to authentic publishing in the very near future. Except Gwen, of course, who was already there. And Emma, who was beginning to publish op-ed pieces in the *Globe and Mail.*

4. *Alive* (Random House, 1987), a translation of *Pour Vivre,* volume one of Danielle Westerman's memoirs. I may appear to be claiming translation as an act of originality, but, as I have already said, it was Danielle, in her benign way, wrinkling her disorderly forehead, who had urged me to believe that the act of shuffling elegant French into readable and stable English is an aesthetic performance. The book was well received by the critics and even sold moderately well, a dense but popular book, offered without shame and nary a footnote. The translation itself was slammed in the *Toronto Star* ("clumsy") by one Stanley Harold Howard, but Danielle Westerman said never mind, the man was *un maquereau,* which translates, crudely, as something between a pimp and a prick.

5. I then wrote a commissioned pamphlet for a series put out by a press calling itself Encyclopédie de l'art. The press produced tiny, hold-in-the-hand booklets, each devoted to a single art subject, covering everything from Braque to Calder to Klee to Mondrian to Villon. The editor in New York, operating out of a phone booth it seemed to me, and knowing nothing of my ignorance, had stumbled on my short story "Icon" and believed me to be an expert on the subject. He asked for three thousand words

4

for a volume (volumette, really) to be called *Russian Icons*, published finally in 1989. It took me a whole year to do, what with Tom and the three girls, and the house and garden and meals and laundry and too much inwardness. They published my "text," such a cold, jellied word, along with a series of coloured plates, in both English and French (I did the French as well) and paid me four hundred dollars. I learned all about the schools of Suzdal and Vladimir and what went on in Novgorod (a lot) and how images of saints made medieval people quake with fear. To my knowledge, the book was never reviewed, but I can read it today without shame. It is almost impossible to be pseudo when writing about innocent paintings that obey no rules of perspective and that are done on slabs of ordinary wood.

6. I lost a year after this, which I don't understand, since all three girls had started school, though Natalie was only in morning kindergarten. I think I was too busy thinking about the business of being a writer, about being writerly and fretting over whether Tom's ego was threatened and being in Danielle's shadow, never mind Derrida, and needing my own writing space and turning thirty-five and feeling older than I've ever felt since. My age—thirty-five—shouted at me all the time, standing tall and wide in my head, and blocking access to what my life afforded. Thirty-five never sat down with its hands folded. Thirty-five had no composure. It was always humming mean, terse tunes on a piece of folded cellophane. ("I am composed," said John Quincy Adams on his deathbed. How admirable and enviable and beyond belief; I loved him for this.)

This anguish of mine was unnecessary; Tom's ego was unchallenged by my slender publications. He turned out to be one of those men we were worried about in the seventies and eighties, who might shrivel in acknowledgment of his own insignificance. Ordinary was what he wanted, to be an ordinary man embedded in a family he loved. We put a skylight in the box room, bought a used office desk, installed a fax and a computer, and I sat down on my straight-from-a-catalogue Freedom Chair and translated

Danielle Westerman's immense *Les femmes et le pouvoir*, the English version published in 1992, volume two of her memoirs. In English the title was changed to *Women Waiting*, which only makes sense if you've read the book. (Women possess power, but it is power that has yet to be seized, ignited, and released, and so forth.) This time no one grumped about my translation. "Sparkling and full of ease," the *Globe* said, and the *New York Times* went one better and called it "an achievement."

"You are my true sister," said Danielle Westerman at the time of publication. *Ma vraie soeur.* I hugged her back. Her craving for physical touch has not slackened even in her eighties, though nowadays it is mostly her doctor who touches her, or me with my weekly embrace, or the manicurist. Dr. Danielle Westerman is the only person I know who has her nails done twice a week, Tuesday and Saturday (just a touch-up), beautiful long nail beds, matching her long quizzing eyes.

7. I was giddy. All at once translation offers were arriving in the mail, but I kept thinking I could maybe write short stories, even though our Glenmar group was dwindling, what with Emma taking a job in Newfoundland, Annette getting her divorce, and Gwen moving to the States. The trouble was, I hated my short stories. I wanted to write about the overheard and the glimpsed, but this kind of evanescence sent me into whimsy mode, and although I believed whimsicality to be a strand of the human personality, I was embarrassed at what I was pumping into my new Apple computer, sitting there under the clean brightness of the skylight. Pernicious, precious, my moments of recognition. *Ahah!—and then she realized;* I was so fetching with my "Ellen was setting the table and she knew tonight would be different." A little bug sat in my ear and buzzed: Who cares about Ellen and her woven placemats and her hopes for the future?

I certainly didn't care.

Because I had three kids, everyone said I should be writing kiddy lit, but I couldn't find the voice. Kiddy lit screeched in my brain. Talking ducks and chuckling frogs. I wanted something sterner and more contained as a task, which is how I came to write *Shakespeare and Flowers* (San Francisco: Cyclone Press, 1994). The contract was negotiated before I wrote one word. Along came a little bundle of cash to start me off, with the rest promised on publication. I thought it was going to be a scholarly endeavour, but I ended up producing a wee "giftie" book. You could send this book to anyone on your list who was maidenly or semi-academic or whom you didn't know very well. *Shakespeare and Flowers* was sold in the kind of outlets that stock greeting cards and stuffed bears. I simply scanned the canon and picked up references to, say, the eglantine (*A Midsummer Night's Dream*) or the blackberry (*Troilus and Cressida*) and then I puffed out a little description of the flower, and conferenced on the phone (twice) with the illustrator in Berkeley, and threw in lots of Shakespearean quotes. A sweet little book, excellent slick paper, US$12.95. At sixty-eight pages it fits in a small mailer. Two hundred thousand copies, and still selling, though the royalty rate is scandalous. They'd like me to do something on Shakespeare and animals, and I just might.

8. *Eros: Essays,* by Danielle Westerman, translation by Reta Winters, hastily translated—everything was hasty in those days, everything still is—and published in 1995. Hugely successful, after a tiny advance. We put the dog in a kennel, and Tom and I and the girls took the first translation payment and went to France for a month, southern Burgundy, a village called La Roche-Vineuse, where Danielle had grown up, halfway between Cluny and Mâcon, red-tiled roofs set in the midst of rolling vineyards, incandescent air. Our rental house was built around a cobbled courtyard full of ancient roses and hydrangeas. "How old is this house?" we asked the neighbours, who invited us in for an aperitif. "Very old" was all we got. The stone walls were two feet thick. The three girls took tennis lessons at *l'école d'été.* Tom went hacking for trilobites, happy under the French sun, and I sat in a wicker chair in the flower-filled courtyard, shorts and halter and bare feet, a floppy straw hat on my head, reading novels day after day, and thinking: I want to write a novel. About something

happening. About characters moving against a "there." That was what I really wanted to do.

Looking back, I can scarcely believe in such innocence. I didn't think about our girls growing older and leaving home and falling away from us. Norah had been a good, docile baby and then she became a good, obedient little girl. Now, at nineteen, she's so brimming with goodness that she sits on a Toronto street corner, which has its own textual archaeology, though Norah probably doesn't know about that. She sits beneath the lamppost where the poet Ed Lewinski hanged himself in 1955 and where Margherita Tolles burst out of the subway exit into the sunshine of her adopted country and decided to write a great play. Norah sits cross-legged with a begging bowl in her lap and asks nothing of the world. Nine-tenths of what she gathers she distributes at the end of the day to other street people. She wears a cardboard sign on her chest: a single word printed in black marker—GOODNESS.

I don't know what that word really means, though words are my business. The Old English word *wearth*, I discovered the other day on the Internet, means outcast; the other English word, its twin, its cancellation, is *worth*—we know what that means and know to distrust it. It is the word *wearth* that Norah has swallowed. This is the place she's claimed, a whole world constructed on stillness. An easy stance, says the condemning, grieving mother, easy to find and maintain, given enough practice. A sharper focus could be achieved by tossing in an astringent fluid, a peppery sauce, irony, rebellion, tattoos and pierced tongue and spiked purple hair, but no. Norah embodies invisibility and goodness, or at least she is on the path—so she said in our last conversation, which was eight weeks ago, the eleventh of April. She wore torn jeans that day and a rough plaid shawl that was almost certainly a car blanket. Her long pale hair was matted. She refused to look us in the eye, but she did blink in acknowledgement—I'm sure of it—when I handed her a sack of cheese sandwiches and Tom dropped a roll of twenty-dollar bills in her lap. Then she spoke, in her own voice, but emptied of connection.

She could not come home. She was on the path to goodness. At that moment I, her mother, was more absent from myself than she; I felt that. She was steadfast. She could not be diverted. She could not "be" with us.

How did this part of the narrative happen? We know it didn't rise out of the ordinary plot lines of a life story. An intelligent and beautiful girl from a loving family grows up in Orangetown, Ontario, her mother's a writer, her father's a doctor, and then she goes off the track. There's nothing natural about her efflorescence of goodness. It's abrupt and brutal. It's killing us. What will really kill us, though, is the day we *don't* find her sitting on her chosen square of pavement.

But I didn't know any of this when I sat in that Burgundy garden dreaming about writing a novel. I thought I understood something of a novel's architecture, the lovely slope of predicament, the tendrils of surface detail, the calculated curving upward into inevitability, yet allowing spells of incorrigibility, and then the ending, a corruption of cause and effect and the gathering together of all the characters into a framed operatic circle of consolation and ecstasy, backlit with fibre-optic gold, just for a moment on the second-to-last page, just for an atomic particle of time.

I had an idea for my novel, a seed, and nothing more. Two appealing characters had suggested themselves, a woman and a man, Alicia and Roman, who live in Wychwood, which is a city the size of Toronto, who clamour and romp and cling to the island that is their life's predicament—they long for love, but selfishly strive for self-preservation. Roman is proud to be choleric in temperament. Alicia thinks of herself as being reflective, but her job as assistant editor on a fashion magazine keeps her too occupied to reflect.

9. And I had a title, *My Thyme Is Up*. It was a pun, of course, from an old family joke, and I meant to write a jokey novel. A light novel. A novel for summertime, a book to read while seated in an Ikea wicker chair with the sun falling on the pages as faintly

and evenly as human breath. Naturally the novel would have a happy ending. I never doubted but that I could write this novel, and I did, in 1997—in a swoop, alone, during three dark winter months when the girls were away all day at school.

10. *The Middle Years,* the translation of volume three of Westerman's memoirs, is coming out this fall. Volume three explores Westerman's numerous love affairs with both men and women, and none of this will be shocking or even surprising to her readers. What is new is the suppleness and strength of her sentences. Always an artist of concision and selflessness, she has arrived in her old age at a gorgeous fluidity and expansion of phrase. My translation doesn't begin to express what she has accomplished. The book is stark; it's also sentimental; one balances and rescues the other, strangely enough. I can only imagine that those endless calcium pills Danielle chokes down every morning and the vitamin E and the emu oil capsules have fed directly into her vein of language so that what lands on the page is larger, more rapturous, more self-forgetful than anything she's written before, and all of it sprouting short, swift digressions that pretend to be just careless asides, little swoons of surrender to her own experience, inviting us, her readers, to believe in the totality of her abandonment.

Either that or she's gone senile to good effect, a grand loosening of language in her old age. The thought has more than once occurred to me.

Another thought has drifted by, silken as a breeze against a lattice. There's something missing in these memoirs, or so I think in my solipsistic view. Danielle Westerman suffers, she feels the pangs of existential loneliness, the absence of sexual love, the treason of her own woman's body. She has no partner, no one for whom she is the first person in the world order, no one to depend on as I do on Tom. She does not have a child, or any surviving blood connection for that matter, and perhaps it's this that makes the memoirs themselves childlike. They go down like good milk, foaming, swirling in the glass.

11. I shouldn't mention Book Number Eleven since it is not a fait accompli, but I will. I'm going to write a second novel, a sequel to *My Thyme Is Up*. Today is the day I intend to begin. The first sentence is already tapped into my computer: "Alicia was not as happy as she deserved to be."

I have no idea what will happen in this book. It is a mere abstraction at the moment, something that's popped out of the ground like the rounded snout of a crocus on a cold lawn. I've stumbled up against this idea in my clumsy manner, and now the urge to write it won't go away. This will be a book about lost children, about goodness, and going home and being happy and trying to keep the poison of the printed page in perspective. I'm desperate to know how the story will turn out.

Nearly

We are more than halfway through the year 2000. Toward the beginning of August, Tom's old friend Colin Glass came to dinner one night, driving out from Toronto. Over coffee he attempted to explain the theory of relativity to me.

I was the one who invited him to launch into the subject. Relativity is a piece of knowledge I've always longed to understand, a big piece, but the explainers tend to go too fast or else they skip over a step they assume their audience has already absorbed. Apparently, there was once a time when only one person in the world understood relativity (Einstein), then two people, then three or four, and now most of the high-school kids who take physics have at least an inkling, or so I'm told. How hard can it be? And it's passed, according to Colin, from crazy speculation to confirmed fact, which makes it even more important to understand. I've tried, but my grasp feels tenuous. So, the speed of light is constant. Is that all?

Ordinarily, I love these long August evenings, the splash of amber light that falls on the white dining-room walls just before the separate shades of twilight take over. The medallion leaves that flutter their round ghost shadows. All day I'd listened to the white-throated sparrows in the woods behind our house; their song resembles the Canadian national anthem, at least the opening bars. Summer was dying, but in pieces. We'd be eating outside if it weren't for the wasps. Good food, the company of a good friend, what more could anyone desire? But I kept thinking of Norah sitting on her square of pavement and holding up the piece of cardboard with the word GOODNESS, and then I lost track of what Colin was saying.

$E=mc^2$. Energy equals mass times the speed of light, squared. The tidiness of the equation raised my immediate suspicion. How can mass—this solid oak dining table, for instance—have any connection with how fast light travels? They're two different things. Colin, who is a physicist, was patient with my objections. He took the linen napkin from his lap and stretched it taut across the top of his coffee cup. Then he took a cherry from the fruit bowl and placed it on the napkin, creating a small dimple. He tipped the cup slightly so that the cherry rotated around the surface of the napkin. He spoke of energy and mass, but already I had lost a critical filament of the argument. I worried slightly about his coffee sloshing up onto the napkin and staining it, and thought how seldom in the last few years I had bothered with cloth napkins. Nobody, except maybe Danielle Westerman, does real napkins anymore; it was understood that modern professional women had better things to do with their time than launder linen.

By now I had forgotten completely what the cherry (more than four dollars a pound) represented and what the little dimple was supposed to be. Colin talked on and on, and Tom, who is a family physician and has a broad scientific background, seemed to be following; at least he was nodding his head appropriately. My mother-in-law, Lois, had politely excused herself and returned to her house next door; she would never miss the ten-o'clock news; her watching of the ten-o'clock news helps the country of Canada to go forward. Christine and Natalie had long since drifted from the table, and I could hear the buzz and burst of TV noises in the den.

Pet, our golden retriever, parked his shaggy self under the table, his whole dog body humming away against my foot. Sometimes, in his dreams, he groans and sometimes he chortles with happiness. I found myself thinking about Marietta, Colin's wife, who had packed her bags a few months ago and moved to

Calgary to be with another man. She claimed Colin was too wrapped up in his research and teaching to be a true partner. A beautiful woman with a neck like a plant stem, she hinted that there had been a collapse of passion in their marriage. She had left suddenly, coldly; he had been shocked; he had had no idea, he told us in the early days, that she had been unhappy all these years, but he found her diaries in a desk drawer and read them, sick with realization that a gulf of misunderstanding separated them.

Why would a woman leave such personal diaries behind? To punish, to hurt, of course. Colin, for the most part a decent, kind-hearted man, used to address her in a dry, admonitory way, as though she were a graduate student instead of his wife. "Don't tell me this is processed cheese," he asked her once when we were having dinner at their house. Another time: "This coffee is undrinkable." He loved pleasure—he was that kind of man—and took it for granted and couldn't help his little yelps of outrage when pleasure failed. You could call him an innocent in his expectations, almost naive on this particular August evening. It was as though he were alone in a vaulted chamber echoing with immensities, while Tom and I stood attendance just outside the door, catching the overflow, the odd glimpse of his skewed but calm brilliance. Even the little pockets under his eyes were phlegmatic. He was not a shallow person, but perhaps he suspected that we were. I had to stop myself interrupting with a joke. I often do this, I'm afraid: ask for an explanation and then drift off into my own thoughts.

How could he now be sitting at our table so calmly, toying with cherries and coffee cups and rolling the edge of his straw placemat, and pressing this heft of information on us? It was close to midnight; he had an hour's drive ahead of him. What did the theory of relativity really matter to his ongoing life? Colin, with his small specs and trim moustache, was at ease with big ideas like relativity. As a theory, relativity worked, it held all sorts of important "concepts" together with its precision and elegance. Think of glue lavishly applied, he said helpfully about relativity; think of the power of the shrewd guess. Such a sweeping perspective had been visionary at the beginning, but had been assessed and reinforced, and it was, moreover, Colin was now insisting, useful. In the face of life's uncertainties, relativity's weight could be assumed and then set aside, part of the package of consciousness.

He finished awkwardly, sat back in his chair with his two long arms extended. "So!" That's it, he seemed to say, or that's as much as I can do to simplify and explain so brilliant an idea. He glanced at his watch, then sat back again, exhausted, pleased with himself. He wore a well-pressed cotton shirt with blue and yellow stripes, neatly tucked into his black jeans. He has no interest in clothes. This shirt must go back to his married days, chosen for him, ironed for him by Marietta herself and put on a hanger, perhaps a summer ago.

The theory of relativity would not bring Colin's wife hurrying back to the old stone house on Oriole Parkway. It would not bring my daughter Norah home from the corner of Bathurst and Bloor, or the Promise Hostel where she beds at night. Tom and I followed her one day; we had to know how she managed, whether she was safe. The weather would be turning cold soon. How does she bear it? Cold concrete. Dirt. Uncombed hair.

"Would you say," I asked Colin—I had not spoken for several minutes—"that the theory of relativity has reduced the weight of goodness and depravity in the world?"

He stared at me. "Relativity has no moral position. None whatever." ("This coffee is undrinkable.")

I looked to Tom for support, but he was gazing with his mild eyes at the ceiling, smiling. I knew that smile.

"But isn't it possible," I said to Colin, "to think that goodness, or virtue if you like, could be a wave or particle of energy?"

"No," he said. "No, it is not possible."

I made an abrupt move to clear the table. I was suddenly exhausted.

Still, I am thankful for the friendship and intellectual ardour of such an unpretentious man as Colin Glass, who despite his suffering and shame really wanted me to understand a key concept of the twentieth century. Or was he simply diverting himself for an hour? This is what I must learn: the art of diversion. He said not one word about Marietta all evening long. Tom and I understand that he is reconstructing his life without her. But a daughter is something different. A daughter of nineteen cannot be erased.

Once

It was understood that I would do the publicity, such as it was, for Danielle Westerman's third volume of memoirs. At eighty-five she was too old, and too distinguished, to handle a day of interviews in Toronto, even though she lives there. I, as the translator, could easily field questions from the press. A very light schedule was organized by the publisher, since Dr. Westerman already possesses a long twilight of faithful readership.

In early September, I drove into Orangetown, down its calm, old-fashioned main street and into the countryside again. The city of Toronto, monumental and lonely, glowed in front of me. Its outskirts are ragged, though its numbered exits pretend at a kind of order. Traffic was light. I drove slowly by the corner of Bloor and Bathurst for a glimpse of Norah. There she was, as always, on the northeast corner, seated on the ground near the subway entrance with her bowl and cardboard sign, even though it was not yet nine o'clock. Had she had breakfast? Did she have nits in her hair? What is she thinking, or is her mind a great blank?

I parked the car and walked over to where she was. "Hello, darling Norah," I said, setting down a plastic bag of food: bread and cheese, fruit and raw vegetables. And, in an envelope, a recent photo of Pet with his straight, proud muzzle and furry ruff. Norah, of all the girls, doted on Pet, and now I was bribing her shamelessly. It was a chilly day, and it iced my heart to see her unreadable immobility, but I was glad to notice that she was wearing warm mittens. Glad? Me glad? The least little signal will gladden my heart these days. Today she looked not quite at me, and nodded. Another wave of gladness struck. I allow myself only one such glimpse a week, since she's made it clear she doesn't want to see us.

It is like watching her through plate glass. All week I will draw expensively on this brief moment of voyeurism, at the same time trying to blot it out with images of Norah on her bicycle; Norah sitting at the kitchen table studying for exams; Norah reaching for her green raincoat; Norah trying on new school shoes; Norah sleeping, safe.

After a while I went to have my eyebrows arched and tinted at Sylvia's, which calls itself a "spirit spa," meaning, it seemed, that while Madame Sylvia swiped at my brow with a little paintbrush, she murmured and sang into my ear. It was now nine-thirty in the morning and I lay on a narrow table in a tiny white room. "You are at the age when you must protect the fine skin around the eyes," she warned. "A woman's face falls, it is inevitable, but the eyes go on and on, giving light. You will be eighty, ninety, and your eyes will still charm."

She knows nothing about my life. I've never been here before and have never thought of having an eyebrow tint. I have perfectly decent eyebrows, nicely shaped and regular, but I did look into a mirror a week or so ago and noticed that the small hairs at the outside corners were coming in grey. There was a little grey at the temples too, but nothing to be surprised about, not for a woman whose forty-fourth birthday is approaching, not for a woman who has never even thought of herself as possessing "temples," such august body parts.

"Are you by any chance a Gemini?" Madame Sylvia asked intimately. Swish went the paintbrush. She stopped, peered at me closely, then swished again, a deft little stroke.

"No," I said, ashamed to acknowledge the astrological universe. "My birthday's in September. Next week, in fact."

"I can tell, yes." She had a touch of the harridan in her voice. "I can always tell."

What could she tell?

"Twenty-four dollars," she said. "Let me give you my card. For next time."

Presumptuous, but yes, there will be a next time. I calculated quickly. My face would make it through the next few weeks, but by November I will probably be back in Madame Sylvia's hushed white cell. I may well become a regular. Eyebrows, lashes, full facials, neck massage. I have led a reflective life, a life of thought, a writer, a translator, but all this is about to change. The delicate skin around my eyes was demanding attention. Has Tom noticed? I don't think so. Christine and Natalie don't really look at me in that way; they just see this watercolour blob that means mother, which is rather how I see myself.

"A woman's charm is with her for life," Madame Sylvia said, "but you must pay attention."

No, I thought an hour later, no. I'm sorry, but I have no plans to be charming on a regular basis. Anyone can be charming. It's really a cheap trick, mere charm, so astonishingly easy to per- form, screwing up your face into sunbeams, and spewing them forth. The calculated lift of the wrist, chin up, thumb and fore- finger brought together to form a little feminine loop, that trick of pretending to sit on a little glass chair, that concentration of radiance, *l'esprit;* little sprinkles of it everywhere, misting the air like bargain scent. Ingenue spritz, Emma Allen calls it.

I know that cheapness so intimately—the grainy, sugary, per- severing way charm enters a fresh mouth and rubs against the molars, sticking there in soft wads, promoting mouth ulcers or whatever it is that's the metaphoric projection of self-hatred. Of all the social virtues, charm is, in the end, the most unreward- ing. And compared to goodness, real goodness, or the unmovable self-abnegation my daughter Norah practises, charm is nothing but crumpled tissue paper, soiled from previous use.

Sincerity? No. Sincerity's over. Sincerity's lost whatever edge it had. It's fine, fine matter but wasted on the press, who all grew up post-Holocaust, devoted readers of *Mad Magazine,* and wouldn't recognize a bar of willed innocence if it came wrapped in foil.

Nor will I ever again be pointlessly, endlessly polite. I got over that two years ago when I did my author tour. It seems I've lost, like a stream of pebbles leaving my hand, the kind of endurance that professional courtesy demands: suck in your breath, let your face go numb, listen to the interviewer's questions, register optimally, let your breath out, evaluate the feelings of those who depend on you (agent, publisher, editor, that nice Sheila person who does publicity, and of course Danielle Westerman), and perform again and again like the tuned-up athlete you are, the fit physical specimen that each new book demands, then move on to the next task.

Mrs. Winters, who has just translated The Middle Years, *the unfolding memoir of Holocaust survivor Danielle Westerman, is a woman of grace and charm, whose thick brown hair is arranged into a bun. Putting down her coffee cup, she shrugs off her beige raincoat and . . .*

I've entered early middle age now and I have a nineteen-year-old daughter who lives on the street. I no longer require a reputation for charm, those saving lilac shadows and contours. Maybe I never did. I won't—not now—tuck the ends of my sentences into little licks of favour, and the next time a journalist pins me down with a personal question, trolling for information—Tell me, Mrs. Winters, how are you able to balance your family and professional life?—I will stare back hard with my newly practised stare. How do I balance my life? Tinted eyebrows up. Just what kind of inquiry is this? Wouldn't you prefer, Mrs. Winters, to pursue you own writing rather than translate Dr. Westerman's work? Please, not that again. How did you and your husband meet? What does he think of your writing?

I will in the future address my interviewer directly, and say with firmness: "This interview is over." There is nothing to lose. Rude and difficult people are more likely to be taken seriously. Curmudgeons are positively adored. I've noticed this. Even the fascinatingly unknowable earn respect.

And when I read in the paper tomorrow that "Mrs. Winters looked all of her forty-three years" and that "Mrs. Winters with

her familiar overbite was reluctant to talk about her work schedule," I will want to phone the editor and complain bitterly. This
from the pen of a small, unattractive man, almost entirely lip-
less beneath a bony, domineering nose, sweating with minor
ambition, head tilted like something carved out of yellow wax.

He interviewed me in a cappuccino bar in mid-Toronto. A
chilly, stooped, round-headed man in his thirties or forties—it
was hard to tell—slow to smile, pathetically in need of human
attention, thinking his superior thoughts. Fluff on his shoulders
begged to be picked off. I, on the other hand, was wearing a soft
jade jacket of cashmere lined with silk, which represented a rare
splurge on my part, but I could be sure this man would over-
look this garment with its crystal buttons and mandarin collar and
concentrate instead on my drab raincoat, beige, and not quite
pristine at the cuffs. In print he will be certain to refer to my
chignon as a bun. It's taken me years to learn to do a glossy little
chignon—I can get my hair brushed back and securely pinned
up each morning in a mere two and a half minutes and I consider
my coiffure one of my major life accomplishments. I really mean
this.

Sheila from publicity had filled me in before the interview, and
I felt the information packet hovering; what to do with it? This
young/youngish man was the newly appointed books columnist
at *Booktimes*. He was well known for holding pious opinions about
the literature of the Great North, about his own role as advocate
of a diverse new outpouring of Canadian voices, the post-colonial
cry of blaming anguish. The stream of current fiction about
middle-class people living in cities was diluting the authentic
national voice that rose from the landscape itself and—

Oh, shut up, shut up.

Cappuccino foam dotted the corners of his undistinguished
mouth. And just one more question, Mrs. Winters—

Of course he didn't call me Reta, even though there might be
only a year or two between us. The "Mrs." gave him power over
me: that vexing *r* rucking things up in the middle and making one

think of such distractions as clotheslines and baking tins. He was the barking terrier, going at Mrs. Winters's ankles, shaking out his fur and asking me to justify myself, wanting me to explain the spluttering, dying, whimpering bonfire of my life, which I would not dream of sharing. He seemed to forget he was interviewing me about Danielle Westerman's new book.

I understand you're working on a second novel, said he.

Well, yes.

Takes nerve.

Uh-huh.

Actually—actually, well, he had a novel on the go himself.

Really! What a surprise!

At the end of the hour he did not ask for the bill. I asked for the bill. "I'll just put it on my Visa," I said, breaking a tenuous breadth of silence. I announced this with all the majesty I could muster over a vinyl table, like a *grande dame,* adding twenty years to my age, and feeling the vowels shifting in my beautifully moulded throat. Such dignity; I surprised myself with my own resonance, and I may have managed a pained smile, displaying, no doubt, that famous overbite. He turned off the tape recorder at the word "Visa."

He had two young children at home, he said. Christ, what a responsibility, although he loved the little bastards. One of them was quite, quite gifted; well, they both were in their separate ways. But the work of raising kids! Never enough time to read the books he had to review, books all over the house with little markers in them, books he would never finish. So much was expected, and of course, like all journalists, he was underpaid.

Oh, shut up.

They also expected him to do a feature on the weekend.

Uh-huh?

And last week he'd actually broken the MacBunna story.

Really? Macumba? Marimba?

Congratulations, said Mrs. Reta Winters from Orangetown.

Thanks.

I should be getting on my way, I said. My parking meter. A lunch date. A long drive home.

I understand you and your family live in a lovely old house near Orangetown . . .

And then, slyly: I understand one of your daughters now lives in Toronto and . . .

I've been here before. There is something about having an established family, a long-lasting spousal arrangement, three daughters in their teens, a house in the country, a suggestion of impermeability, that draws the curiosity of others so that they can, as Tom says, probe with probity.

But no, this man across the table will not be feeding on my flesh, nor will his colleagues—though one can tell that he has no colleagues; there is no possibility of colleagues. He has no context for friends or co-workers, though there are the kids and there's the wife; he's referred to her three times now. Nicola. She has her professional life, too, he tells me, as though the matter were in dispute.

I can't resist. "Does Nicola—is she a journalist too?"

"Journalist?"

"Like you, I mean."

His hand jumps, and for a moment I think he's going to turn the tape recorder on again. But no, he's reaching into his pocket and now he's releasing two coins onto the table. The tip. They lie there, moist from his hand. Two dimes. I focus on them with what I hope is a cool, censorious gaze.

But he's not looking at me. He's looking across the room where a silver-haired man is seating himself gracefully at a table. "I'm not sure, but I think that's Gore Vidal," my interviewer whispers in a hungry voice. "He's here for the writers' festival, you know."

I rise and exit, as though led by a brass quintet.

The charming Mrs. Winters slips on her comfortable beige raincoat . . .

Wherein

It is late afternoon, early October, the sky darkening, and the lights in the old Orangetown Library already on. The smell of waxed floors is particularly sharp at this hour; it must be the heating system that triggers it.

Today, as always, the librarians, Tessa Sands and Cheryl Patterson, are helpful. I've dropped by to pick up Dennis Ford-Helpern's *The Goodness Gap*. I am not, by the way, unaware of the absurdity of believing one can learn goodness through the medium of print. Bookish people, who are often maladroit people, persist in thinking they can master any subtlety so long as it's been shaped into acceptable expository prose.

I could easily have bought the Ford-Helpern book last week when I was in Toronto. But no, if I am sincere about achieving genuine goodness in my life and thereby finding a way to reconnect with Norah, this means dealing with issues large and small, or else shifting my finite dispersal of goodness to goodish places such as the public library. At the moment I am attempting to be a good citizen who supports her local library, which is dramatically underused by the community and in danger of closing.

Aside from a part-time custodian, these two librarians, Tessa and Cheryl, are the only full-time employees of the Orangetown Library; everyone else got the boot a year ago when the town council announced the library cutbacks.

Tessa and Cheryl have known our family for years. I've been a member of the Library Board forever, and Tessa remembers Norah from when she was four years old, attending Saturday-morning story hour, able to sit cross-legged and absolutely still, wearing only a nametag, not a sign saying GOODNESS. She was capable at that age of an exquisite shiver when listening to the adventures of Bluebeard and ready to shed tears over the fate of the twelve dancing princesses, a story that Tessa always reshapes for her young audiences. Happy endings are her specialty.

Tessa, in her fifties—married to a classical guitarist, mother to one adolescent child—is big, starchy, and pedagogic and getting more so every year. She possesses several lolloping chins, which shift as she talks, each one a millisecond out of sync with the movement of her surprisingly small mouth. She was a biologist before she decided to get her librarian's qualifications. Her voice is clear and elocutionary.

Cheryl, divorced, in her late thirties, leans toward me today with both elbows on the desk, her chin cupped in her hands; her look is hunched and quizzical and surprisingly chic. Today she has a stick-on bindi in the middle of her forehead; I find it hard to avoid staring at this little colourful spot, which is in honour, I can only suppose, of the man she is currently seeing, a dentist trained in Bombay who has hung up his shingle at the Orangetown Mall, a shy young bespectacled man whose Indian wife couldn't deal with small-town Ontario and went back to her parents after six months.

They are great friends, Tessa and Cheryl—colleagues—and they have the good sense to be proud of the generation-stretching bond they've devised. Snobbishness of a particular kind attends them, a case of old-style womanhood kissing up with the new— they've actually done it. It's almost like love. They're each so proud of the other, and like to express this reciprocal pride aloud. *She knows exactly where to find things. Well, she's the best there is when it comes to following up on the Internet.* What they share is their dominion over this granite building, whose brown stones hint at the colour of the earth beneath, that good rich agricultural land so wisely set aside for the public good. Another serious budget cut, though, and this place will be a tea room–slash–gifte shoppe.

Tessa and Cheryl are united in their passion for books, books like Ford-Helpern's, which they are happy enough to provide, but especially novels, novels that describe the unwrittenness of unremarkable men and women. Their instinct is to keep these books flowing toward those who have lost touch with the "real world." I'm their number-one project these days. "Here's the new Atwood," Tessa tells me today, patting the book's cover. "It came in yesterday, and I moved your name to the top of the waiting list."

"It's been nominated for the Booker, you know."

"Thanks," I say in an immaculate tone, "both of you."

They beam. And wait for more.

"How's Norah? Any news? Is she coming home soon?"

No, she will not be home soon. That is perfectly clear. "I'm not sure when she'll be home. Nothing much has happened."

The fact is, Tom and I don't use the library nearly as much as we used to. Tom orders his books—mostly about trilobites—through Amazon.com, and I tend to pick up what I need in Toronto.

"How's she doing?" From Cheryl.

"Reasonably well. As far as we know."

Ah! They exchange glances. Tessa, who has some of the rough, shaggy manners of our own Pet, reaches awkwardly over the counter and embraces me. "She'll get through this nonsense." She fixes me with a snagging look of determination and strength, that "carry on" look that brings tears to my throat.

It was Tessa who alerted us to Norah's whereabouts last April. We hadn't heard from her for over a week. Tom thought Norah had quarrelled with her boyfriend, but I knew better. When we tried to phone we could never get through. Her last visit home at the end of March had been deeply disturbing. I thought several times of getting in touch with the university, but the idea seemed ridiculous, parents checking up on a grown daughter. We were worried, worried sick. Springtime depression. The thought of suicide. Only recently a Muslim woman had set herself on fire in

Toronto. I read something about it in the paper. Then Tessa happened to go into the city to visit her elderly mother, and there she caught a glimpse of Norah when she came up out of the subway. Norah, sitting on the sidewalk, begging.

"Norah?" Tessa said.

Norah looked up. Of course she recognized Tessa at once, but she said nothing. She firmed her grip on the little square of cardboard and thrust it at Tessa. It must have been a cool day, Tessa remembers, because Norah was wearing a pair of old gardening gloves, far too big for her small hands.

"Norah," softly, "do your parents know you're here?"

Norah shook her head.

Around the corner, Tessa opened her bag, fished out her cell phone, and reached me in Orangetown. Luckily, Tom was home. We got straight into the car and drove to Toronto. All the way, my chest was convulsed with pain. The air we breathed was shaking like a great sail.

I'm supposed to be Reta Winters, that sunny woman, but something happened when her back was turned. Reta's dropped a ball in the schoolyard, she's lost that curved, clean shell she was carrying home from the beach. And these two women—Tessa and Cheryl—know what I am, standing here juggling my cascading images of before and after, all my living perfume washed off because my oldest daughter has gone off to live a life of virtue. Her self-renunciation has even made her choose a corner of Toronto where the pickings are slim. I had to explain the situation to my other daughters, how their sister Norah was in pursuit of goodness. I remember that I sketched in the picture fast, using the simplest and shortest words I could find, as though a summary would take the sting and strangeness away. *Yes, a life of goodness, that's what she's chosen.*

They've been expecting me at the library; I always phone ahead. They have six books stacked on the counter, *The Goodness Gap* on top, then the Atwood, then a biography and a couple of slender new mysteries for my mother-in-law, Lois, and a copy of

The Waves for Christine, who has just discovered Virginia Woolf. These books have been carefully chosen. Just the right degree of narrative packing for me, nothing too dark or New Agey; literary novels, but not postmodernly so; no "poetic" novels, please; no insulting trash. An exotic setting is always nice. But nothing about rich people or people who go to lunch—that is, people who know "where" to go to lunch, those smart-edged professionals who "want a life," as if they weren't getting one. Nothing hip. No family sagas, no male bonding with nature stuff. No horses. No poetry or short stories, not for the moment; they don't work.

Cheryl slides the little tower of books toward me slowly, as though they were gathered treasure aboard the deck of a schooner. Their bright new covers gleam in plastic library coats, catching warm bars of light from overhead. I dig into my bag for my library card, grateful.

The reading room today is, as usual, lightly scattered with housewives and seniors, a few students, several of whom I recognize, and one or two strangers. These people move through the stacks or sit quietly at the old oak tables, turning the pages of reference books, poring over newspapers, glancing up when the door opens or closes, looking around and observing the quiet activity, and then retreating to print. This might be a private club, with everyone so relaxed and polite and obeying the rules.

No one actually stares, but they know who I am. I'm Reta Winters, the doctor's wife (that fine man!), the mother of three daughters, the writer. I live five miles out of town, in what used to be the countryside but is now becoming more and more a part of Orangetown, almost a suburb, if a town of five thousand can have a suburb. In our big old house, it could be said, we live the life we long ago chose: abundant, bustling, but with peaceful intervals, islands of furniture, books, music, soft cushions to lean into, food in the fridge, more in the freezer. I work as a writer and translator (French into English). And I am the mother of Norah Winters, such a sad case. They remember seeing her around town, a striking girl with fine features, tall like Tom, sometimes riding her bike up Main Street or sitting with her friends in front of the high school, that long straight blonde hair of hers, those strong slender legs testifying to the loose agility of the young. She had a smile that cut like a crescent through her whole body. She went away to university in Toronto, where she had a boyfriend, then she went missing for a few days last spring, then she turned up on a Toronto street corner. The word's got around.

They nod in my direction or else they utter greetings under their breath. "Afternoon." Blessings that I return with a congenial dip of my head as though I were sniffing a nosegay. I'm braced by people's steady repeatable gifts of acknowledgement, and am reminded of what I seem to be waiting for, what all of us wait for: that moment of grace or surprise that has left us but will certainly return. It always does. I believe this, more or less.

In half an hour—I will be gone by then—Cheryl will ring a little bell and move from table to table, announcing in her tender girl's voice that the library will be closed in five minutes. She will say this with a plunge of apology; she is genuinely sorry to break through the thread of her clients' thoughts and regretful about disturbing the concentration of perception and silence that the library has promised each of its visitors and that has accumulated during the long sleepy afternoon. There is no longer enough money to keep the library open on weekday evenings. This is not Cheryl's fault, but she feels sorry about the situation and hopes that they will understand.

I glance around at my fellow citizens as I deposit the books in my sack, and I feel a surge of love for the arbitrariness of our arrangements, that we should be assembled here together in this particular compartment of time, sharing public space, at one with each other in our need for retreat and for the printed word. There's Mrs. Greenaway, with her impossibly narrow nose bridge, smiling perpetually, an intelligent woman with no place to stow her brand of originality. Mr. Atkinson, retired teacher, his tie sunk into the fat of his neck, the *Britannica* opened on the table before him, to a map of some sort. There's a bearded man whose name I don't know but who seems to be scribbling a novel or a memoir into a series of spiral notebooks. There's Hal (Swiftfoot) Scott, who pumps gas and plays hockey, or at least he did before he got caught in a drug bust last year. He's reading *Maclean's*, probably the sports section.

This is a familiar yet unique scene. The precise pattern will occur only once—us, here, this moment engraved in a layer of memory—a thought that stirs me to wonderment.

Such feelings come easily to me these days, and I know enough to distrust myself with these little ironic turnings, these fake jewels. The string section comes on somewhere behind my eyes. There is a sense of buoyancy, as though I'm being carried along on a tidal wave of sensation, borne forward. Precious and precarious, a bending, subtle wand of desire making itself known. Followed by a tightening of the throat, moistening of the eyes, awe for the beauty of ongoing life. Et cetera. Oh, God. This is insane, these errands, these visions, my stepping into cantilevered space and allowing myself to be tipped from skepticism to belief. Twin babies in snowsuits. People hugging at the airport. Pet with his golden fur and brown-socketed eyes sniffing endearingly into the corners of the house, knowing something is wrong, something is missing. Boo hoo.

"She is such a lachrymose woman." I once heard a man say that disdainfully about his sister; he might have been talking about me in my present state. But it's just me, Reta Winters, pushing against what has become an observant loyalty to my habit of sadness. Stupid or shrewd; one or the other. It's only temporary, a warped sense of rejoicing, *une déformation*—so says Danielle Westerman—but it's somehow true, too. For here we are, together in this room at the public library with its old, worn wooden floors, held inside a little tick-tock of time.

And each of us has a life we'll soon be going back to. Dinners will be waiting for us; what an odd and consoling thought. Elaborate full-course affairs or plates of Kraft Dinner or Greek salad from a Safeway tub. I've got two chickens roasting in the

oven right now, enough for leftovers tomorrow; a potato cas-
serole that just needs heating up, and the makings of a salad. My,
my, such a good woman, so organized, too.

Enough of that!

Yes, I must get home. A long day, yes. Rain, rain. The weather
forecast. Goodbye. My umbrella, good heavens, I almost forgot.
Yes, busy, busy. Parked just outside. Don't really need. Still have
the dog to walk. Yes, I will, of course I will. Thank you again,
thank you both. You must be glad to see the end of a long day.

I want, I want, I want.

I don't actually say these last words; I just bump along on their
short, stubbed feet, their little dead declarative syllables—while
buttoning up my coat and making my way home.

Nevertheless

We live on a steep hill. This is rolling country on the whole, so our rocky perch is a geological anomaly, chosen no doubt because it offered a firm foundation as well as a view. The house is a hundred years old, a simple brick Ontario farmhouse that has been much added on to by its several previous inhabitants, and by us. It has weathered into durable authenticity, withstanding the scorchings and freezings of the Ontario climate.

People often ask me—I don't know why—how many rooms we have, and each time this happens I go blank. This is something I should know, but don't. It depends on what you call a room. Is a vestibule a room? Ours has a bright Indian rug, a bench, an engraving on the wall, a number of hooks for coats. The large square entrance hall has a Swedish wood-burning stove on the left-hand side, which we installed during the bitter winter of 1986 and which provides the kind of good, dry radiant heat required in our climate. And there's space in this "hall" for several easy chairs, a telephone table, the oak floor laid with a soft, faded kilim, and in the corner a big blocky desk that Tom uses for personal correspondence—and yet this is not really a room. A hall is not a room; any real estate agent will tell you that. The dining room, off to the right, has a tiny sunroom adjoining it, which is more a cupboard than a room, a wicker settee, a tiny table, some hanging plants, a large squashy ottoman, a sense of opalescence and purity. The living room to the left has a deep bay window, almost a room in itself. Everything's green and white or shades of teal, clear and, at least to my eye, luminous. There's a screened porch off the den, and above it another screened porch, what used to be called a sleeping porch. The room where I work is the old box room in the attic, also not officially a room, though the new skylight and cunningly suspended bookshelves make it feel like one. My office is what I call this space, or else my cubby—or, most often, the box room. My life as a writer and translator is my back story, as they say in the movie business; my front story is that I live in this house on a hill with Tom and our girls and our seven-year-old golden retriever, Pet.

Each of our three daughters has a room of her own, Natalie in the south room and Christine in what we call the raspberry room, not because of the colour of the walls but because her window overlooks our flourishing raspberry patch. Norah, the eldest, has her bedroom at the end of the hall (she is not home at the moment, hasn't been for months, in fact). The sweetest smell hovers in this room, wafting from the tulip-printed duvet or the warm white linen curtains at the windows. Tom and I have the north bedroom, which could really be called two rooms because of the little L-shaped anteroom off the end where Tom keeps his precious trilobite collection in a locked glass case. When the girls were babies they slept here in a crib, to be close to us at night. That crib is now in the basement, occupying a corner of another non-room, a half-finished space with rather sooty knotty-pine walls and painted cement floor, built probably in the late fifties by the McGinn family.

The McGinn House; that's what our place is still called locally, though three or four tenants intervened between them and us, short-term renters who left scarcely any impression of themselves and, in fact, let the house go halfway to ruin.

The McGinns were the first non-farming family to live here. Mr. McGinn ran a second-hand furniture store in town, not very successfully by all accounts. It was during his tenure that the farm acreage was sold off, leaving just four acres for us, woods mostly, maple, sycamore, and a few ancient oaks, and a small apple orchard. I read recently that an English oak takes three hundred years to grow, then lives for three hundred years, then spends three hundred years dying. This thought gave me pause, or at least a lash of sentimental static that was not quite elaborated into a thought: the wonder that living oaken tissue could be so patient and obedient to its built-in triadic rhythm, responding to the tiny distortions of its oversized cells. Did it matter at which moment an oak heart decided to wither and call it a day?

I often think about the McGinn family. I never met them, but they linger nevertheless. They left traces. I've asked Lois about the family, but she had little to do with them, not being one for neighbourliness. She is a great believer in "not imposing," and at that time Tom was a very small boy, too young to play with the McGinn children. The two houses were well separated in those days by ghostly old lilacs and springy untrained stands of spirea.

When we moved in, the half-finished basement room had a freestanding bar at one end with a dark slate top, and we can only think they left it behind because it was too heavy for them to move, not worth the effort. In the deep drawer behind the bar we found a single large cocoa bean, waxed and beautiful and smelling exotically of oily dust. We kept it for years, though now it seems to have vanished. There was also an ancient cardboard box of Dance Dust. If you sprinkled a little on the floor, it made it slippery, just right for a sliding foxtrot. The McGinns, mum and dad, must have had parties, we think—other couples over to dance to records on the wind-up Victrola, something else they left behind. People have probably been happy in this house.

The family had several children—teenagers—and I sometimes wonder if these children were affected by the political tumult of the early sixties, if they got themselves into trouble and worried their parents. They would be approaching late middle age now, these children, keeping an eye on their eroding health and their aging marriages and the doings of their grandchildren, and it seems entirely likely to me that their thoughts must turn occasionally to the house where they grew up. Probably they recall the immense built-in gun cupboard (tongue-and-groove) in the upstairs hall, for which we have never had any use. They may, when they get together for family reunions, reminisce about the tiny crawl space under the porch, which is entered by a concealed door on the wall and which, for my children, became a secret clubhouse.

Someone in the McGinn family left a sealed envelope behind a bathroom radiator, one of those old-fashioned, many-ribbed hot water affairs with ornamental spines. I discovered the envelope when I was painting the room. Reaching down behind the radiator with my paintbrush, I encountered something papery. I had to be careful to dislodge it in one piece. I put down my brush and looked around for a wire coat hanger that I could poke through the grooves of the radiator. The envelope, intact and still sealed after all this time and only lightly smudged with dirt, had the name "Mrs. Lyle McGinn" written across it. Blue ink, faded. It felt crisp in my hands, even after lying hidden all those dateless winters with the furnace clanking off and on and sending heat through the pipes and baking and rebaking it. Should I open it? I wondered. Yes, of course I would open it. I only pretend to have moral scruples about such things. Just touching the envelope brought on a rush of sweet religious melancholy. Yes, I most certainly would open it.

The thought came to me that it might be a suicide note. Or a child's admonishing report card. Or a confession of some sort. *I am so sorry to tell you that I have fallen in love with . . .* The neighbours in back of us, when we first moved in, had hinted at tragedy in the McGinn family, an event of some kind that precipitated the move, years of happiness overcome by sorrow. (My mother-in-law, who hadn't liked Mrs. McGinn, had nothing to contribute in the way of information.) I hadn't paid attention to these rumours, but I also reasoned that any family who surrendered such a house must have had serious cause.

What I found inside the ancient envelope was a simple, rather cheap invitation. A baby shower to be held March 13, 1961. (I would have been four years old.) Pink and blue flowers dangled on their short stems from a rustic cradle suspended from a tree branch. "Please bring a small toy or article of clothing," the invitation read in svelte, arched handwriting, the same handwriting as on the envelope, "not exceeding $3. Please also bring a 'mother's hint' for Georgia."

What happened to the pregnant Georgia who was to be honoured at the party? What happened to her baby when it was born, and was the shower a happy success? These questions opened up for me like rooms along a dim corridor, and these rooms possess doorways to other rooms. I remembered Danielle Westerman asking me once what a shower was; as a transplanted Frenchwoman, a woman in her mid-eighties, she had trouble understanding the concept. But I've been to dozens of such events and find it not at all difficult to imagine an early-sixties living room ringing with high-pitched women's laughter that never seems to let up, though always, beneath it, there is the deeper sound of one particular woman hooting. This person would be famous among her acquaintances for her much-praised, infectious laugh. She, with her boldly printed home-sewn shift dress—I imagine a geometric design, black against red—would be the sort of person who enlivened any gathering and who was always welcome. Mrs. McGinn, on the other hand, would have a tiny, whispery laugh, and would often draw her hand up against her mouth.

Was it Mr. McGinn who owned the rifle collection housed in the specially built cupboard, and did one of those guns go off accidentally? Was it he who attempted to insulate the attic and made a terrible botch of it? How did Mrs. McGinn—I've never discovered her first name, and Lois was no help here, but I speculate it might be Lillian or Dorothy or Ruth, something like that—occupy herself, and was it she who decided to install the green steel kitchen sink with its green enamel basin? Today the sink has reached a kind of antique status, too much a curiosity to part with, and, in any case, it still functions perfectly. I can imagine Lillian/Dorothy/Ruth standing at this sink, cutting wax beans into one-inch pieces and covering them with water, sighing and looking at the clock. Almost suppertime. The clock—postwar plastic—would have been shaped like a teapot or a frog. She is a woman of about my size and age, a medium frame, still slim, but widening at the hips. Middle forties with a lipsticked pout. Some essence has deserted her. A bodily evaporation has left her with nothing but hard, direct questions aimed in the region of her chest, and no one would ever suspect that she might be capable of rising to the upper ether of desire, wanting, wishing.

I love this house. Tom and I—we've been together for twenty-six years, which is the same as being married—moved here in 1980, next door to the red-shingled house he grew up in and where his mother still lives, a seventy-year-old widow, rather gaunt these days, and increasingly silent. Tom, like his father before him, has a family practice in Orangetown, a quick ten minutes away, but he spends at least a third of his time working on trilobite research, his hobby, his avocation, he would tell you in a kind of winking way so that you understand trilobites are his real work.

What's confusing to people is that I've taken his name. I grew up as Reta Summers and when I was eighteen with long straight brown hair down to my waist and enrolled in French studies, I met a medical student named Tom Winters, and so we had on our hands a "situation." We could become a standing joke or else one of us could change seasons. At the time this name business seemed an enormous problem, and it's only recently that I've been able to reel off a fast and funny account of the dilemma and how we solved it. I went to court and signed some papers; that was it, but you would have thought at the time that I'd sacrificed body parts. (I grew up, after all, listening to Helen Reddy singing "I Am Woman.") We are, both of us, *soixante-huitards* in spirit, and I suppose we will remain so all our lives. In truth, I was only twelve years old in 1968, but the potential of rebellion had spiked me even then, what it could be used for or stored against and how we have to live inside the history we're given, but must resist, like radicals, being made into mere creatures of a mere era.

Our house is full of rough corners that seem to me just about to come into their full beauty. I often think of how Vicente Verdú, the Spanish writer, spoke of houses as existing between reality and desire, what we want and what we already have. Probably this old house is not as lovely as I believe. My eyes are curtained over. I used to be able to see the separate rooms with their colours and spaces, but now I can't. I've overvalued its woody, whorled coves and harbours, convincing myself of an architectural spaciousness and, at the same time, coziness, when I really, long ago, should have pursued some professional decorating advice. The word *cozy* cannot be translated into French; I've often had this discussion with Danielle Westerman, not that *cozy* is a word that crops up frequently in her stern essays. There is no French word for *reckless,* either, which is curious when you think that the French are, stereotypically at least, a reckless people.

It's highly unlikely that Mrs. McGinn went to that 1961 baby shower for her friend Georgia. The envelope was still sealed, after all, when I discovered it. No one in the family would have deliberately hidden the note from her. It simply went astray as small bits tend to do in a busy house, getting separated from the rest of the mail, carried into this unlikely room where it became lost and, curiously, preserved.

It mattered so little, this 1961 women-only social evening. John Fitzgerald Kennedy was President of the United States. The country was exploding with consciousness and guilt. There were marches in the streets; intelligent, responsible people were willing to spend months in jail. Around the world the political forces eclipsed an event as neutral and trivial and minuscule as a baby shower in a small Canadian town; a lost invitation weighed nothing at all on the scale of human concerns.

But maybe, if Mrs. McGinn happened to be a certain kind of woman, then maybe she had a good, affectionate friend who phoned to remind her of the event. March is a dreary month in our part of the world, with its blackened snow and random melts. The faint feminism of the early sixties had not yet ignited for women like Lillian (?) McGinn. Feminism was in its chrysalis stage, and Lillian was adrift between generations and between seasons. Probably she still wore a girdle and used a diaphragm to prevent further pregnancies. The house was drafty and the children were churlish. An evening social occasion would be welcome. Mrs. McGinn, standing at the green sink and slicing her beans, might be thrilled to be invited out for a shower and to know that an invitation had been sent, even though it had been mislaid somehow. She would be grateful for the telephone reminder and feel relief from the thoughts that preyed on her. She would rush her family through dinner and make a stab at the supper dishes, getting them soaking in Ivory Liquid at the very least. Or maybe, just this once, a teenaged daughter, overburdened with her own unhappiness and her concern about tomorrow's biology test, would pitch in and offer to help. "Let me," she would say to her featureless (to her) mother. "You go to your thingamajig." The daughter, who in my mind rather resembles Natalie, would feign disinterest but be moved at the same time by her own curiosity about the communal lives of adult women. And perhaps, if she were at all sensitive, she would feel the invisible wave of distress in the house; something was wrong with her mother, some element unanswered.

She would be a daughter who understood nothing about the care of a house. Her bedsheets in that upstairs bedroom—the same room Natalie has occupied all these years, going straight from a crib into a junior bed—were changed regularly, delivered crisp and fresh, but she has never considered the notion of domestic maintenance, and why should she?

"Leave the kitchen to me," Mrs. McGinn's daughter might have commanded her mother in March of 1961, speaking in an exasperated tone, exactly like Christine's, wanting to prod a troubling root of kindness that she feels but can't yet quite claim. "I'll look after the dishes."

A house requires care. Until recently the Merry Maids came and cleaned our house twice a month, but now I call on them less and less frequently. Their van rolling into our driveway, the women's muscles and buoyancy and booming equipment wear me out. I mostly look after the house myself. I deal with the dust and the dog hairs, wearing my oldest jeans and a cotton sweater coming unknit at the cuffs. Cleaning gives me pleasure, which I'm reluctant to admit and hardly ever do, but here, in my thoughts, I will register the fact: dusting, waxing, and polishing offer rewards. Quite a lot of people would agree with this if pressed, though vacuuming is too loud and cumbersome to enjoy. I especially love the manoeuvring of my dust mop over the old oak floors. (It is illegal to shake a dust mop out of a window in New York, and probably even in Toronto; I read that somewhere.) Those Buddhist monks I saw not long ago on a TV documentary devote two hours to morning meditation, followed by one hour of serious cleaning. Saffron-robed and their shaved heads gleaming, they actually go out into the world each day with buckets and rags, and they clean things, anything that needs cleaning, a wall or an old fence, whatever presents threat or disorder. I'm beginning to understand where this might take them.

With my dampened dust cloth in hand I'm keeping myself going. I reach under the sink and polish that hard-to-get-to piece of elbow pipe. Tomorrow I'm planning to dust the basement stairs, swiftly, but getting into the corners.

I'm not so thick that I can't put the pieces of my odd obsession together, wood and bone, plumbing and blood. To paraphrase Danielle Westerman, we don't make metaphors in order to distract ourselves. Metaphors hold their own power over us, even without their fugitive gestures. They're as real as the peony bushes we observe when we're children, lying flat on the grass and looking straight up to the undersides of leaves and petals and marvelling: Oh, this is secret territory, we think, an inverted world grown-ups can't see, its beetles, its worms, its ant colonies, its sweet-sour smell of putrefaction. But, in fact, everyone knows about this palpable world; it stands for nothing but the world itself.

I dust and polish this house of mine so that I'll be able to seal it from damage. If I commit myself to its meticulous care, I will claim back my daughter Norah, gone to goodness. The soiling sickness that started with one wayward idea and then the spreading filaments of infection, the absurd notion—Tao?—that silence is wiser than words, inaction better than action—this is what I work against. And probably, especially lately, I clean for the shadow of Mrs. McGinn, too, wanting to drop a curtsey in her direction. Yes, it was worth it, I long to tell her, all that anxiety and confusion. I'm young enough that I still sigh out: what is the point? but old enough not to expect an answer.

I hurry with this work. I hurry through each hour. Every day I glance at the oak banister. Hands have run up and down its smoothed curves, giving it the look of a living organism. This banister has provided steady support, all the while looking graceful and giving off reflected light, and resisting with its continuity the immensity of ordinary human loneliness. Why would I not out of admiration stroke the silky surfaces now and then; every day, in fact? I won't even mention the swift, transitory reward of lemon spray wax. Danielle Westerman and I have discussed the matter of housework. Not surprisingly, she, always looking a little *dérisoire*, believes that women have been enslaved by their possessions. Acquiring and then tending—these eat up a woman's creativity, anyone's creativity. But I've watched the way she arranges articles on a shelf, and how carefully she sets a table, even when it is just me coming into Toronto to have lunch in her sunroom.

Her views often surprise me, though I like to think I know her well, and despite the forty years between us. Dr. Westerman: poet, essayist, feminist survivor, holder of twenty-seven honorary degrees. "It might be better," I said once, pointing to a place in her first volume of memoirs and trying not to sound overly expository, "to use the word *brain* here instead of *heart*."

She gave me a swift questioning look, the blue-veined eyelids sliding up. Now what? I explained that referring to the heart as the seat of feeling has been out of fashion for some time, condemned by critics as being fey, thought to be precious. She considered this for a second, then smiled at me with querulous affection, and placed her hand on her breast. "But this is where I feel pain," she said. "And tenderness."

I let it go. A writer's *partis pris* are always—must be—accommodated by her translator. I know that much after all these years.

There are other things I could do with my time besides clean my house. There's that book on animals in Shakespeare, the companion volume to my *Shakespeare and Flowers*. Or I could finish my translation of the fourth and final volume of Westerman's memoirs, which would take me about six months. Instead I'm writing a second novel, which is going slowly because I wake up in the morning anxious, instead, to clean my house. I'd like to go at it with Q-tips, with toothpicks, every crack and corner scoured. Mention a new cleaning product and I yearn to hold it in my hand; I can't stop. Each day I open my eyes and comfort myself with the tasks that I will accomplish. It's necessary, I'm finding, to learn devious means of consoling oneself and also necessary to forgive one's own eccentricities. In the afternoon, after a standing-up lunch of cheese and crackers, I get to my novel and produce, on a good day, two pages, sometimes three or four. I perch on my Freedom Chair and think: Here I am. A woman seated. A woman thinking. But I'm always rushed, always distracted. Tuesdays I meet my friends for coffee in Orangetown, Wednesdays I go to Toronto, every second Thursday afternoon is the Library Board meeting.

Last Friday, after days spent at home waiting for a phone call from Mrs. Quinn at the Promise Hostel—which yielded nothing but the fact that nothing had changed—I went into Toronto with Tom to a one-day trilobite conference at the museum, and even attended a session, thinking it might provide distraction. A paleontologist, a woman called Margaret Henriksen, from

Minneapolis, lectured in a darkened room, and illustrated her talk with a digital representation of a trilobite folding itself into a little ball. No one has ever seen a trilobite, since they exist only in the fossil record, but the sections of its bony thorax recorded in stone were so perfectly made that, when threatened, these creatures were able to curl up, each segment nesting into the next and protecting the soft animal underbodies. This act is called enrolment, a rather common behaviour for arthropods, and it seems to me that this is what Tom has been doing these past weeks. I clean my house and he "enrols" into a silence that carries him further away from me than the fleeting figure of Mrs. McGinn, who rests like a dust mote in the corner of my eye, wondering why she was not invited to her friend's baby shower on that March evening back in 1961. It nags at her. She is disappointed in herself. Her life has been burning up one day at a time—she understands this for the first time—and she's swallowed the flames without blinking. Now, suddenly, this emptiness. Nothing has prepared her for the wide, grey simplicity of sadness and for the knowledge that this is what the rest of her life will be like, living in a falling-apart house that wishes she weren't there.

After the conference in Toronto, some trilobite friends from England wanted to go for a meal at a place called the Frontier Bar on Bloor Street West, where the theme is Wild West. They'd read about it in a tour guide and thought it might be amusing.

Everything's in your face at the Frontier Bar—from the cowhides nailed to the walls to the swizzle sticks topped with little plastic cowboy hats. The drinks have names like Rodeo Rumba and Crazy Heehaw, and we felt just a little effete ordering our bottle of good white wine. Before we said goodnight at the end of the evening, I excused myself to go to the women's washroom (the Cowgals' Corral), and there I found, on the back of each cubicle door, a tiny blackboard supplied with chalk, a ploy by the management to avoid the defacing of property.

I've often talked to Tom about the graffiti found in public bathrooms; we've compared notes. The words women write on walls are so touchingly sweet, so innocent. Tom can hardly believe it. "Tomorrow is cancelled," I saw once. And another time, "Saskatchewan Libre!" Once, a little poem. "If you sprinkle / when you tinkle / Please be a sweetie / and wipe the seatie." I love especially the slightly off witticisms, the thoughts that seemed unable to complete themselves except in their whittled-down elliptical, impermanent forms.

I'd never before felt an urge to add to the literature of wash-room walls, but that night, at the Frontier Bar, I picked up the piece of chalk without a moment's hesitation, my head a ringing vessel of pain, and my words ready.

First, though, I wiped the little slate clean with a dampened paper towel, obliterating "Hi, Mom" and "Lori farts" and leaving myself a clear space. "My heart is broken," I wrote in block letters, moved by an impulse I would later recognize as dramatic, childish, indulgent, grandiose and powerful. Then, a whimsical afterthought: I drew a little heart in the corner and put a jagged line through it, acutely aware of the facile quality of the drafts-manship.

At once I felt a release of pressure around my ribs. Something not unlike jubilation rubbed against me, just for a moment, half a moment, as though under some enchantment I was allowed to be receptor and transmitter both, not a dead thing but a live link in the storage of what would become an unendurable grief. I believed at that instant in my own gusto, that I'd set down words of revealing truth, inscribing the most private and alarming of visions instead of the whining melodramatic scrawl it really was, and that this unscrolling of sorrow in a toilet cubicle had all along been my most deeply held ambition.

I went to join the others gathered on the pavement outside the bar. They hadn't noticed I'd been away so long, and perhaps it really had been only a moment or two. Everyone was topped up with good wine and bad food and they were chattering about Toronto and how strange that such campy curiosities as the Frontier Bar continued to exist. Tom slid an arm around my waist, oh so sweetly that I half believed I'd left my poison behind. The night air was bitingly cold, close to freezing, but for the first time in weeks I was able to take a deep breath. *My Heart Is Broken.* My mouth closed on the words, and then I swallowed.

So

"So-oo-oo?" my daughter Norah once asked me—she was about nine years old. "Why exactly is it that you and Daddy aren't married?"

I had been waiting for the question for some years, and was prepared. "We really are married," I told her. "In the real sense of the word, we are married." She and I were in Orangetown on a Saturday morning, in the only shoe store in town not counting the ones out at the mall, and Norah was trying on new school shoes. "We're married in that we're together forever."

"But," she said, "you didn't have a wedding."

"We had a reception," I told her cheerily. This diversion from wedding to reception had always been part of my plan. "We had a dinner for friends and family at your father's apartment."

"What kind of reception?"

How easily I managed to lead her sideways. "We had pizza and beer," I said. "And champagne for toasts."

"Was Grandma Winters there?"

"Well, no. She and Grandpa Winters had another reception for us later. Sort of a tea party."

"What did you wear?"

"You mean at the pizza party?"

"Yes."

"I had a caftan that Emma Allen made out of some African cotton. A blue and black block print. You've seen the picture. Only she was Emma McIntosh then."

"Was she your bridesmaid?"

46

"Sort of. We didn't use that word in those days."

"Why not?"

"This was back in the seventies. Weddings were out of style back then. People didn't think they were important, not if two people really loved each other."

"I hate these shoes." She wiggled in the chair.

"Well, we won't buy them, then."

"What kind of shoes did you have?"

"When?"

"At the pizza thing."

"I'm not sure I remember. Oh, yes I do. We didn't have shoes. We were barefoot."

"Barefoot? You and Daddy?"

"It was summertime. A very hot summer day."

"That's nice," she said. "I wish I'd been there."

This was much too easy. "I wish you'd been there too," I said, meaning it. "That would have made the day perfect."

"So, is there anything new?" It was Emma Allen phoning a week ago from Newfoundland. She has been a friend since high-school days in Toronto. There is no need for reference points between Emma and me. Our brains tick over in the same way. She is a writer, a medical journalist, a redhead, tall and lanky, who once lived, briefly, in Orangetown with her husband and kids and was part of the same writers' workshop. We speak at least once a week on the phone. When she asks if there's anything new, she is talking about Norah, about Norah living on the street.

"She's still there. Every day."

"That has to be some comfort," she said in her measured way. "Though it's not bloody much."

"I worry about the cold."

It was October, and we were having a frost almost every night. We'd even had a fall of snow, which had since melted.

"Thermal underwear?" Emma asked.

"Good idea."

"On the other hand—"

"Yes?"

"The cold may bring her home. You know how a good cold snap makes people wake up and look after themselves."

"I've thought of that."

"I thought probably you had."

Tom's father was a family physician in Orangetown, so Tom became a family physician in Orangetown. It's not really as simple as that, but the fallout is the same. When he was a student he was in rebellion against the established order, way over to the edge of the left. He didn't attend his own university graduation, because the ceremony involved wearing academic dress. For ten years the only trousers he wore were jeans. He doesn't own a necktie and doesn't intend to, not ever—the usual liberal tokens. His instincts are bourgeois, but he fights his instincts. That is, he lives the life of a married man but balks at the idea of a marriage ceremony. Mostly, he is a different kind of doctor than his crusty, sentimental father. Tom is a saint, some people in Orangetown think, so patient, so humane, so quietly authoritative. He works at the Orangetown Clinic with three other doctors, one of whom is an obstetrician who looks after most of the births in the region. Tom misses that, attending births. He sees a lot of sick people and a lot of lonely people. It's through Tom that I've found out about the ubiquity of loneliness. I wouldn't have believed it otherwise.

It's my belief that he thinks about trilobites all the time. While he's checking out a prostate gland or writing a prescription for asthma drugs, a piece of his mind holds steady to the idea of 500 million years ago—unfathomable to me—and the extinct, unlovely arthropods that occupied every sea and ocean in the world. They hung around for a long time, something like a hundred million years. Some were half the size of a thumbnail and some were a foot long. Recently, a giant trilobite was found near the shores of Hudson Bay, a monster measuring 70 centimetres—that's two feet, four inches. Ugly but adaptable creatures, trilobites, and obliging with their remains. A head with bulging eyes, a thorax, a tail of sorts; a little three-part life that once was. Tom loves them, and so we all love them.

"So what!" says Christine when I confront her with a bent cigarette that I found in the pocket of her winter parka. "So why were you going through my parka anyway?"

"I was putting it in the washer and so I checked the pockets."

"I'm not addicted, if that's what you're worried about."

"That is what I'm worried about, yes."

"Well, I'm not. I've just had a few. With friends."

"When I was pregnant with you, Chris, I never had a drop of wine for nine months. I never took so much as an aspirin. I drank three glasses of milk, every day, and you know I hate milk."

"Wow! You were a real martyr to the cause of motherhood."

"I wanted you to be healthy."

"So you could lay a guilt trip on me when I got older."

"I just hoped—"

"No wonder Norah—" She stopped herself.

No wonder Norah left home. I looked into her stricken face and could read the words she had come so close to engraving on the air.

"It's all right," I said, gathering her in my arms.

"I hate smoking anyway," she whispered. "It was just something to do."

"Sooo-ooo-oo!"

That's what people say when they are about to introduce a narrative into the conversation or when they are clearing a little space so that you can begin a story yourself. It can be sung to different tunes, depending on the circumstances.

"So!"

That's usually the first word uttered when I sit down to have coffee with Sally Bachelli and Annette Harris and Lynn Kelly. So! Meaning, here we are again at the Orange Blossom Tea Room. We're the Orangetown coffee "lie-dies" getting together on a Tuesday morning. What's new? So! So is like the oboe, signalling the A pitch to the strings. So, where do we go from here?

Aside from Emma Allen, and Gwen Reidman, with whom I'm rather out of touch, these three—Sally, Annette, Lynn—are my closest friends. We are all about the same age but are wildly different in size. Sally is a large woman, queenly. She has a round mouth in a round face and wears thick, round, plastic-rimmed eyeglasses. A former actress who now runs an after-school drama group, she's brilliant with accents: Scottish, German, East Indian; she can do anything. Even her shoulders are theatrical, even her elbows and wrists. Her clothes, which she designs and makes herself, are extraordinary in their roomy, fluttering, brightly coloured and gathered shapes.

"So," says Lynn Kelly, who wears matched pantsuits in muted tones with department store jewellery and flat shoes. She is the shortest of us, under five foot and very wiry. How she produced two children from those tiny hips is a mystery. She has large hair, though, to make up for lack of body size, thick, dark, luxurious hair all in a tangle. Every sentence she utters seems to have a full stop attached. She was born and educated in North Wales.

Annette Harris came to Orangetown from Toronto, and before that from Jamaica. When she says the word *so,* she makes a circle of it. Of all of us, she has the best figure, a model's figure, slim-waisted, deep-breasted, wonderful legs, and beautiful hands. She dresses with austerity except for her collection of handmade silver bracelets and earrings. I met Annette in the writers' group I once belonged to. She was writing poetry in those days, and still is. Her book *Lost Things* was published a year ago and has done very well. She gave a reading in Toronto, and people were fighting to get in.

So, what do the four of us talk about as we gather at the Orange Blossom Tea Room? We never think about the aboutness of talk; we just talk.

Today Lynn was talking about trust. She is an avid cyclist, and her bike was leaning against a lamppost just out of view of the window. "How do I know it won't be stolen?" she asked us. "Why is it I'm absolutely sure it's safe?"

"Because this is Orangetown," Sally said.

"Because school's in session," I suggested.

"Because it's a twenty-year-old bike." From Annette. "Not that it isn't a terrific model."

"And why is it," Lynn went on, "that I'm not afraid of riding my bike down Borden Road and turning on to Main Street? I've got my helmet on and I'm trying to keep way over on the margin of the road, but what if a driver suddenly decides to go into road rage and ram straight into me?"

"I don't think there's that much road rage in Orangetown at this hour," I said, remembering that I had left my own house unlocked.

"Don't believe it," Annette said. "There's rage every-where."

"Someone could walk into this café right this minute brandishing a sword. I read about a man who went into a church in England and started slicing up people."

"He was insane."

"It could never have been predicted."

"Like being struck by lightning. You can't go around worrying about lightning."

"Or planes crashing into your house."

"If someone came in here with a sword," Lynn said coolly, "we wouldn't have a chance."

"We'd be helpless."

"We could duck under the table."

"No, we'd be helpless."

"Trust. We've had it drilled into us at birth. Or rather, we emerge from the womb already trusting. Trusting the hand that's about to hold us."

"So?" Lynn said. "When are we disabused of this notion?"

"When does doubt cut in, you mean?"

"Immediately," I said. "One second after birth. I'm sure of it."

So, the days go by, early fall, middle fall. Natalie and Chris both got small parts in *The Pajama Game* that the high school is putting on, and at home they're always bursting into *Pajama Game* songs, which, after all these years, are still good songs. "Hernando's Hideaway," "Seven and a Half Cents." *I've got ssss-steam heat.* That's Natalie's favourite; she belts it out, descending the stairs as she sings, going from one side to another, leaning over the banister, stretching her arms wide; Chris, just behind her on the stairs, chants a subtle boom-de-boom in accompaniment. Tom is writing a paper for the trilobite conference next year in Estonia. "Wouldn't you like to go to Estonia?" he asks me. I don't know. It depends on Norah, what happens to Norah. I'm trying to work on my new novel but am often derailed. Danielle's new book is selling well even without an author tour, even with minimal promotion. So it goes.

Otherwise

Two years ago I inhabited another kind of life in which I scarcely registered my notion of heartbreak. Hurt feelings, minor slights, minimal losses, small treacheries, even bad reviews—that's what I thought sadness was made of: tragedy was someone not liking my book.

I wrote a novel for no particular reason other than feeling it was the right time in my life to write a novel. My publisher sent me on a four-city book tour: Toronto, New York, Washington, and Baltimore. A very modest bit of promotion, you might say, but Scribano & Lawrence scarcely knew what to do with me. I had never written a novel before. I was a woman in her forties, not at all remarkable looking and certainly not media-smart. If I had any reputation at all it was for being an editor and scholar, and not for producing, to everyone's amazement, a "fresh, bright, springtime piece of fiction," or so it was described in *Publishers Weekly*.

My Thyme Is Up baffled everyone with its sparky sales. We had no idea who was walking into bookstores and buying it. I didn't know and Mr. Scribano didn't know. "Probably young working girls," he ventured, "gnawed by loneliness and insecurity."

These words hurt my feelings slightly, but then the reviews, good as they were, had subtly injured me too. The reviewers seemed taken aback that my slim novel (200 pages exactly) possessed any weight at all. "Oddly appealing," the *New York Times Book Review* said. "Mrs. Winters's book is very much for the moment, though certainly not for the ages," *The New Yorker* opined. Tom advised me to take this as praise, his position being that all worthy novels pay close attention to the time in which they are suspended, and sometimes, years later, despite themselves, acquire a permanent lustre. I wasn't so sure. As a long-time editor of Danielle Westerman's work, I had acquired a near-crippling degree of critical appreciation for the severity of her moral stance, and I understood perfectly well that there was something just a little bit *darling* about my own book.

My three daughters were happy about the book because they were mentioned by name in a *People Magazine* interview. ("Mrs. Winters lives on a farm outside Orangetown, Ontario, is married to a family physician, and is the mother of three handsome daughters, Natalie, Christine, and Norah.") That was enough for them. Handsome! Norah, the most literary, the most mercurial of the three—both Natalie and Chris are in the advanced science stream at Orangetown High School—mumbled that it might have been a better book if I'd skipped the happy ending, if Alicia had decided on going to Paris after all, and if Roman had denied her his affection. There was, my daughter postulated, maybe too much over-the-top sweetness in the thyme seeds Alicia planted in her window box, and in Alicia's listless moods and squeaky hopes. And no one in her right mind would sing out (as Alicia had done) those words that reached Roman's ears—he was making filtered coffee in the kitchen—and bound him to her forever: "My thyme is up."

It won the Offenden Prize, which, though the money was nice, shackled the book to minor status. Clarence and Margot Offenden had established the prize back in the seventies out of a shared exasperation with the opaqueness of the contemporary novel. "The Offenden Prize recognizes literary quality and honours accessibility." These are their criteria. Margot and Clarence are a good-hearted couple, and rich, but a little jolly and simple in their judgments, and Margot in particular is fond of repeating her recipe for enduring fiction. "A beginning, a middle, and an ending," she likes to say. "Is that too much to ask?"

At the award ceremony in New York she embraced Tom and

the girls and told them how I shone among my peers, those dabblers in convolution and pretension who wrote without holding the reader in mind, who played games for their own selfish amusement, and who threw a mask of noir over every event, whether it was appropriate or not, who put a doorway, say, or a chair in every chapter, just to be baffling and obscure. "It's heaven," Margot sang into Tom's ear, "to find that sunniness still exists in the world." I was interviewed for television, sitting in a Vasily chair with a cat on my lap; someone, the director or producer, had insisted on the cat. Something to do with image.

I don't consider myself a sunny person. In fact, if I prayed, I would ask every day to be spared the shame of dumb sunniness. Danielle Westerman, her life, her reflection on that life, has taught me that much. Don't hide your dark side from yourself, she said to me once, it's what keeps us going forward, that pushing away from the blinding brilliance. She said that, of course, in the tough early days of feminism, and no one expected her to struggle free to merriment. I remember that I did feel, starting my mini-tour, the resident anxiety you develop when you know you've been too lucky; at any moment, maybe next Tuesday afternoon, I would be stricken with something unbearable.

After the New York event, I said goodbye to the family and got on a train and travelled to Washington, staying in a Georgetown hotel, which had on its top floor, reserved for me by my publisher, something called the Writer's Suite. A brass plaque on the door announced this astonishing fact. I, the writer in a beige raincoat, Ms. Reta Winters from Orangetown, entered this doorway with small suitcase in tow and looked around, not daring to imagine what she might find. There was a salon as well as a bedroom, two full baths, a very wide bed, more sofas than I would have time to sit on in my short stay, and a coffee table consisting of a sheet of glass posed on three immense faux books stacked one on the other. A large bookshelf held the tomes of the authors who had stayed in the suite. "We like to ask our guests to contribute a copy of their work," the desk clerk had told me, and I was obliged to explain that I had only a single reading copy with me but that I would attempt to find a copy in a local store. "That would be most appreciated," she said with deep sincerity.

The books left behind by previous authors were disappointing, inspiration manifestos or self-help manuals, with a few thrillers thrown in. I am not a snob—I read the Jackie Onassis biography, for example—but my close association with writers such as Danielle Westerman has conditioned me to hope for a degree of ambiguity or nuance, and there was none here.

In the great, wide bed I had a disturbing but not unfamiliar dream—it is the dream I always have when I am away from Orangetown, away from the family. I am standing in the kitchen at home, producing a complicated meal for guests, but there is not enough food to work with. In the fridge sits a single egg and maybe a tomato. How am I going to feed all those hungry mouths?

I'm aware of how this dream might be analyzed by a dream expert, that the scarcity of food stands for a scarcity of love, that no matter how I stretch that egg and tomato, there will never be enough of Reta Winters for everyone who needs her. This is how my old friend Gwen, whom I was looking forward to seeing in Baltimore, would be sure to interpret the dream, if I were so foolish as to tell her. Gwen is an obsessive keeper of a dream journal—as are quite a number of my friends—and she also records the dreams of others if they are offered and found worthy. She is, she claimed in a recent letter, an oneirocritic, having completed an extension course in dream interpretation.

I resist the theory of insufficient love. I understand dreams to be an alternative language and one we don't necessarily need to learn. My empty-fridge dream, I like to think, points only to the abrupt cessation, or interruption, of daily obligation. For more than twenty years I've been responsible for producing three meals a day for the several individuals I live with. I may not be conscious of this obligation, but surely I must always, at some level, be calculating and apportioning the amount of food in the house and the number of bodies to be fed: Tom and the girls, the girls' friends, my mother-in-law, and various passing acquaintances. And then there's the dog to feed, and water for his bowl by the back door. Away from home, liberated from my responsibility for meals, my unexecuted calculations steal into my dreams like engine run-on and leave me blithering with this diminished store of nurture and the fact of my unpreparedness. Such a small dream crisis, but I always wake with a sense of terror.

Since *My Thyme Is Up* was a first novel and since mine was an unknown name, there was very little for me to do in Washington. Mr. Scribano had been afraid this would happen. The television stations weren't interested, and the radio stations avoided novels, my publicist told me, unless they had a "topic" like cancer or child abuse.

I managed to fulfill all my obligations in a mere two hours the morning after my arrival, taking a cab to a bookstore called Politics & Prose, where I signed books for three rather baffled-looking customers and then a few more stock copies, which the staff was kind enough to produce. I handled the whole thing badly, was overly ebullient with the book buyers, too chatty, wanting them to love me as much as they said they loved my book, wanting them for best friends, you would think. ("Please just call me Reta, everyone does.") My hair had come unpinned—this happens only rarely—and was dangling in my hot face. My impulse was to apologize for not being younger and more adorable, like Alicia in my novel, and for not having her bright ingenue voice and manner. I was ashamed of my red pantsuit, catalogue-issue, and wondered if I'd remembered, waking up in the Writer's Suite, to apply deodorant.

From Politics & Prose I took a cab to a store called Pages, where there were no buying customers at all but where the two young proprietors took me for a splendid lunch at an Italian bistro and also insisted on giving me a free copy of my book to leave in the Writer's Suite. I had the afternoon free, a whole afternoon, and nothing to do until the next morning when I was to take my train to Baltimore. Mr. Scribano had warned me I might find touring lonely.

I returned to the hotel, freshened up, and placed my book on the bookshelf. But why had I returned to the hotel? What homing instinct had brought me here when I might be out visiting museums or perhaps taking a tour through the Senate chambers? There was a wide springtime afternoon to fill, and an evening too, since no one had suggested taking me to dinner.

I decided to go shopping in the Georgetown area, having spotted from the taxi a number of tiny boutiques. My daughter Norah's birthday, the first of May, was coming up in a week's time, and she longed to have a beautiful and serious scarf. She had never had a scarf in all her seventeen years, not unless you count the woollen mufflers she wore on the school bus, but since her grade-twelve class trip to Paris, she had been talking about the scarves that every chic Frenchwoman wears as part of her wardrobe. These scarves, so artfully draped, were silk, nothing else would do, and their colours shocked and awakened the dreariest of clothes, the wilted navy blazers that French-women wear or those cheap black cardigans they try to get away with.

I never have time to shop in Orangetown, and, in fact, there would be little available there. But today I had time, plenty of time, and so I put on my low-heeled walking shoes and started out.

Georgetown's boutiques are set amid tiny-fronted houses, impeccably gentrified with shuttered bay windows and framed by minuscule gardens, enchanting to the eye. My own sprawling, untidy house outside Orangetown, if dropped into this landscape, would destroy half a dozen or more of these impeccable brick facades. The placement of flowerpots was ardently pursued here, so caring, so solemn, and the clay pots themselves had been rubbed, I suspected, with sandpaper, to give them a country look.

These boutiques held such a minimum of stock that I wondered how they were able to compete with one another. There

might be six or seven blouses on a rod, a few cashmere pullovers,
a table strewn casually with shells or stones or Art Nouveau
picture frames or racks of antique postcards. A squadron of very
slender saleswomen presided over this spare merchandise, which
they fingered in such a loving way that I suddenly wanted to
buy everything in sight. The scarves—every shop had a good half
dozen—were knotted on dowels, and there was not one that was
not pure silk with hand-rolled edges.

I took my time. I realized I would be able, given enough shopping time, to buy Norah the perfect scarf, not the near-perfect and
certainly not the impulse purchase we usually settled for at home.
She had mentioned wanting something in a bright blue with perhaps some yellow dashes. I would find that very scarf in one of
these many boutiques. The thought of myself as a careful and
deliberate shopper brought me a bolt of happiness. I took a deep
breath and smiled genuinely at the anorexic saleswomen, who
seemed to sense and respond to my new consumer eagerness.
"That's not quite her," I quickly learned to say, and they nodded
with sympathy. Most of them wore scarves themselves around
their angular necks, and I admired, to myself, the intricate
knotting and colours of these scarves. I admired, too, the
women's forthcoming involvement in my mission. "Oh, the scarf
absolutely must be suited to the person," they said, or words
to that effect—as though they knew Norah intimately and
understood that she was a young woman of highly defined tastes
and requirements and biddable spirits that they were anxious
to satisfy.

She wasn't really. She was, Tom and I always used to think, too
easily satisfied and someone who too seldom considered herself
deserving. When she was a very small child, three or four, eating
lunch at the kitchen table, she heard an airplane go overhead and
looked up at me and said, "The pilot doesn't know I'm eating an
egg." She seemed shocked at this perception of loneliness, but
was willing to register the shock calmly so as not to alarm me.
She, the girl she was two years ago, would be grateful for any

scarf I brought her, pleased I had taken the time, but for once I wanted, and had an opportunity to procure, a scarf that would delight her heart.

As I moved from one boutique to the next I began to form a very definite notion of the scarf I wanted for Norah, and began, too, to see how impossible it might be to accomplish this task. The scarf became an idea; it must be brilliant and subdued at the same time, finely made, but with a secure sense of its own shape. A wisp was not what I wanted, not for Norah. Solidity and presence were what I wanted, but in sinuous, ephemeral form. This was what Norah at seventeen, almost eighteen, was owed. She had always been a bravely undemanding child. Once, when she was four or five, she told me how she controlled her bad dreams at night. "I just turn my head around on the pillow," she said matter-of-factly, "and that changes the channel." She performed this act instead of calling out to us or crying; she solved her own nightmares and candidly exposed her original solution— which Tom and I took some comfort in but also, I confess, some amusement. I remember, with shame now, telling this story to friends, over coffee, over dinner, my brave little soldier daughter, controlling her soldierly life.

I seldom wear scarves myself, I can't be bothered, and besides, whatever I put around my neck takes on the configuration of a Girl Guide kerchief, the knot working its way straight to the throat and the points sticking out rather than draping gracefully downward. I am not clever with accessories, I know that about myself, and I am most definitely not a shopper. Although I possess a faltering *faiblesse* for luxury, I have never understood what it is that drives other women to feats of shopping perfection, but now I had a suspicion. It was the desire to please someone fully, even oneself. It seemed to me, in that stupidly innocent time, that my daughter Norah's future happiness now balanced not on acceptance at McGill or the acquisition of a handsome new boyfriend but on the simple ownership of a particular article of apparel, which only I could supply. I had no power over McGill or the boyfriend or, in fact, any real part of her happiness, but I could provide something temporary and necessary: this dream of transformation, this scrap of silk.

And there it was, relaxed over a fat silver hook in what must have been the twentieth shop I entered. The little bell rang; the now-familiar updraft of potpourri rose to my nostrils, and Norah's scarf flowed into view. It was patterned from end to end with rectangles, each subtly out of alignment: blue, yellow, green, and a kind of pleasing violet. And each of these shapes was outlined by a band of black and coloured in roughly as though with an artist's brush. I found its shimmer dazzling and its touch icy and sensuous. Sixty American dollars. Was that all? I whipped out my credit card without a thought. My day had been well spent. Then, looking around, I bought crescent-shaped earrings for Natalie, silver, and a triple-beaded bracelet for Christine. I made all these decisions in one minute. I felt full of intoxicating power.

In the morning I took the train to Baltimore. I couldn't read on the train because of the jolting between one urban landscape and the next. Two men seated in front of me were talking loudly about Christianity, its sad decline, and they ran the words *Jesus Christ* together as though they were some person's first and second name—Mr. Christ, Jesus to the intimates.

In Baltimore, once again, there was little for me to do, but since I was going to see Gwen at lunch, I didn't mind. A young male radio host wearing a black T-shirt and gold chains around his neck asked me how I was going to spend the Offenden Prize money. He also asked what my husband thought of the fact that I'd written a novel. Then I visited the Book Plate (combination café and bookstore) and signed six books, and then, at not quite eleven in the morning, there was nothing more for me to do until it was time to meet Gwen.

I hadn't seen her since the days of our old writing group back in Orangetown, when we met twice monthly to share and "workshop" our writing. Poetry, memoirs, fiction; we brought photocopies of our work to these morning sessions, where over coffee and muffins—this was the early eighties, the great age of muffin—we kindly encouraged each other and offered tentative suggestions, such as "I think you're maybe one draft from being finished" or "Doesn't character X enter the scene a little too late?" These critical crumbs were taken for what they were, the fumblings of amateurs. But when Gwen spoke we listened. Once she thrilled me by saying of something I'd written, "That's a fantastic image, that thing about the whalebone. I wish I'd thought of it myself." Her short stories had actually been published in a number of literary quarterlies, and there had even been one near-mythical sale, years earlier, to *Harper's*. When she moved to Baltimore five years ago to become writer-in-residence for a small women's college, our writers' group fell first into irregularity and then slowly died away.

We'd kept in touch, though, Gwen and I. I wrote ecstatically when I happened to come across a piece of hers in *Three Spoons* that was advertised as being part of a novel-in-progress. She'd used my whalebone metaphor; I couldn't help noticing and, in fact, felt flattered. I knew about that novel of Gwen's—she'd been working on it for years, trying to bring a feminist structure to what was really a straightforward autobiographical account of an early failed marriage. Gwen had made sacrifices for her young student husband, and he had betrayed her with his infidelities. In the late seventies, in the throes of love and anxious to satisfy his every demand, she had had her navel closed by a plastic surgeon because he complained that it smelled "off." This complaint, apparently, had been made only once, a sour, momentary whim, but out of some need to please or punish she became a woman without a navel, left with a flattish indentation in the middle of her belly, and this navel-less state, more than anything, became her symbol of regret and anger. She spoke of erasure, how her relationship to her mother—with whom she was on bad terms anyway—had been erased along with the primal mark of connection. She was looking into navel reconstruction, she'd said in her last e-mail, but the cost was criminal. In the meantime, she'd retaken her unmarried name, Reidman, and had gone back to her full name, Gwendolyn.

She'd changed her style of dress too. I noticed that right away when I saw her seated at the Café Pierre. Her jeans and sweater had been traded in for what looked like large folds of unstitched, unstructured cloth, skirts and overskirts and capes and shawls; it was hard to tell precisely what they were. This cloth wrapping, in a salmon colour, extended to her head, completely covering her hair, and I wondered for an awful moment if she'd been ill, undergoing chemotherapy and suffering hair loss. But no, there was her fresh, healthy, rich face. Instead of a purse she had only a lumpy plastic bag with a supermarket logo. That did seem curious, especially because she put it on the table instead of setting it on the floor as I would have expected. It bounced slightly on the sticky wooden surface, and I remembered that she always carried an apple with her, a paperback or two, and her small bottle of cold-sore medication.

Of course I'd written to her when *My Thyme Is Up* was accepted for publication, and she'd sent back a postcard saying, "Well done, it sounds like a hoot."

I was a little surprised that she hadn't brought a copy for me to sign, and wondered at some point, halfway through my oyster stew, if she'd even read it. The college pays her shamefully, and I know she doesn't have money for new hardcover books. Why hadn't I had Mr. Scribano send her a complimentary copy?

It wasn't until we'd finished our salads and ordered our coffee that I realized she hadn't mentioned the book at all, nor had she congratulated me on the Offenden Prize. But perhaps she didn't know. The notice in the *New York Times* had been tiny. Anyone could have missed it.

It became suddenly important that I let her know about the prize. It was as strong as the need to urinate or swallow. How could I work it into the conversation?—maybe say something about Tom and how he was thinking of putting a new roof on our barn, and that the Offenden money would come in handy. Drop it in casually. Easily done.

"Right!" she said in her hearty, unimpeded voice, letting me know she already knew. "Beginning, middle, end." She grinned then.

She talked about her "stuff," by which she meant her writing. She made it sound like a sack of kapok. There were always little linguistic surprises in her work, but more interesting to me were the bits of the world she brings to what she writes, observations or incongruities or some sideways conjecture. She understood their value. "He likes the fact that my stuff is off-centre and steers a random course," she said of an admirer. Her eyes looked slightly pink at the corners, but it may have been a reflection from the headwrap, which cut a sharp line across her forehead.

She had always claimed she had little imagination, that she wrote out of the material of her own life, but that she was forever on the lookout for what she called putty. By this she meant the arbitrary, the odd, the ordinary, the mucilage of daily life that cements our genuine moments of being. I've seen her do wonderful riffs on buttonholes, for instance, the way they shred over time, especially on cheap clothes. And a brilliant piece on bevelled mirrors, and another on the smell of a certain set of wooden stairs from her childhood, wax and wood and reassuring cleanliness accumulating at the side of the story but not claiming any importance for itself.

She looked sad over her coffee, older than I'd remembered, and I could tell she was disappointed in me for some reason. One can always feel this sense of non-delivery. Every encounter sets us up for success or failure. It occurred to me I might offer Gwen a piece of putty by telling her about the discovery I had made the day before, that shopping was not what I'd thought, that it could become a mission, even an art if one persevered. I had had a shopping item in mind; I had been presented with an unasked-for block of time; it might be possible not only to imagine this artifact but to realize it.

"How many boutiques did you say you went into?" she asked, and I knew I had interested her at last.

"Twenty," I said. "Or thereabouts."

"Incredible."

"But it was worth it. It wasn't when I started out, but it became more and more worth it as the afternoon went on."

"Why?" she asked slowly. I could tell she was trying to twinkle a gram of gratitude at me, but she was closer to crying.

"To see if it existed, this thing I had in mind. This item."

"And it did."

"Yes."

To prove my point I reached into my tote bag and pulled out the pale, puffy boutique bag. I unrolled the pink tissue paper on the table and showed her the scarf.

She lifted it against her face. Tears glinted in her eyes. "It's just that it's so beautiful," she said. And then she said, "Finding it, it's almost as though you made it. You invented it, created it out of your imagination."

I almost cried myself. I hadn't expected anyone to understand how I felt.

I watched her roll the scarf back into the fragile paper. She took her time, tucking in the edges with her fingertips. Then she slipped the parcel into her plastic bag, tears spilling freely now, wetting the pink kernel of her face. "Thank you, darling Reta, thank you. You don't know what you've given me today."

But I did, I did.

But what does it amount to? A scarf, half an ounce of silk, maybe less, floating free in the world, making someone happy, this person or that person, it doesn't matter. I looked at Gwen/ Gwendolyn, my old friend, and then down at my hands, a little garnet ring, a gift from Tom back in the seventies, one week after we met. I thought of my three daughters and my mother-in-law, and my own dead mother with her slack charms and the need she had to relax by painting china. Not one of us was going to get what we wanted. I had suspected this for years, and now I believe that Norah half knows the big female secret of wanting and not getting. Norah, the brave soldier. Imagine someone writing a play called *Death of a Saleswoman*. What a joke. We're so transparently in need of shoring up that we're asking ourselves questions, endlessly, but not nearly sternly enough. The world isn't ready for us yet; it hurts me to say that. We're too soft in our tissues, even you, Danielle Westerman, feminist pioneer, Holocaust survivor, cynic, and genius. Even you, Ms. Reta Winters, with your new old, useless knowledge, your erstwhile charm. We are too kind, too willing—too unwilling too—reaching out blindly with a grasping hand but not knowing how to ask for what we don't even know we want.

Instead

I need to speak further about this problem of women, how they are dismissed and excluded from the most primary of entitlements.

But we've come so far; that's the thinking. So far compared with fifty or a hundred years ago. Well, no, we've arrived at the new millennium and we haven't "arrived" at all. We've been sent over to the side pocket of the snooker table and made to disappear. No one is so blind as not to recognize the power of the strong over the weak and, following that, the likelihood of defeat. It was only last Sunday, I think, that old What's-his-crust was on Channel 2, the *Literary Lights* program, he of the square, bony, well-made head and the transparent ears clasped tight to his skull, and the look of being eighty and impish about it. "Who would you say your major influences were?" he was asked.

"Hmm." This required some careful literary thought, but not too much thought. "Chekhov, definitely," he replied, his face softening to dough. "And Hardy. And, of course, Proust, that goes without saying."

What's the matter with this man? Hasn't he ever heard of Virginia Woolf? Isn't he brave enough to pronounce the names: Danielle Westerman or Iris Murdoch? But of course it's not a matter of bravery in his case; the idea simply does not occur.

But, wait!—here comes the "woman" question, delivered by the rumpled, anxious chairperson, coiffed, suited, sweating, consulting her script with a swift, fearful eye: "What about (pause) women writers? Surely women have reshaped the discourse of our century." "Hmm." More heavy thinking, more doughy pinching of the eyebrow between thumb and forefinger, then he looks with hope into the camera and says, "Now the nineteenth century—there were some interesting women writers back then." Yes, but. The program is over in thirty seconds and he's not about to bring a woman's name to his stately fadeout.

Women have been impeded by their generative responsibility, he might have gone on to say had he been given time or encouragement from the chairperson, or had he been sufficiently embarrassed at drawing such an immense public blank. Women were busy bearing children, busy gathering edible grasses or bulbs. You see, he could have said, his little finger waving, it comes down to biology and destiny. Women have been hampered by their biology. Hampered: such a neutral and disingenuous concept and one that deflects blame.

Emma Allen sent me an e-mail from Newfoundland yesterday. She and her daughter and her widowed daughter-in-law were off to a health spa for the weekend, she wrote, and she was looking forward to being utterly "hampered" for a change.

Hampered; obviously a typo, not the kind of linguistic or cultural cross-wiring I sometimes experience when talking to Danielle Westerman, whose volume four memoirs I will eventually be translating. *Traduction* she insists on calling this process, even though she's lived in an English-speaking milieu for forty years now. When am I going to be finished with the *traduction* of chapter two, she wants to know. This is the chapter in which she takes a long back view and deals with her ex-husband's insane jealousy following the publication of her first book of poetry, which came out to ravishing reviews in France in 1949. It was titled *L'Île*, and published in Paris by Éditions Grandmont. I found the poems themselves very tricky to translate (poetry is not my specialty), but I was younger then and willing to stretch myself and be endlessly patient about moving words back and forth, singing them out loud under my breath as translators are told to do, attempting to bring the fullness of the poet's intention to the work. The poems were like little toys with moving parts, full of puns and allusions to early feminism, most of which I let fall into a black hole, I'm sorry to say.

We agreed to change the title to *Isolation*. The direct translation, *Island*, didn't quite capture the sense Danielle had at that time in her life of being the only feminist in the world. She also wanted me to change the name of her original publisher, from Éditions Grandmont to Big Mountain Press, on the copyright page. She can be emphatic and stubborn, as everyone knows, but there's sometimes a bead of logic beneath her obduracy. "This is a translation, dear God," she breathed from beneath her bright pink makeup, "why not give those pretentious French *éditeurs* a nice name from the New World, something with a gasp of oxygen and a glossy new liver?"

"Generally," I told her quietly, "it's not good translation practice to alter the names of foreign publishers."

Who makes these rules, she wanted to know, but I could tell she was going to trust my judgment in the long run. Loving life as she does, she has no patience with puritans. She and I have worked together for years now, but even in those early days we'd come to understand each other, dangling our little proposals and resistances gracefully so that they veered away from actual confrontation. We disagree on quotation marks but are in accord when it comes to levels of usage. For instance, she refuses to employ the word *ass* when referring to someone's rear end, and I am with her there. Oh, how the two of us hate that word! Ass, ass, ass. We get along, and there's no reason we shouldn't. We each know, but in slightly separate ways, about the consolation of the right word perfectly used.

We're two women *au fond*—this is how she frequently expresses the intellectual gas that surrounds and binds our separate energies—and each of us is equipped with women's elemental anatomy, women's plumbing and deployment of soft tissue, with women's merciless cycles that bring on surprisingly similar attacks of inquietude. In addition, the two of us share a love for the hard bite of language and a womanish (in my opinion) tolerance for the moments when words go swampy and vague. She knows the importance of rigorous scholarship, and, at the same time, how to keep her intellect uninflated.

But her life is not my life. She's worked harder and been braver because she's had to, and for a long time she hid her political agenda behind a lace of literary conventions. Suddenly, her traditional phase terminated, and she was left with her rucksack of hard questions, some of them aimed straight at me. How do I permit myself to live with a man? she's asked me more than once. She'll never understand how I've come to accept the tyranny of *pénétration*. This word, for some reason, is always pronounced as though it doesn't exist in English. She gives it full front-of-the-mouth fervour, even though she's grown to be quite fond of Tom, and even though she is no stranger to penetration herself— but that was another chapter of her life.

And our three daughters; she knows each of them, and loves them fully, but has no real idea of my investment in their lives, how my body, my consciousness, has never, even for a moment, been separated from them. She worries about Norah's homeless state, phoning me every second day to see whether she's returned. She's even taken a taxi to Norah's corner at Bloor and Bathurst, alighting with a giant basket of fruit and addressing her loudly, as though through a megaphone, calling her foolish and misguided, a stupid girl who is keeping her mother from getting ahead with her work. Norah refused to lift her head, Danielle reported with an exhausted shrug. *Qu'est-ce qu'on peut faire?*

At least Danielle Westerman does not, like many of my acquaintances, refer to Norah's behaviour as a "developmental stage." She believes that Norah has simply succumbed to the traditional refuge of women without power: she has accepted in its stead complete powerlessness, total passivity, a kind of impotent piety. In doing nothing, she has claimed everything.

"Say that again," I said. And she did.

"Say it in French," I pressed her, wanting to be sure of what she said.

She obliged at once. *"Norah s'était tout simplement laissée aller vers ce refuge traditionnel des femmes qui n'ont aucun pouvoir. Elle avait ainsi fait sienne cette totale impuissance, cette passivité absolue. Ne faisant rien, elle avait revendiqué tout."*

I half agree with her, but belief slips away. I don't want to think Norah is concerned with power or lack of power, not as we usually describe that essence. She's in a demented trance of some kind, and any minute—next week, next month—she'll snap her fingers and bring herself to life again. Yes, yes, says Danielle Westerman, Norah is too intelligent for extravagant fantasy, especially the clever inversion she has devised, claiming her existence by ceasing to exist. Nevertheless she can't understand why I'm not getting on with the translation of her memoirs or why, instead, I'm writing another novel. She has, though she would never confess to it, a deep, almost eighteenth-century suspicion of fiction.

I'm not sure I understand myself why, at such a troubled time, I'm headed off in the frivolous direction of comic fiction. It was Mr. Scribano at Scribano & Lawrence who urged me to get started on another novel. And, difficult as it is to believe, he wasn't thinking of publishing profits to be made in the wake of *Thyme*'s success. *Profit* is not a word that would come out of his distinguished old fleshy mouth. He is a fragment that's drifted away from a lost world that honoured, perhaps too worshipfully, the act of writing. An old-fashioned publisher, an old-fashioned man, he was thinking, instead, that a woman with a disturbed daughter would do well to distract herself with a project that occupies and consumes another plane of existence. "Something airy," he said on the telephone from New York. "Something, dear Mrs. Winters, to take you away from your sadness for an hour a day. Perhaps two hours." And then he said, "The world is hungry for amusement."

I write now in the afternoons, carrying a pot of tea and a mug up to my box room. I am trying to be more disciplined about this. Natalie and Chris have basketball practice after school today. Tom will bring them home around six o'clock. Pet has settled down for a nap in the kitchen sunlight. He loves to lie on his back like a big hairy rug, back legs splayed, front paws neatly folded in, while gazing at you with a coyly wolfish grin. I try to breathe lightly as I climb the stairs, as though a willed quietness in my chest might connect with the points and edges of all I'm attempting to put out of my mind. Then I switch on my computer and get down to work. I have the sense that if I am serious about this business of "being good," this is the only place in the world I can begin, snug in my swivel chair, like a hen on her nest.

I'm not interested, the way some people are, in being sad. I've had a look, and there's nothing down that road. I wouldn't reply, as Anna Karenina does when asked what she's thinking about: "Always about my happiness and my unhappiness." The nakedness of that line of thought leads to a void. No, Ms. Winters of Orangetown much prefers the more calculated protocols of dodging sadness with her deliberate manoeuvres. She has an instinct for missing the call of grief. Scouring the separate degrees of innerness makes her shy. A reviewer writing about *My Thyme Is Up* two years ago charged its author—me—with being "good" at happy moments but inept at the lower end of the keyboard. Well, now! What about the ripping sound behind my eyes, the starchy tearing of fabric, end to end; what about the need I have to curl up my knees when I sleep? Whimpering.

Ordering my own house calms me down, my careful dusting, my polishing. Speculating about other people's lives helps, too. These lives hold a kind of tenancy in my mind, tricking the neural synapses into a grand avoidance of my own sorrow. The examined life has had altogether too much good publicity. Introversion is piercingly dull in its circularity and lack of air. Far more interesting, at least to a fiction writer going through a bad time, is the imaginative life projected onto others. Gwendolyn Reidman in Baltimore has just come out as a lesbian; the news arrived via a note from a bed-and-breakfast place called the Inglenook, and so far I've put off my reply. And there's Emma Allen off with her daughter and daughter-in-law to a spa, where the two younger women will give themselves over to mud wraps and massages and leave Emma, who's forty-four, the same as me, to feel guilty about falling into the vanity trap. Then there is Mrs. McGinn, who whispers her loneliness through the floorboards and who, in all probability, shook her dust mop on the same porch railing I banged on this morning, doing my daily rounds. There's the violet late-afternoon autumn transparency entering the box room from the skylight, precise and square, and the creak of ancient tree trunks bending in the gusty October wind. Up here, on the third floor of the house, my senses sharpen and connect me with that other Reta, young Reta, not really so far away.

There's my dead mother, who taught me French and also thrift. Every day her image rises up in one form or another, brushing against me with a word or gesture or sometimes the remembrance of a simple recipe: *mousse au citron,* Chantilly cream. *Doucement, doucement,* I hear her say; use the fork and only the fork, be gentle, be patient. Who else? There's Lois, my still-living but silent mother-in-law, and this is a silence I must deal with soon, or get Tom to deal with. And, of course, there is the immense, hovering presence of Danielle Westerman with her European-based culture, her thin, distinguished chin, her boxy knuckles and long crimson nails. Would Danielle approve? I scarcely ever budge from my habitual stances or perspectives without causing that stern question to flap against my ear. Last week I disappointed her by using the word *veggies.* She had thought better of me, I could tell.

These human mysteries—cleaning my house, fantasizing about the lives of other people—keep me company, keep me alert.

But more than anything else it is the rhythm of typing-and-thinking that soothes me, what is almost an athlete's delight in the piling of clause on clause. Who would have thought this old habit of mine would become a strategy for maintaining a semblance of ongoing life, an unasked-for gift, *une prime*. On days when I don't know which foot to put in front of the other, I can type my way toward becoming a conscious being. Writing a light novel is very much as Mr. Scribano promised: a diversion, a forgiving place with fine air and moisture and attractive people seen through nicely blurred light. I can squeeze my eyes shut, pop through a little door in the wall, and stand outside my child's absence. I can hush the critical voice in my head that weighs serious literature against what is merely entertainment. A quick read. A beach book. Light, lightly. The kind of shallow invention this particular genre demands is as healing as holy oil. "Deep down we're all shallow"—who said that?

The pages of the new manuscript add up quickly, though narrative coherence is in short supply in the early chapters. I've already blocked in the happy ending, but now I have to throw a few hurdles in the way. Roman and Alicia have set the date for their wedding. The invitations have already been mailed to their families and friends, beautifully lettered on rice paper by Alicia herself, who has a gift for calligraphy. But there are complications, and some of these I have yet to work out. I don't want to overburden my people with neuroses; I want to suggest a rumple of complication disturbing their psychic normalcy. Alicia has one or two remaining doubts about marriage to Roman. She's seen the way he gets itchy and feverish when he's around her friend Suzanne. This is her second marriage, after all, and she's been warned that musicians are unstable. Roman plays trombone in the Wychwood Symphony, Wychwood being my fictional city, a self-important, swaggering cousin to Toronto. Alicia has noticed that Roman is inattentive to his personal hygiene, and has to remind herself that his odour of musk was attractive to her in the early days. His forthright chin suggests conceit. When he's in the presence of men who are taller than he is, he becomes faintly obsequious, and touches his mouth rather a lot, like the Mrs. McGinn of my imagination. This is beginning to get on Alicia's nerves, and she's thinking of mentioning it to him. Meanwhile

Suzanne—Suzanne does something, something unpardonable, but finely modulated in its intent. Or perhaps it is Sylvia, the symphony's bassoonist. The details must be worked through.

In all probability Roman is having second thoughts about the marriage, too, but I am not inside Roman's massed angular head. It is Alicia's skin I wear. I see through her woman's eyes, reach with her woman's fingers, stroking the thick and rather sticky wool of Roman's brushed-back hair. Should something be said to him about his brand of hair gel? Soon. And how painstakingly must I describe Alicia's apartment? Fiction demands such pitiless enumeration; I'll try to get away with light wood furniture, tall windows, a palette of sunny colours, and a few pieces of Polish amber scattered here and there just so, catching the natural light. And the matter of cars? This has to be settled. Alicia doesn't own a car; she thinks a car is too expensive to keep in a city like Wychwood. Roman has a car, a Honda Civic, a model from the early nineties. He looks after it beautifully. Just a week ago he replaced the rubber floor mats instead of scrubbing the old ones.

I can deconstruct Alicia's acute feminine sensibility for an hour or more, depending on whether I can keep myself from coasting into a secondary fiction, the compacted imaginative ravellings that collect around the end of each writing hour. A fantasy of mine: Norah is sleeping downstairs in her bedroom. In my mental movie she has come home, exhausted, hitching a ride from Toronto. Every rerun is the same. She appears, suddenly within the protection of our walls. She is slightly feverish with flu, but nothing serious, nothing a few days in bed won't fix. In a few minutes I'll take her some lemon tea. My daughter, my sick daughter. I don't want to wake her, though. Waking a sleeping person seems to me a particularly violent act. This is how political prisoners were tortured in China—or was it Argentina?—with an intricate and automatic alarm system cutting in five minutes after sleep commenced so that the already tormented bodies were shocked by sleep deprivation and whipped with chronic distrust.

No, let her sleep. Punch the delete key. I must get back to

Roman and Alicia, my two lost children, and their separate branches of selfishness.

Tom often speaks about the oddness of trilobite evolution. No one knows a thing about the trilobite brain or even how they reproduced sexually. All the beautiful soft-tissue evidence has rotted away, leaving only the calcium shell. But it is known that most trilobites developed huge and complex eyes on the sides of their slick heads. The fossil remains are clear, right down to the smallest lens. All trilobites possessed eyes, except for one species which is blind. In this case the blindness is thought to have been a step forward in evolution, since these eyeless creatures lived in the mud at the bottom of a deep body of water. It seems that nature favours getting rid of unused apparatus. The blind trilobites were lightened of their biological load, their marvellous ophthalmic radar, and they thrived in the darkness. When I think of this uncanny adaptation, I wonder why I can't adapt too. All I wanted was for Norah to be happy; all I wanted was everything. Instead I've come to rest on the lake bottom, stuck there in the thick mud, squirming, and longing to have my eyes taken away.

Two years ago, off to Washington for a book tour, I was an innocent person, a mother worried about nothing more serious than whether her oldest daughter would qualify for McGill and whether she would find a boyfriend. The radio host in Baltimore asked me—he must have been desperate—what was the worst thing that had ever happened to me. That stopped me short. I couldn't think of the worst thing. I told him that whatever it was, it hadn't happened yet. I knew, though, at that moment, what the nature of the "worst thing" would be, that it would be socketed somehow into the lives of my children.

Thus

"Goodness is an abstraction," Lynn Kelly said last Tuesday when the four of us met for coffee. "It's an imaginative construct representing the general will of a defined group of people." As always she speaks with authority, using her strong Welsh accent to crispen each word. "Goodness is a luxury for the fortunate." As always we occupied the window table at the Orange Blossom Tea Room on Main Street. Only once or twice have we arrived to find someone already at "our" table, which is why, years ago, we decided to assemble at nine-thirty sharp. By ten the place is packed.

"'Goodness but not greatness,'" I said to Annette and Sally and Lynn, quoting from Danielle Westerman's memoirs.

Whenever, and for whatever reason, those famous words fall into my vision, I feel my breath stuck in my chest like an eel I've swallowed whole.

"How can she go on living her life knowing what she knows, that women are excluded from greatness, and most of the bloody time they choose to be excluded?"

"Going on their little tiny trips instead of striking out on voyages."

"The voyage out, yes."

"After all Danielle's efforts to bring about change." From Lynn. "She's still not included in the canon."

"Except in the women's canon."

"Inclusion isn't enough. Women have to be listened to and understood."

"Men aren't interested in women's lives," Lynn said. "I've asked Herb. I've really pressed him on this. He loves me, but, no, he really doesn't want to know about the motor in my brain, how I think and how—"

"I've only had a handful of conversations with men," I said. "Other than with Tom."

"I've had about two. Two conversations with men who weren't dying to 'win' the conversation."

"I've never had one," Sally said. "It's as though I lack the moral authority to enter the conversation. I'm outside the circle of good and evil."

"What do you mean?"

"I mean that most of *us* aren't interviewed on the subject of ethical choices. No one consults us. We're not thought capable."

"Maybe we're not," Annette said. "Remember that woman who had a baby in a tree? In Africa, Mozambique, I think. There was a flood. Last year, wasn't it? And there she was, in labour, think of it! While she was up in a tree, hanging on to a branch."

"But does that mean—?"

"All I'm saying," Annette continued, "is, what did we do about that? Such a terrible thing, and did we send money to help the flood victims in Mozambique? Did we transform our shock into goodness, did we do anything that represented the goodness of our feelings? I didn't."

"No," I said. "I didn't do anything."

"Me neither," Sally said. "But we can't extend acts of goodness to every case of—"

"I remember that now," Lynn said slowly. "I remember waking up in the morning and hearing on the radio that a woman had given birth in a tree. And I think the baby lived, didn't it?"

"Yes," Annette said. "The baby lived."

"And remember," Sally said, "that woman who set herself on fire last spring? That was right here in our own country, right in the middle of Toronto."

"In Nathan Phillips Square."

"No, I don't think it was there. It was in front of—"

"She was a Saudi woman, wearing one of those big black veil things. Self-immolation."

"Was she a Saudi? Was that established?"

"A Muslim woman anyway. In traditional dress. They never found out who she was."

"A chador, isn't it?" Annette supplied. "The veil."

"Or a burka."

"Terrible," I said. I was toying with the plastic flowers in the middle of the table. I was observing the dog hairs on my dark blue sleeve.

"She died. Needless to say," Annette said.

"But someone did try to help her. I read about that. Someone tried to beat out the flames. A woman."

"I didn't know that," I said.

"It was in one of the papers."

"And what about that other young woman in Nigeria who got pregnant and was publicly flogged? What did we do for her?"

"I was going to write a letter to the *Star*."

"A lot of people did write, they got quite excited about it—for Canadians, I mean—but she was flogged anyway."

"God, this is a brutal world."

Annette, born and brought up in Jamaica, is a poet and economist, divorced from her husband, who turned violent after his bankruptcy. She lives alone in a tiny cottage-like house in Orangetown, working part-time for a dot-com, shuffling statistics on her screen.

Lynn lives with her mensch of a husband, Herb, and their two children in a sparkling new house on the edge of town. She has a busy law practice, but she still takes off two hours every Tuesday morning to come to coffee.

And Sally is at home for a year with a baby son, born on her fortieth birthday, a miracle baby, a sperm bank success. She used to bring Giles in a backpack thing, but now he's weaned and she gets a Tuesday-morning sitter. She's thought about suing her obstetrician—Lynn advises against it—because he wouldn't let her wear her glasses during the delivery, and so she missed most of what happened. The doctor said it wasn't safe to wear glasses, but she's convinced herself it was a matter of aesthetics, that she and her "eyewear" disturbed his painterly vision of what the Birth of a Child should look like.

The four of us have been meeting like this for ten years now. We order cappuccinos; three out of four of us ask for decaf. Once in a while we order a scone or a croissant.

We don't have a name; we're not a club; there's no agenda. We prefer not to think of ourselves as holders of opinions, that is, we do not "hold forth" on our opinions, because such opinions are arbitrary and manufactured in an unreal world with only fifty per cent participation. We know almost everything there is to know about each other. We talk about all kinds of topics, although we don't talk about our sex lives—I think we avoid this subject out of a very old taboo, the need to protect others. Nor do we do much cooing over children because of Annette, who doesn't have any. If Annette happens to be travelling, as she sometimes does, Sally, Lynn, and I get in our kid stuff then. Sometimes we drop in gender discoveries: the fact that men like wind but women don't very much, they find it worrying. The observation that men won't, if they can help it, sit in the middle seat of a sofa, but women don't seem to care. In France it's thought that menstruating women are incapable of making a good mayonnaise. No! Surely, not anymore. We discuss the public library crisis, since both Annette and I sit on the board. Has our old friend Gwen, now Gwendolyn Reidman, always been a lesbian or is this a discovery of her middle age? And will Cheryl Patterson, the librarian, marry Sam Sondhi, the dentist out at the mall? Art is a courtship device, Annette says, at least poetry is. We wonder if the innocence we are born with is real, and try to imagine a case in which it isn't destined to be obliterated. What then?

Tom has asked me once or twice what it is we talk about on Tuesday mornings, but I just shake my head. It's too rich to describe, and too uneven. Chit-chat, some people call it. We talk about our bodies, our vanities, our dearest desires. Of course the three of them know all about Norah being on the street; they comfort me and offer concern. A phase, Annette believes. A breakdown, thinks Sally. Lynn is certain the cause is physiological, glandular, hormonal. They all tell me that I must not take Norah's dereliction as a sign of my own failure as a mother, and this, though I haven't acknowledged it before, is a profound and always lurking fear. More than a fear—I believe it. They tell me it's all right to be angry with Norah for giving up, but I can't seem to find the energy for anger.

We know what we look like: four women in early middle age, hunched over a table in a small-town coffee shop, leaning forward, all of us, the way women do when they want to catch every word. Two years ago when I went to New York to receive the Offenden Prize, the three of them gave me a send-off gift of purple underpants in real silk. I wore these to the ceremony under my white wool suit, and all evening, every time I took a step this way or that, shaking hands and saying "Thank you for coming" and "Isn't this astonishing," I felt the rub of silk between my legs, and thought how fortunate I was to have such fine, loving friends. Lynn, coming from Wales, calls underpants knickers, and now we all do. We love the sound of it.

I have been careful to give Alicia a few friends. It's curious how friends get left out of novels, but I can see how it happens. Blame it on Hemingway, blame it on Conrad, blame even Edith Wharton, but the modernist tradition has set the individual, the conflicted self, up against the world. Parents (loving or negligent) are admitted to fiction, and siblings (weak, envious, self-destructive) have a role. But the non-presence of friends is almost a convention—there seems no room for friends in a narrative already cluttered with event and the tortuous vibrations of the inner person. Nevertheless, I like to sketch in a few friends, in the hope they will provide a release from a profound novelistic isolation that might otherwise ring hollow and smell suspicious.

Alicia's best friend is Linda McBeth. Linda, an art consultant who toils at the same magazine where Alicia works, had a role in *My Thyme Is Up*, and so she also appears in the sequel. The two women have side-by-side cubicles at work, and they go together to a yoga class every Thursday night, and then out for a drink. They talk and talk and sometimes get a little drunk. Linda has a weight problem. She has a man problem too, a lack-of-man problem, that is. She requires Alicia to reinforce her self-confidence. But she's funny, gifted at her work, and highly perceptive when it comes to other people. "I don't know about Roman," she says to Alicia at one point. "He's such a great guy, but sometimes he comes on just the tiniest bit kingly."

"You mean sitting-on-a-throne kind of kingly?" Alicia asked.

"Yes," Linda said. "He always seems to be sort of surveying his vast domain, if you know what I mean. And looking over the heads of his subjects, who are bowing down before him."

"Hmm," said Alicia. "Yes."

Roman has a good friend too, I've seen to that. Michael Hammish will be best man at Roman and Alicia's wedding, which is coming up soon, unless I do something quickly to prevent it. He was Roman's roommate at Princeton, a slightly menacing stockbroker and weekend soccer player, married to the demure blonde Gretchen, who does publicity for the Wychwood Dance Company. Michael Hammish, who has hamlike thighs and big square mannish knees, has taken Roman aside and warned him about this marriage he's about to enter. "If there's anything you want to do, do it now, Roman, because once you're married you haven't a hope in hell, even married to a great woman like Alicia. Things get in the way, couple-type things. You'll see. It happens all the time, it's even happened to Gretch and me to a certain extent. But you've got a chance to think this over. You've been wanting for months to find out where your family comes from. I've noticed, I've taken note of it. Albania, Albania, that's all you talk about. Take my advice, pal, and do it now. You won't be getting another chance."

Yet

Norah was accepted at McGill back in 1998. Of course she was, with her marks. There had never been any doubt about it. Our foolish worries were only a test of our certainty. The letter of acceptance glowed with welcome. But by then "the boyfriend" had come along, a twenty-two-year-old named Ben Abbot who was a second-year philosophy student at the University of Toronto. Of course that changed everything. She cancelled McGill, enrolled at Toronto, moved into a basement apartment off Bathurst with Ben, and opted for a major in modern languages. Good girl. After her mother's heart.

But I worried: because she wasn't under our roof any longer, like Natalie and Christine, and because I didn't know if she was having a decent breakfast in the mornings and because she was having sex all the time with a person who had been a stranger a short while ago and who now was intimate with every portion of her body; just thinking of this brought on a siege of panic. First they were together a month, then six months, then a year, then a year and a half. I was beginning to get used to it. But not really, not completely. I recognized that I was one of those mothers who has difficulty with her child's becoming a woman.

Almost through her second year, the first day of April, she was home for a weekend, drinking a cup of coffee at the kitchen table while I, snug in my warmest robe, stirred up some eggs for breakfast. The kitchen in this ancient house is exceptionally airy and bright, and I was reminded of all the mornings of Norah's childhood when she sat here at the window overlooking the bare brown winter woods, eating her buttered toast and chattering about the day ahead. She had been wakened in those days with a buzz from her own small wind-up alarm clock, a gift for her tenth birthday, something she had particularly asked for. Being woken by an alarm clock one has set for oneself was a sign of maturity, she believed, and she was anxious, perhaps, as the oldest child in the family, the big sister of Natalie and Christine, about maturity—what it meant and how she could get there fast. More important than being good and pleasing and adorable was the wish, early in her life, to be mature. That little plastic clock became a part of her perpetualism, a doctrine, as in the Church, of everlastingness. She took it with her to camp as a child, and then she carried it back and forth in her backpack to the basement apartment in Toronto where she and her boyfriend lived. Had she set the alarm last night?

Yes, probably she had, even just coming home to Orangetown for the weekend—and here she was, awake—while Tom and the other girls were barely stirring upstairs. No one asked her to be this intense; no such demands were ever made on her by anyone other than herself.

I enjoyed having company in the kitchen in the early morning. I loved her sleepy, yawning, mussed look, merging with what I thought of as the careless use of herself in the world—the untidy Bathurst apartment, Ben, the passion for Flaubert—all of which I would never understand completely because it was unhinged from my own frame of time, the sixties child, the nineties child. For the moment, though, she was home; I had her to myself. She was wearing one of my cast-off robes that zipped up the front, that awful burgundy colour, her body lending grace to the awkward lines. But I was suddenly alerted to something about her presence: the fact that her face looked oddly fallen. Her eyes were swollen, filled, though not with tears. What I glimpsed there was something hard, fixed, chitinous. What was it? "We are real only in our moments of recognition"—who said that? I was recognizing something now. I put on my reading glasses and looked at my daughter again, closely. I made her turn toward the window so that the light fell across her eyes and on her hard little upper lip. She blinked at last, then closed her eyes against the light and against me.

"Is it Ben?"

"Partly."

"You don't love him the way you did."

"I do. And I don't. Don't enough."

"What do you mean, not enough?"

She shrugged and made a grab for my waistline, just hooked her thumb over the belt of my robe and hung on, with her forehead pressed into my stomach. I would give anything to have that moment back.

"Try to explain," I said.

"I can't love anyone enough."

"Why not?"

"I love the world more." She was sobbing now.

"What do you mean, the world?"

"All of it. Existence."

"You mean," I said, knowing this would sound stupid, "like mountains and oceans and trees and things?"

"All those things. But the other things too."

I had eased myself into a chair and was massaging the tender place between her shoulder blades. My thumb fit there perfectly, doing its little circular motion. I had no way of knowing this would be her last visit home, that she was about to disappear. "Go on."

"There's literature," she said. "And language. Well, you know. And branches of languages and dead languages and forgotten dead languages. And Matisse. And Hamlet. It's all so big, and I love all of it."

"But what—?"

"And whole continents. India. Especially those places like India that I've never seen. Every little trail running off every hidden dirt road branching off from every major trade route. The shrubbery, the footpaths. The little town squares. There must be millions of town squares. I'll never see them all, so what is the point?"

"You could spend a year travelling, you know, Norah." I could hear Natalie and Christine moving about upstairs, shouting from bedroom to bedroom, tuning a radio to the local rock station.

"And the tides," Norah said. "Think of the tides. They never forget to come and go. The earth tipping in space. Hardly anyone understands them."

"Has Ben moved out?"

"No."

"What, then?"

"I don't know."

"Where are you living?"

"I'm still there. For the time being. But I'm thinking about going on my own."

"Your classes. Your spring courses. What about them?"

"What about them?"

"You've dropped out of university." I couldn't believe this thought that popped into my head so suddenly and had to say it again. "You've dropped out of university."

"I'm thinking about it. About not taking my exams."

"Why?"

"It's just—you know—sort of pointless."

"What about your scholarship?"

"I don't need any money. That's what's so astonishing. I can give up my scholarship—"

"Does Ben know what you're thinking of?"

"Moving out or not taking exams?"

"Both."

"No."

"You don't intend to tell him."

"No."

"Will you talk to your father?"

"God, no."

"Please, Norah. He went through some—some phases—when he was younger. Way back. Please talk to him."

"No. I can't."

"Please, Norah."

"All right."

Injury, when it comes, arrives from so many different directions that I don't even attempt to track it. News from Indonesia or Jerusalem, Bush heating up for the election, breakthrough advances in cancer research—none of this had anything to do with this beautiful first daughter of mine with her light, fine hair, who was good, who was clever, who spoke in a low musical voice unusual for her age, who was living obediently and reading Flaubert and provoking no one who might do her damage.

I felt the kitchen walls swell outward, everything curved as in a TV cartoon, and then shrink inward, pressing against the two of us. "You do realize this is serious," I said to her. "You are in a serious psychological state and you need help. It is very likely that you are depressed. It may be you have some mineral or vitamin deficiency, something as simple as that."

"It's not one big thing. I know that much. It's a lot of little things. I'm trying to get past the little things, but I can't."

"Norah," I tried. "The world often seems to be withholding something from us. We all feel that way at times, but especially at your age. You have to face up to it—"

"But that's exactly what I want to do. I'm trying to face up to it. But it's too big."

"Has something happened, something you haven't told us about?"

"No. It's just—everything."

I heard myself shouting into her face, making a rough knothole in the centre of the world, rude and out of control. "You have to talk to your father today," I told her. "Today."

"I said all right."

"But you must talk to someone else as well. Someone in the counselling area. Today."

Did I really say that: "in the counselling area"? No wonder she stared at me.

"It's Sunday," she said.

"We'll go to the hospital. Emergency will be open."

"It's not an emergency."

"Norah, you need help."

"I'm trying to find where I fit in."

She held on to me desperately then. I was thinking quickly. Drugs. Some awful mix-up with drugs. Or a cult. I tried to picture cult members I'd seen hanging around the university, grey robes, sandals. Or those awful born-again Christians who won't let women wear makeup and cut off their hair if they talk back. I stared at Norah's mouth: no lipstick. But, no, it was breakfast time; no one would be wearing makeup at this hour. Still, there had to be some perfectly logical explanation if I could just think my way through to it. Something had scrolled backward in her consciousness, giving her a naked naïveté about life, that it can be brought to a state of perfection, though we know this can never happen. Or maybe it was a temporary imbalance of the inner ear. I'd read about that recently. Mononucleosis, the old bugaboo, the particular enemy of students; people used to think it was passed around by kissing. Or maybe a brain tumour, massive but not inoperable. A misalignment in the spine, which would require the merest adjustment by an expert in Boston—we could fly down there in less than two hours, a breeze.

These were sensible ideas, examples of the kind of sideways thinking I've learned from Tom. My heartbeat, though, kept drilling straight through my calm speculations. I knew. Right away I knew this was the beginning of sorrow. In fact, it must have been less than an hour later that Norah left the house, just slipped out the front door with her orange backpack, hitching a ride, probably, into Toronto. I couldn't believe she left without saying goodbye. I looked all over the house for her and for her things. No one. Nothing. Then I knew how wildly out of control she was, how she'd become dangerous to her own being. She was lost.

Lost. A part of my consciousness opened like the separation of a cloud onto scenes of abrupt absence. Sunlight fell with a thud on streets that Norah would never walk down, the stupid, dumb, dead sun. Her birthdays would go on without her, the first of May, ten years from now, or twenty. Somehow she had encountered a surfeit of what the world offered, and had taken an overdose she is not going to be able to survive.

Or else not a surfeit, but its opposite, as Danielle Westerman seems to understand. A trick of perception may have fooled Norah into believing that life is too full to be embraced and too beautiful to bear. But the truth is something very different, and I am trying to figure out what that truth might be. Sometimes I am close to knowing.

Other times I feel I'm just another anxious mother who quarrelled with her daughter, a daughter who was merely depressed, fed up at the end of a long winter and probably worried about her first love affair going stale. I've overreacted, that's all. And projected my own fears and panics onto Norah. What evidence do I have? None. She will be fine in a few days, home again, feeling a little foolish and apologetic.

I go back and forth between complacency and worry. No one gets through this time of life unruffled. It's impossible. On the other hand, I remember the look in her eyes as she sat at the kitchen table, and my thoughts become more and more reckless. It sometimes occurs to me that there is for Norah not too much but too little; a gaping absence, a near-starvation. There is a bounteous feast going on, with music and richness and arabesques of language, but she has not been invited. She is seeing it for the first time, but now she will never be able to shake it from view. A deterioration has occurred to the fabric of the world, the world that does not belong to her as she has been told. Again and again and again. She is prohibited from entering. From now on life will seem less and less like life.

No, I am not ready yet to believe this.

Insofar As

October 8, 2000

Dear Sirs:

I was feeling more than usually depressed last night over personal matters and I happened to be sitting in a big armchair skimming through the latest issue of your magazine, which my spouse thoughtfully picked up for me at the local Mags & Fags. (We don't subscribe, because we already feel there is too much paper flowing into our house, and we do try to be good citizens and only take the occasional nick off the planet.)

I couldn't help noticing that you have sold one of your very expensive advertising pages to what appears to be a faux institution of some kind. The density of the typography and its brown uncurling script are attempting to avoid the usual four-colour commercial blast, but without success. There's actually a lot of hustle on this page. The product, in any case, is Great Minds of the Western Intellectual World: Galileo, Kant, Hegel, Bacon, Newton, Plato, Locke, and Descartes. Small but very authentic-looking engravings of these gentlemen's heads form a tight (let us say *impregnable*) band across the top of the page, and what is suggested is a continuum of learning, a ceaseless conveyor belt of noble thought, extracts of which are recorded, as you explain further down on the page, in eighty-four (84) half-hour lecture tapes, which one may listen to as he [assumed pronoun] walks or jogs or commutes or does the CHORES [my emphasis].

That's a great number of half-hours given over to learning, you will agree, but at least a subscriber will be saved, according to the advertising copy, "years of intense reading and study" and, even worse, "complete withdrawal from active life." You can awaken your mind "without having to quit your job or become a hermit." A hermit! The scholar will be guided in his study by the Faculty; that's Darren (skipping last names), Alan, Dennis, Phillip, Jeremy, Robert, another Robert, Kathleen (Kathleen?), Louis, Mark, and Douglas. My question is: How did Kathleen make it to this race?

I might as well admit that I am troubled these days (and nights) by such questions. I have a nineteen-year-old daughter who is going through a sort of soak of depression—actually her condition has not yet been diagnosed—which a friend of mine suspects is brought about by such offerings as your Great Minds of the WIW, not just your particular October ad, of course, but a long accumulation of shaded brown print and noble brows, reproduced year after year, all of it pressing down insidiously and expressing a callous lack of curiosity about great women's minds, a complete unawareness, in fact.

You will respond to my comments with a long list of rights women have won and you will insist that the playing field is level, but you must see that it is not. I can't be the only one who sees this.

I realize I cannot influence your advertising policy. My only hope is that my daughter, her name is Norah, will not pick up a copy of this magazine, read this page, and understand, as I have for the first time, how casually and completely she is shut out of the universe. I have two other daughters too—Christine, Natalie —and I worry about them both. All the time.

Yours,
Reta Winters
The Hermitage,
Orangetown, Canada

Thereof

There is a problem all fiction writers must face if they want to create unique and substantial characters. Characters, at least those personages who are going to be important to the developing narrative, require context. They can't simply be flung onto the page as though they had metamorphosed from warm mud. Darwin put an end to that. Freud too. Parthenogenesis doesn't work for human beings, not yet and probably never, unless being human becomes something other than what we know. Characters in books need to be supplied with a childhood of some sort, with parents at the very least, sometimes even grandparents. These genealogical antecedents may be dead or lost, in which case they need not be introduced into the ongoing narrative but simply alluded to. Ancient Granddad Barney with his war medals. Grandma Foster and her fixation on bodily functions. The old genetic mutterings press directly or subtly on the contemporary character and how he/she responds to life's vicissitudes. The distinctions may be shaded in with a rub of graphite: WASP or Jewish, old money or new; a novelist must recognize that the gene pool is part of the plot, and that even my spacey, romantic Alicia is a bundle of chromosomes, precisely engineered. Parents influence children, stiffening or weakening their resolve, and no credible novelist is going to reverse that assumption. Even in the most Kafkaesque dreamscape there are certain elements that cannot be subtracted from substance, geography, family, blood. Everyone is someone's child, and a novel, in the crudest of terms, is a story about the destiny of a child. There is always a bank of DNA pressing its claim. The question is: How far back does a novelist have to go in order to stabilize a character and achieve solidity?

In my view, it's not necessary to provide a complete genealogical chart; hardly any contemporary readers have the patience for that heft of information. Only a few vital family traces are required, the sense that the character isn't self-invented or arbitrary. Jane Austen, even though she is pre-Darwinian, always goes back at least one generation, and sometimes two. She knew the importance of grounding.

I am working on my sequel to *My Thyme Is Up* (which I am titling *Thyme in Bloom,* reserving *Autumn Thyme* in the event I decide to go for a trilogy) and am struggling with how much hereditary infill I need to secure Alicia and Roman in time. I've gone for simplicity—and symmetry: each of them is the only child of loving parents. Alicia's family is medium wealthy; Roman's is second-generation Albanian working class but on the way up (all the men have heads of thickly woven hair; the women are sharp-voiced, sexy). At first I was going to have their parents all dead, but now I want them involved in the wedding preparations, and also taking part in a farcical restaurant scene when they come together for the first time. Alicia's father (lawyer? No, I've already got him down in *My Thyme Is Up* as a mechanical engineer, too bad) cannot believe there is a single man anywhere on earth worthy of his darling daughter. Just hearing of possible suitors, he offers an angry, offended face and some highly specialized grunts of disapproval. Meanwhile, Roman's mother (a futurist, a top-drawer futurist, working for a think-tank in the middle of Wychwood) announces that no living woman is capable of appreciating her sweet boy. She smiles, but slyly, lips pressed tight. Her sturdy cheerfulness repudiates any real feeling. Secretly she believes that the pursuit of happiness is a selfish act, something only children can take seriously. Children, in her opinion, are untamed savages waiting to be shaped by civilizing hands.

I didn't know Tom as a child, and this has always seemed

an incalculable loss. As an adult he is patient and preoccupied, a somewhat melancholy hedonist, also on occasion barbed, twitchy, and dishevelled; as a medical student in the seventies he was outrageous and was twice arrested for political demonstrations and, in partnership with his classmates, jailed for bandaging up the statues of esteemed Canadian heroes around Queen's Park, putting splints on former prime ministers and blood-coloured paint on their muscular bronze chests. But what was he really like, that skinny kid running out into the yard after dinner with a football tucked under his arm, the screen door banging after him, the grass growing green and long-shadowed and in autumn dotted with wet yellow leaves? This imagined scene speaks of security and wood smoke and encrusted sunlight, and oh, I think, those swarming, uncaptured moments were stolen from me, snatched away by a mismatch of the primal timeline.

But it's not just Tom; my own childhood is missing the same kind of specific content. "The trouble with children," Danielle Westerman once said, "is that they aren't interested in childhood" ("Autoreflections," private interview, 1977). Yes, and when they do finally develop sufficient curiosity, it's too late. (She rejects entirely her childhood at La Roche-Vineuse, her father, her mother. Both of them neglected their only child, she confesses. But there must be more to it than that, I suspect, something sharper and more hurtful and sudden.)

Most of what I remember from the early years is my own appalling ignorance. A partial view of the world was handed to me, a row of houses in the Kingsway area of Toronto, and the rest I had to pretend to know. Like all children, I was obliged to stagger from one faulty recognition to the next, always about to stumble into shame. It isn't what we know but what we don't know that does us in. Blushing and flushing, shuffling and stuttering—these are surface expressions of a deeper pain. The shame of ignorance is killing. "I nearly died," grown-ups say of their early dumb misunderstandings, and they mean that the revealing of their ignorance feels like a stoppage of the heart.

At least this is how I, Reta Winters (née Summers), felt as a child, rummaging through an even younger child's mind and seeing nothing but a swirl of images before words and grammar arrived, a sort of fingerpainting, wet and vivid smears of colour that signalled, mostly, danger. I recognized from the beginning that I was unhinged from what I assumed everyone else in the world knew. I was obliged to regulate the world, but in secret. Why was the sky blue if you looked up but not when you looked at it sideways? What if the moon fell down into our garden or, worse, onto the roof? These questions, more like miracles in their phenomenological shapes, gathered around me and formed the oxygen I breathed, and what they whispered to me was: You will very possibly be killed because of your ignorance. It could happen at any moment.

Someone entered our garden, when I was a child, and carried away every blossom from my mother's three hydrangea bushes. My mother took this assault with remarkable good humour, as though she didn't know the real danger we were in. I knew, though. I knew our family had been chosen and that the missing flowers signified a greater evil and a part of a larger design, which might ultimately lead to death, but I was unable to turn my fears into words, since I knew at a completely other level that I was being ridiculous.

Such gaps of comprehension, such incompletions, had to be lived with silently—that seemed the natural law. A child is suspended in a locked closet of unknowing, within the body's borders, that dark place. To name a perplexity is to magnify it. At the same time—I recognized the calumny for what it is—children's natural observations are often thought to be whimsical, even adorable, and their sayings, their mild queries, much quoted and smiled over, but there is no guarantee of an answer. Why do children risk disclosure at all? It must be out of desperation or unsupportable fear. It's a wonder they don't throw themselves out of windows in fits of confusion.

Our sunny daughter Norah teased us with curious notions.

Voices talking in her head, she said. All the time. But we understood at once that this meant nothing, only that she had become conscious of the lifelong dialogue that goes on in a person's head, the longest conversation any of us has. Oh hello, it's me again. And again. The most interesting conversation we'll ever know, and the most circular and repetitive and insane. Please, not that woman again! Doesn't she ever shut up? (This is why I read novels: so I can escape my own unrelenting monologue.)

I suspect that little Reta Summers was slower than most in accepting the unknotting of earthly matter and manifestation, or else she was more afraid of ridicule. I tried to puzzle things out for myself. There was a war, for instance, and everyone talked about it, how awful it was with people getting killed, even babies, who were horribly burned. But what was a war exactly? What was napalm? How far away was Vietnam? No one told me, but I figured out it must be in the lane behind the Bloor Street delicatessen because I'd once heard loud noises coming from the store's back wall. I cried when I was taken to this place, even though my mother and father were holding my hand. They didn't ask me why I was crying. Probably they thought I was scared of Mr. Hopkins, who had a moustache and cut meat with a black blade as long as his arm.

I understood that people had two names or sometimes three. I was really Reta Ruth Summers. Before I went to school I'd learned to recite my address, 555 Strath Avenue, and my telephone number, and everyone thought this was amazing for a child of my age. Once in a while I was allowed to hold the phone up to my ear and talk to Grandma or Aunt Judy. "But Aunt Judy isn't a real aunt," my mother told me carefully. I knew what real meant. You could touch it or see it, it wasn't made up like the stories I invented.

The angels are moving their furniture, they said when the thunder roared on a summer night; *Le tonnerre,* my mother whispered dramatically, making her eyes big and letting me know this was a splendid thing, nothing to be frightened of. But the angel part was nonsense. Even they knew it was nonsense, the way their lips came together as they said the words, confessing that they loved their own piece of whimsy dearly, but I must have loved it too when I think of the way I swallowed down its easy comfort.

My mother always spoke to me in French and my father in English, and I was allowed to reply in either language. This was part of a pact the two of them had made before my birth, that any child of theirs would grow up in two languages, and that they would share responsibility for this plan. My mother, a *pure laine* Marteau from Montreal, spoke a musical French, and my father a crisp Edinburghian English, only slightly eroded by his years in Canada.

Oddly, the epic confusion of my early years was not caused but rather mitigated by immersion in two languages; doubleness clarified the world; *la chaise,* chair; *le rideau,* curtain; *être,* to be; *le chien,* dog. Every object, every action, had an echo, an explanation. Meaning had two feet, two dependable etymological stems. I swam in English, a relaxed backstroke, but stood up to my hips in French. The French-English dictionary with its thready blue cover was our family bible, since we were a family unattached to formal religious practice.

Nevertheless, they taught me to say a prayer at bedtime. "Dear Jesus, bless Mummy and Daddy and Grandma and the two grandpas and Aunt Judy and make me a good girl." What I knew of Jesus I plucked from the air. Jesus was invisible, but he could hear everything I thought or said. He could see me even when I sat on the toilet, which was humiliating. He was like God but not as old as God. He didn't stop loving me when I was bad, not that I believed this for a moment. He wore a brown gown and liked to have kids climbing on his lap. He wasn't invisible then. Nails were driven through his hands and feet; I couldn't bear to think of that, the tearing of flesh.

I learned to say the prayer perfectly. "The way she enunciates!" my father, the lapsed Presbyterian, said, his voice full of warm minerals. This was a mere trick, and I'd learned how to do it, and in so doing I had made them love me even more. "Isn't she the clever one," they said, and every time they said it, it was as if they handed me a flower. *Bien douée,* said my mother, who had not been inside a Catholic church since her marriage. I remember how she shook her head with wonder, the proud young mother, the way she stood so buoyantly on the front porch in her lime-coloured pedal-pushers and squeaky Mexican sandals—there is a word for those woven leather shoes: huaraches. She loved her early married life, her little mock-Elizabethan Toronto house and rectangular patch of garden, and that period of time before she became discouraged.

From my mother I developed my love of flowers. Their shapes came folded inside tiny seeds, so small that fifty of them filled the bottom of a flat seed packet. They were miraculously encoded from the beginning, little specks of dark matter that we shook into our hands, then sowed into flower beds. They sprouted, then opened out in a studied and careful program of increments. Now, that was astonishing, all those compressed unfoldings and burstings, but no one said so. No one made a fuss when the seeds actually performed: sprouts, leaves, the long rivery stems, and finally the intricacy of blossoms. I liked to tear the silk of the petals between my fingers, rubbing the pollen into my hands. "But that isn't nice, Reta," my mother said. "Why would you want to hurt a beautiful flower?" I didn't believe this, that flowers hurt, but nevertheless I didn't do it again. I was the inept child searching for those moments of calm when I would find adult validation or at least respite from my endless uncertainty.

I once scratched the banister with a spoon. My mother rubbed it with butter, and the scratch went away. She had no idea I had done it, her little girl wouldn't do a thing like that. With great good nature they laughed when I said eggshells were made of plastic, and also when I asked my father if we could buy some icicles to hang from our roof. Our neighbours, the McAndrews, had icicles, long sculptured fingers of silvery ice that lasted all winter. "Our little Reta," they said, laughing. "Our little one." I was afraid of drowning in their approbation. There was nothing hard to hang on to. Any minute I would lose my balance and then I wouldn't be little Reta anymore. Like Norah, I wouldn't be anything.

I had no siblings, but I closely observed small babies who entered our house, the children of my parents' friends. There they lay, tiny, bundled, smelling like spoiled milk, wound tight in fleece blankets. From the beginning I saw that they possessed a patient evenness of curiosity that reduced and simplified the mysteries thronging our household. They didn't worry as I did about the halo around the head of the baby Jesus, what it was made of, what kept it hovering over his head and travelling along with him wherever he went. They put their small hands on the plastic-ribbed face of the radio in the kitchen and laughed at the vibrations that poured out. I could see that they accepted simple electrical transmission for what it was, whereas I had special knowledge available to me: I knew there were little people living inside the radio's shell, the obliging citizens of a miniature village that clung to a steep dark mountain. No one else knew this, and there was no one I trusted enough to tell.

It wasn't neglect that spawned the ignorance I was captive to. Adults were too busy to deliver complicated explanations. In fact, it was partly the busyness of my parents that frightened me, the frantic responsibility that preoccupied them. Their job was to keep us alive. It never occurred to them that I worried about the fact that I could see through my nose when I looked to the left or right, straight through, except for the fleshly blurred outline. And certainly neither of them stopped to express their own bafflement about the universe they inhabited, that they too might be swamped by barely grasped concepts. My slender, long-legged father patrolling the garden, swinging a cigarette in his hand, leaning down to inspect an iris; he possessed a gardener's watchfulness and did not appear to reel with wonder at this serenely formal flower, that its cape and collar opened out of a tightly packed bulb, every part of it predestined and perfectly in place. He was a dealer in early Canadian pine furniture and as a sideline worked as a distresser; that is, he took modern limited editions of books and battered their pages and their boards into decent old age, giving them the tact and smell of history.

The moon followed me. When I staggered, seven years old, across the grass in the backyard, my head thrown back, willing myself to be dizzy, I could see how the moon lurched along with my every step, keeping me company as I advanced toward the peony bed. Why, out of all the people in the world, had I been chosen as the moon's companion? What did this mean? Honour, responsibility, blame, which?

I confided to my friend Charlotte this curious business about the moon. But she insisted that, on the contrary, the moon followed her. So back to back, at the end of the lane we paced off steps, she one way, I the other. Immediately I grasped the fact that the moon followed everyone. This insight came mostly as a relief, only slightly tarnished with disappointment.

Charlotte was the child of a Danish-Canadian family who ran a sign-painting business on Bloor Street. The secret at the centre of her heart was her father's first name: Adolph. Knowing the evil associations of that blunt, harsh Adolph (none of this was clear to me), he went by the name of Chris Christiansen. I promised I would never tell anyone his true name, and I never did. Charlotte had yellow hair, cut squarely, severely. She was exceptionally docile and obedient. Some other, older, child said to me, speaking of Charlotte, that the good die young, and that that would be Charlotte's fate. This was uttered with such authority—nonchalantly, nonchalantly, accepting, accepting—that I believed it absolutely, without any evidence either of Charlotte's essential goodness or of the kind of early death she might expect to be honoured with. Charlotte's goodness and her presumed punishment were entered on the roll of confusion that made up my bank of assumptions, and the problem of goodness—what is it? where does it come from?—occupies me still.

Confusion has kept me from staring back at childhood through drifts of longing. Danielle Westerman says much the same thing in her piece "Sentimentality." She is the other voice in my head, almost always there, sometimes the echo, sometimes the soloist. Who would wish, the renowned Dr. Westerman says, a return to such grunting incomprehension, when, *mon Dieu,* we are all struggling to keep up a brave front, pretending to know how the world works? The fact is, I didn't need to know everything, and no one expected it of me in the first place.

It seems I have a knack for self-forgiveness. This is one of the very few easy comforts still available to me at age forty-four—that there is no need to suffer that degree of guttered fear and ignorance again. I've kept a steady eye on my own growing children, watching for signs of a similar disorientation and hoping I can jump in and rescue them with assurance and knowledge. Norah, of course, has temporarily been lost. She's got my disease, only worse. She's been listening too avidly, too seriously, caring too much, so that harm has come up upon her by surprise. As for Natalie and Chris, they seem, so far, in a state of calm, despite what's happened to their sister. There's an excellent possibility, however, that they're bluffing.

Every

"Thank you for releasing me from your loins," my middle daughter, Christine, said to me today, October twelfth, which happens to be her seventeenth birthday.

Loins. Where had she got a word like loins? "It's from Tom Wolfe's novel," she explained. "It means uterus. Or else womb."

She was standing in the kitchen and eating a breakfast of left-over pizza and washing it down with a mug of apple juice.

"You're welcome," I said, and then, to keep the rhythm of our conversation going, I added, "It was a pleasure."

"You don't mean that," she said. She had exactly two minutes to put on her jacket and run down to the road for the school bus. "Giving birth cannot be filed under one of life's pleasures."

"Well," I said, working for a noncommittal tone, "now how do you know that, Chris? How exactly?" I glanced at the clock over the stove and she watched me glance at the clock and I watched her watching me. Her mouth was stretched with half-chewed pizza crust, her strong, healthy teeth going at it. Not a pretty sight, though I adore this slightly chunky daughter of ours and attempt every day of my life to keep her affectionate and close to us.

"Well, really," she said, exasperated, "I did watch that video on home birth. And so did you. And so did your husband."

Lately, when she speaks of her father, she refers to him not as Dad or Daddy but as my "husband," sometimes my "erstwhile husband," employing an exaggerated, plummy English accent. And when she speaks to him of me, it is always "your wife."

"Your wife has a weakness for chocolate," she told him last night as I scraped up the last of my cake crumbs. "Your wife promised to go over my essay on *Twelfth Night*." "Your wife needs some interesting new shoes to replace those running shoe things she's been wearing for the last hundred years." Tom and I understand that this shift of rhetoric is meant to be ironic, and that our old familial names—Mummy, Daddy—can no longer be produced without a wince of embarrassment.

"So I wanted to thank you," she said, and now she really was putting on her jacket and mitts and moving toward the door. "God! Twenty hours of labour to push me out of your womb." She pronounced it *"womb*ah," giving comic voice to the final *b*.

"Twelve hours."

"You forget."

"Shouldn't I remember? Of all people?"

"You have this thing about revising history," she said. "You and your husband want us to believe we girls arrived in the world without causing too much fuss and bother. Why are you smiling like that?"

"It's that phrase, fuss and bother. It makes me think of your grandmother. Grandma Winters. You know how she always wants to spare the world fuss and bother."

"But demanding it at the same time. Ha!"

Now she really is out the door, flying down the lane. "Anyway," she yelled after me, "thank you."

Two thank-yous in one day. Only this morning, colliding with Natalie, our youngest daughter, in the vicinity of the bathroom door, she had breathed out the words, "Just wanted to thank you for not naming me Ophelia."

"Ophelia!"

"We have this new girl at school, a transfer from Prescott."

"And her name is—"

"Ophelia."

"Now that is"—I looked for the word—"unusual. As a name."

"A ditz name."

"Well, it's not a name everyone would choose." Why am I obliged to bring diplomacy to even the most minor of exchanges? "I suppose they thought it was lyrical," I said. "Her parents, I mean."

"Most of the kids don't know. They don't connect, I mean. We don't do *Hamlet* till next year."

"I don't think I've ever met anyone named—"

"Ophelia? So Mr. Fosdick asked me to look after her for a day or two, give her a tour of the school and introduce her around. Can you picture it?—I'd like you to meet, ahem, Ophelia. And trying to keep a straight face."

I smiled at Natalie, aged fifteen, one eye taking in the delicacy of her jaw, admiring its lovely shape. The other eye, my mother eye, worried: Was she too thin? What forms of knowledge were erupting in her innocent body cells?

"But otherwise you like her. Ophelia, I mean."

"Like her? I suppose so."

"Do you want to invite her home? To dinner? Not today. But, well, tomorrow."

"I guess so. I could ask her."

"Okay."

"Remember Nestia? From grade four? That's a weird name, Nestia. But we were so young, nine years old. We never thought Nestia was odd. We never, like, teased her about it."

I waited a beat before answering. Natalie, of all our children, is the most suggestible, always eager to find an excuse for disaffection. "I guess we learn to live with our names," I said finally.

Now it was her turn to pause. "So you don't mind being called Reta, then?" She clutched tightly to her own effusiveness now that had started in. "I mean, your mother and father did this to you and you were just a baby. Grandma and Papa. They named you Reta."

"It could have been worse."

"At least they could have spelled it right. With an *i*."

"They just liked the sound of it."

"And we went and named our dog Pet. Not very original of us."

"It was Norah who—"

"She was twelve. I remember. She wanted A Pet."

"We called him A Pet for a few days. Then just Pet. Then we got used to it. A generic name. Instead of something embarrassingly literary."

She gave me a look of disdain, and I thought she was going to say: "I've-heard-that-story-a-million-times." But she drew back and smiled thinly. She and Chris are determined not to bring grief, not even a crackle of static, into our pulverized family.

"So I'll ask Ophelia to come tomorrow night, okay? You won't burst out laughing when I introduce her?"

"I promise."

"Okay, then."

When she looks back on her life, when she's a fifty-year-old Natalie, post-menopausal, savvy, sharp, a golf player, a maker of real estate deals, or eighty years old and rickety of bone, confined to a wheelchair—whatever she becomes she'll never remember this exchange between the two of us outside the bathroom door, her embarrassment about a girl with an unfortunate name, and her attempt to challenge me, her mother, about my own name, what it means to me. Her life is building upward and outward, and so is Chris's. They don't know it, but they're in the midst of editing the childhood they want to remember and getting ready to live as we all have to live eventually, without our mothers. Three-quarters of their weight is memory at this point. I have no idea what they'll discard or what they'll decide to retain and embellish, and I have no certainty, either, of their ability to make sustaining choices.

They are trying so hard, Natalie and Chris, to keep the noise of the house alive. It pierces my heart, their little entr'actes, their attempts to amuse or divert Tom and me, to assure us that they are still here, willing to be regulation daughters, to keep up with the daughterly routines, school, friends, family dinners, basketball practice, the swim team. Why is it so reassuring to have children who are part of a school swim team? Because the sight of those sleek wet skins shivering at the edge of the pool and the scent of chlorine clinging to their hair combine to ward off infection.

What the two girls *have* given up is volleyball, which at Orangetown High School takes place on Saturday morning.

Instead, on Saturday morning Tom drives Chris and Natalie into Orangetown before dawn. There the two of them catch the bus into Toronto, disembarking at the old bus station downtown. From there they walk a block to catch the subway to Bloor and Bathurst and they spend the day with Norah on her patch of sidewalk in downtown Toronto, returning to Orangetown in the late afternoon. They've been doing this since we first found out where she was.

The first time, they went without telling us. We were worried to have them gone all day, never mind that they were in their teens. We insisted on an explanation. They were embarrassed, reluctant. "We just sort of thought we'd go see her," Chris said finally.

They take mats to sit on. And blankets, now that the weather's turned. They pack sandwiches, bottles of water, a thermos of tea, a stack of magazines and books, toilet paper and tampons; they've thought of everything. They've ransacked Norah's dresser drawers for socks, underwear, sweaters. They're dying to take Pet, but he's not allowed on the bus. They're convinced that one look at Pet—slobbering and sniffing and wagging his tail—would bring her home. Tom and I are hesitant; we worry about putting pressure on her, about blackmail.

Neither one of us is clear about what the girls do at Bloor and Bathurst for all those long hours. We've only had hints.

"We just hang out," Natalie says.

"We're like visitors," says Chris.

I hold my tongue. To ask too much might unsettle the exceedingly fragile arrangements they've worked out.

Passivity has the capacity to arouse violence, and this is what I worry about mostly, that Norah will not be able to defend herself. I'm deluded enough to believe that Chris's and Natalie's Saturday excursions help to keep her safe, though at a risk to their own safety. I go along with it, the Saturday visitations, and wave the girls off for the day blithely, as though this new routine might succeed, actually rescuing a portion of what's been lost.

The first time they went they threw their arms around her and pleaded and cried.

"She smiled at us," Chris reported. "Just sat there and smiled horribly and said she was happy to see us."

"She stank," Natalie said another time. "Kronk City. They do have showers at the hostel. You'd think she'd remember how to use a shower."

"She doesn't stink," Chris said, anxious to reassure me. "It's just that street smell."

"She doesn't really talk to us," Natalie says.

"At first we sat about ten feet away from her. We didn't want to freak her out."

"As if she isn't already—"

"Now we sit right next to her. Natalie sits on one side and I sit on the other."

"She doesn't mind. She just keeps smiling and people keep giving her money."

"Or not giving her money."

"She gets more money than anyone else on that corner, and there are about four other guys. People just seem to like her, people going by."

"No one gives us money, but then we don't have a board or a sign or anything."

"There was that one man who gave me a dollar. He just sort of dropped it into my lap. But he was weird."

"It gets awfully boring, but she seems to be used to it."

"It's like she's hibernating. Everything about her is slowed down."

"Just sitting, not even reading, not even watching."

"We took her a toothbrush. In case she didn't have one."

"We took her her old peacoat. We just put it down next to her before we left."

"We wrapped it up in a plastic bag."

"We always tell her we'll be back next week. That's the last thing we say to her."

"We don't hug her or anything. It's like she doesn't want us to."

"But she doesn't seem to care one way or another about us being there. It's like she thinks it's our right to be there if we want to be there."

Natalie is sleeping badly. Chris is falling behind in math. But neither of them will admit it. They want to believe, and they want us to believe it too, that nothing more has happened than a detour from "the story thus far." They are co-conspirators in this effort of faith.

For Norah, the story of a childhood won't become human ballast as it will (maybe) for Chris and Natalie, and even for my idiotic two-dimensional pop-fiction airhead, Alicia. Norah seems lodged in childhood's last irresponsible days, stung by the tang of injustice, nineteen years old, with something violent and needful beating in her brain. It's like a soft tumour, but exceptionally aggressive. Its tentacles have entered all the quadrants of her consciousness. This invasion happened fast, when no one was looking.

Regarding

October 17, 2000

Dear Alexander Valkner:

I've been feeling somewhat despondent lately (general malaise, concern over a teenaged daughter, and so on) and it was a relief to come across your long, brilliant piece in a recent issue of *Comment,* namely "The History of Dictionaries." The material felt exceptionally fresh and was set out with vigour and irreverence. I, too, love words and spend my working day chasing after synonyms. Particularly diverting was the way you leapt up and down from the lecturing platform, speaking sometimes with thrilling historical echoes booming from the page and other times whispering like the curly-bearded man who sits in our public library and tries to write novels with a thesaurus at his elbow. From intimacy you travelled to grandeur, then back and forth, like a marvellously controlled metronome. I admired the way your essay builds on itself so meticulously, and the way it is anecdotal, accessible, and, finally, shading toward the confessional. I recognized only too well the moment in which you were tempted to approach some of our great writers to see whether or not they "indulge," keeping a thesaurus hidden in their desk drawer, the equivalent of a mickey of gin. John Updike, Saul Bellow, Richard Ford, Tom Wolfe, Anthony Lane are some of the names you suggested—wouldn't that lot be taken by surprise to be questioned about their dictionary usage or non-usage! Just imagine their abashed scramble to hide the volume from view! And who else?—Calvin Trillin,

William F. Buckley, Robert Lowell, Anthony Burgess, Julian Barnes.

That's quite a list. A high list and also, you will agree, a rather low list. I am sure you realized when you were reading over your proofs that you had neglected to mention Danielle Westerman or Joyce Carol Oates or Alice Munro, but perhaps it was too late by then. I'm sure you felt a tickle at the scalp; a little stick figure shaking a finger at you saying—*something is missing here, Mr. Valkner.* You might have dropped in the name of Sylvia Plath? It's well known that she really did use a thesaurus in the composing of her poetry, which seems rather shocking when you think about it. You don't imagine poets leaping up from their chairs and consulting a mechanical device, which a thesaurus ultimately is.

Perhaps you were tired when you ran through your testicular hit list of literary big cats; trying to even out the numbers may have seemed too much of a reach or too obvious in its political correctness. But did you notice something even more significant: that there is not a single woman mentioned in the whole body of your very long article (16 pages, double columns), not in any context, not once? As though these great literary men came into the world through their own efforts. Bean counting is tiring, and tiresome, but your voice, Mr. Valkner, and your platform (*Comment*) carry great authority. You certainly understand that the women who fall even casually under your influence (mea culpa) are made to serve an apprenticeship in self-denigration.

This will explain my despondency, and why I am burbling out my feelings to you. I am a forty-four-year-old woman who was under the impression that society was moving forward and who carries the memory of a belief in wholeness. Now, suddenly, I see it from the point of view of my nineteen-year-old daughter. We are all trying to figure out what's wrong with Norah. She won't work at a regular job. She's dropped out of university, given up her scholarship. She sits on a curbside and begs. Once a lover of books, she has resigned from the act of reading, and believes she is doing this in the name of goodness. She has no interest in cults, not in cultish beliefs or in that particular patronizing cultish nature of belonging. She's too busy with her project of self-extinction. It's happening very slowly and with much grief, but I'm finally beginning to understand the situation. My daughter Christine grinds her teeth at night, which is a sign of stress. Another daughter, Natalie, chews her nails. Women are forced into the position of complaining and then needing comfort. What Norah wants is to belong to the whole world or at least to have, just for a moment, the taste of the whole world in her mouth. But she can't. So she won't.

Yours,
Renata Winters,
The Orangery, Wychwood City

Hence

My daughter is living like a vagabond on the streets of Toronto, but even so I had to have four yards of screened bark mulch delivered to the house this morning, $141.91, including haulage. The last weeding's done in the garden, and now we'll spread this dark woody-smelling stuff between the shrubs and perennials, raking it as evenly as we can, inhaling the slightly unnatural scent, which is pitched halfway between rot and freshness. By spring it will have worked its way into the soil, all the splintery bits reduced to fine dust.

This thought brings on a metaphor blitz that cracks my head in two, so I get rid of it in my usual way. Think of something else, do something else. Immediately.

I wrote a cheque for the deliveryman, a boy, really, with a fine face and lovely straight teeth. I've been too preoccupied to pay attention to the calendar lately, and I had to ask him to remind me of the date.

"It's my birthday," he beamed. "I'm twenty-eight today."

"That's a good age," I said, for what else really was there to say?

"Yeah, I think so," he agreed. Mr. Amiability. "I'm hoping they'll take me on regular." He nodded in the direction of his truck. "Then I can quit my night job delivering the *National Post* and that'll make it easier to see my girlfriend, who's out in Lake Inlet, and then we can think about getting married and having a family, yeah."

I could see, if I had nodded or smiled, that he would tell me everything, every little wavelet of thought that lapped between his ears and kept him alive. What power I had over him; I could turn him on and off like a radio; it shamed me somewhat. He stood, his arms crossed over his chest, bursting with his life chronicle and the importance of this particular day to him and how much he hoped for—which was really so little, so pathetically little. It wasn't until he was walking back to the truck that I noticed something wrong with his legs; they twisted inward, kneeing together oddly, producing a bounce instead of a smooth stride.

"Have yourself a good one," he called back to me in his outrageously happy voice.

Tom and I spread the mulch late in the afternoon. The clean look of it was pleasing, as though we'd done the earth a good deed. We stopped and observed the tussle of dark and light on the few remaining leaves, and then went together into the warm, orderly kitchen, which seemed like a rebuke of some kind. We had failed in our effort to live our happy life. Never mind our careful arrangements, we were about to be defeated. This despite the sweet burnt-tomato smell of lasagna rising from the oven. Chris was playing the piano in the living room, Mozart, absorbed for once in the music's deepening repetitions. Natalie was sprawled on the floor in front of the TV in jeans. Tom settled down on the chair next to her, and Pet, who willingly serves as a footstool, seemed to be saying: isn't this heaven!—why isn't it like this all the time? They were watching the six-o'clock news, not avidly, not with eagerness, but attentively enough. They were amiable and groggy. Natalie regarded the screen with her where-have-all-the-flowers-gone? look, while Tom actually registered what was being announced. A federal election had been called at the insistence of the prime minister, and this tiny election news, not unexpected, fluttered alongside the immensity of the Gore-Bush dance in the States. "I don't like him anymore," Natalie said lazily from the floor. Jean Chrétien, she means. She spoke with an astringency that was almost asexual. "Pompous. A kronkhead."

Chris in the next room launched into another round of Mozart, knowing that any minute she'd be called to set the dinner table and wanting me to know that she was more usefully employed getting prepared for her lesson tomorrow. I checked the oven and set the table.

Seven o'clock. I reached in the oven and removed the foil from the lasagna, then shut the red kitchen curtains, which is my signal to my mother-in-law next door to put on her coat and walk up the hill and across the leaf-strewn lawn for dinner. She takes her evening meals with us, and we have used the curtain signal for close to twenty years. She'll be watching from her darkened sunroom, waiting patiently, her nose already powdered, a dash of lipstick applied, her bladder emptied, her house keys in her pocket, and it will take her exactly four minutes to travel the hundred yards uphill to our back door, which I leave unlocked. Why do I have red curtains in my kitchen? Because Simone de Beauvoir loved red curtains; because Danielle Westerman loves red curtains out of respect for Beauvoir, and I love them because of Danielle. They serve, when nothing else quite does, as the sign of home and comfort, ease, companionability, food and drink and family.

I set the steaming lasagna on the table along with a green salad in my mother's old mahogany bowl from Brazil, that time she and my father had attended a conference in São Paulo—when was that? Back in the early seventies when I was young, left alone with Aunt Judy. "Dinner," I called. And then, louder: "Dinner!"

They are well trained. Mozart faded at once with a spill down the keyboard. Grandma Winters came through the door bearing an apple crumble for dessert. She shed her good fall coat, sighing, and, as usual lately, gave no word of greeting. The TV died, and we all sat down together, Chris with a baseball cap on backwards as though she were intent on driving her grandmother mad.

We were in the midst of family love; I breathed it in gratefully, despite its mixture of disorder and unreckoning. On this fall evening I had lit candles in the dining room, and we were sitting down as though we were an ordinary family, as if our small planet was on course, as though the seasons would continue, autumn about to move into winter, and outdoors the new mulch, like a coat of fleece, protecting and warming the ground. Snow was forecast even though it's only October.

Natalie, always one to take responsibility for dinnertime silences even though she's the youngest, was chattering about her history teacher, Mr. Glaven, who announced to the class today that he was gay. "Big fat surprise," she said, "as though we didn't have an inkling." "Oh, him," Chris said. "We knew he was gay two years ago." Grandma Winters blinked, and then attacked her lasagna, carrying soft forkfuls of food straight into her mouth. She is proud of her appetite but would never say so. What has she eaten today? Toast and coffee for breakfast and toast and tea for lunch. No wonder she has an appetite at the end of the day. Tom serves himself last. His hands are shaking. When did that start? Thank God for Chris, thank God for Natalie, for their inane high-school gossip, their naive willingness to lunge forward and expand on tiny particulars of the quotidian, Mr. Glaven who was spotted in Toronto in a gay bar over the weekend, holding hands with another man, kissing him on the lips. "Oh no, not on the lips!" From Chris. They strained to compensate for Norah's absence, keeping up the volubility quotient but without quite catching Norah's murmuring reflectiveness or her perfectly judged pause when she is asked a question. "Don't forget the salad," I reminded them, and this was my only real contribution to the dinner conversation, a reflex embedded in my role as mother, the provider of nutrition, the server of balanced meals.

I was thinking about Alicia in my novel who has gone on a no-carb diet so she can fit into the size-eight wedding dress she has ordered. What a vapid woman she is. What does Roman see in her really? Such fatal vanity, such a lack of suffering—either that or the suffering hasn't quite reached her. It's got blocked in her marrow, it never moves from her flesh up into her brain stem.

Suddenly it was clear to me. Alicia's marriage to Roman must be postponed. Now I understood where the novel is headed. She is not meant to be partnered. Her singleness in the world is her paradise, it has been all along, and she came close to sacrificing it, or, rather, I, as novelist, had been about to snatch it away from her. The wedding guests will have to be alerted and the gifts returned. All of them, Alicia, Roman, their families, their friends —stupid, stupid. The novel, if it is to survive, must be redrafted. Alicia will advance in her self-understanding, and the pages will expand. I'll start over tomorrow. This thought pulsed in my throat. Tomorrow.

The telephone rang at that moment. A call from New York and the news that my editor, Mr. Scribano, had died during the afternoon.

Next

Dear Mr. Scribano died in hospital, after a fall down the stairs the previous day. The small private funeral will be held in three days and there is to be a special tribute in next week's *New York Times Book Review*. Someone from the paper phoned me at home in Orangetown and asked how I had found him as an editor.

I was not composed and certainly not eloquent. I explained: Mr. Scribano had been Danielle's editor, and Danielle had directed me toward him with my first novel. This had been fortunate for me, being handed *une courte échelle,* and publishing my first novel in my forties. How had I found him to work with? We met only twice; talked on the telephone perhaps a dozen times; corresponded occasionally, erratically. I signed a contract in his presence, in his large, sparsely furnished, over-bright office on the sixty-second floor in the middle of Manhattan. He had apologized for not taking me to lunch, something publishers were expected to do, but he was a man whose habit was to have a sandwich sent up from the ground-floor deli at twelve sharp. It was noon now. Would such a common everyday sandwich do for me? Yes, I had said, and in a few minutes we were munching our way through dense rye bread, cheese, and lettuce. He ate with daintiness, was careful about the crumbs getting into his moustache, and sipped his hot tea searchingly. His laughter was short, deep, and unforced, and I could see that he might be attractive to women. I sat on a little chair. He sat in his big father bear chair.

Much later, he raised the subject of writing a second novel, a sequel, though I remember he did not use that word, and now he was suddenly dead. "I admired him greatly," I heard myself saying into the phone, and then, incomprehensibly, "I had no idea."

Tom says that people who fall down stairs don't usually die. They get themselves covered with bruises and sometimes they break their arms or legs. Death occurs only if the head strikes something hard with a particular force or angle, and all day I've been thinking of how he might be alive this minute if only—if only he hadn't pitched forward so helplessly, if only he hadn't insisted on bare uncarpeted stairs, if only his head hadn't banged on the large chunk of granite he kept on the landing, a souvenir from a lecture tour in Italy back in the fifties.

He died within hours without suffering, his secretary, Adrienne, said, phoning to give a full report, as though this information was owed to me as one of the firm's listed novelists. Yes, she said, all the Scribano & Lawrence authors were to be personally contacted and informed of the death, just as Mr. Scribano would have wished. All the variables had been in place, Adrienne said: disorientation on the dark stairway, the headlong fall, the stony weapon waiting. He was probably going down to the kitchen to make tea, some herbal potion to help him sleep.

But I didn't know he was troubled, that he lived alone, that he'd ever lectured in Italy, that he had sleep problems; I didn't even know how old he was, but I was told, and later I read it in his obituary. He was seventy-seven. His death should not have come as the shock it did. It seemed to me, when I first got the news, that I would not be continuing the novel, that Mr. Scribano alone had instigated the project and kept it alive. (I did know that there was no Mr. Lawrence, that he had died decades ago, that his name was kept for the sake of euphony.)

The news about Mr. Scribano was worse for Danielle Westerman, who has known him for more than forty years and who has led me to believe that he was not only her editor but, for a brief period in the early sixties, a lover. She calls him by his first name, Andreas. She took the news badly. A good many of her friends have died in the last year or two. For one's editor to die, she told me over the phone, is to understand what an artifice writing really is. "Without editors, writers are nothing but makers of lace."

I didn't agree with this notion, not for a moment, but lacked the energy for a quarrel. If the truth were known, worry over Norah took so much of my concern that it was hard to feel genuine sorrow over the death of a seventy-seven-year-old man who had died in a rather careless manner. My grief for Mr. Scribano was cut short, a modest mourning; it was over and done with in a matter of days; I sent flowers for the funeral, which was held in St. Patrick's Cathedral—that did impress me!—wrote a note to his secretary—he had no family—and then I forgot about him, put him out of my mind. I had only so much concentration for sadness.

Danielle seemed baffled by this hierarchy of concerns or what she perceived as my hardness of heart. "Such a grand life. Such a presence. So great a contribution. It will be impossible to replace such a person."

Yes, I said, but he had a long life. What I meant was: he had more than Norah is going to get.

Early November—I hate this time of year. Dark mornings, broken jack-o'-lanterns on the roadway. Winter's harder, I keep thinking, but harder than what? Snow flurries in the headlights. The trees, all bare, divide the sky into segments. A short, sunless Wednesday, the air stretched out on every side like sheets of muslin.

On Wednesdays I drive to Toronto. This is not as easy as it sounds. I have been awake since six o'clock. Shower, dress, twist my hair back. I've wakened Chris and Natalie and alerted Tom to a spot on his sweater. Breakfast: coffee for Tom and me and tea for the girls. Toast, butter, jam. Crumbs around the toaster. Plates and cups in the dishwasher. Urge girls to hurry so they won't miss the school bus. Natalie hasn't eaten a thing, how long can she live on milky tea? Hug girls. Wish them luck on whatever: math quiz, chem lab, basketball. Unplug coffee maker. Help Tom find his calendar, which is under yesterday's mail. Hug, hug, and he's off. Let the dog out for a few minutes. Phone Tom's mother to see if she slept well. Check outdoor temperature, minus ten. Finally, back car out of the garage, drive into Toronto.

The drive is endless, repetitive, the colour of cement. It takes an hour—now it's ten-thirty, and I park near Norah's corner.

I walk around and around the block where she sits, trying to keep a little distance. I don't want to threaten her in any way. *O my love, what have they done to you?* Her face: I don't dare get close enough to see her face clearly, but what I imagine is a passive despair, a mingling of contempt and indifference that projects silence but is ready to incinerate whatever is offered. In this oppressive weather—snow in the air, a driving wind—she is more isolated than ever. This is a nervous, feverish corner of the city, rowdy, cheap, and lonely. Across the street is Honest Ed's, an immense and eccentric discount department store with uneven flooring and everything on sale, from clothes pegs to TV sets. But Norah's posture excludes everything around her, as though nothing is real except for her bent head and neck. The fact that I am unseen—that I can remain unseen—is oddly comforting, as though I am giving her something of value but which is really just my steady, resolute, useless anxiety. I wander into the local shops and observe her through the windows. I circle the street and count how many people walk by her, how many give her a coin or two. Sometimes I feel she is aware of my presence. When I finally approach her with a parcel of food, she doesn't look up.

At noon I go to Danielle Westerman's Rosedale apartment and eat small sandwiches at a table set up in her sunroom, wonderful catered sandwiches, crabmeat, artichoke, curried chicken. These days I am almost her only visitor. A beautiful cloth covers the little table, and small ladylike napkins, professionally laundered, standing up in crisp points. We drink very strong tea from Russian glasses; this is one of Danielle's affectations. Her hair has been dyed so often it has grown into a soft rust and purple turban. One of her hands touches her hair, which is coming unpinned and threatening to fall over her eyes. Once, years ago, she wore her hair brushed straight back from her forehead and ears and caught in a shining chignon—which is how I wear my hair now; a tribute—and not unconscious at all—to young Danielle, early Danielle, that vibrant girl-woman who reinvented feminism. Nowadays she wears tiny gold and white shoes that look like bedroom slippers, and her bare legs are much marked with bruises and spots. Her pleated grey skirt and cardigan are part of her daily uniform, as they have been for years. Where does she find such terrible cardigans? I marvel at the number of years locked up in her body, all she has seen and thought, all the words she has lined up on the page, the weather she's endured, the lovers she's encountered, the suffering during the war. We talk about volume four of the translation, which I am not, to her consternation, doing, and then, after a little while, we discuss the problems of Alicia and Roman in my new novel, which is finally on the trajectory it was meant to have. We raise our tea glasses to the memory of Mr. Scribano, and Danielle wonders for the thousandth time whether Scribano can possibly have been his real name or one adopted when he found his vocation. I rise, finally, bend down to hug her fragile body, and insist that I will let myself out the door. I can see that she is nodding off to sleep.

After that I take one more slow drive past Bloor and Bathurst before heading for the highway and home, looking for that familiar gallant self in its navy peacoat, that bent head, wrapped now in a scarf, awarding myself the easy pleasure that people invite when nothing has improved but at least nothing has changed. Still there. Still there. A dithering reassurance that pulls against the gravity of mourning. Never mind the car behind me impatiently honking. I take my time.

Notwithstanding

Tom and I still have sex—have I mentioned this?—even though our oldest daughter is living on the street, a derelict. This happens once or twice a week. We actually lie on our queen-size bed together; it will be midnight, the house quiet, our faces close together, the warm, felt cave beneath Tom's jaw at my cheek, his breath. The specificity of his body keeps me still, as though I'm listening for a signal. He reaches for me; I respond, sometimes slowly, lately quite slowly. Spirals of transcendence drift through me like strands of DNA, always rising upward. Concentrate, concentrate; yes, concentration helps. Soon we are rocking together like a pair of hard-breathing lunatics, and afterwards one or the other of us will cry. Sometimes we both cry. Our ongoing need for sex lies between us like something we don't dare pick up. It's as though we have struggled to enter an interior sleep-room where the capacity for suffering has withered. The hum in our ears is our own history, and that hum never goes away.

Do we still love each other? We must if we're still having sex after twenty-plus years. Of course we have our quarrels, but never anything we can't find our way back from. The question of love is not relevant in our case, not for the moment. The question can be postponed. We live in each other's shelter; we fit. We're together after all this time; that's what matters. When we go for a walk together, his arm is locked into my arm, his hand is locked into my hand. Since I'm several inches shorter, this requires a lifting of my shoulder and a slight stoop on his part. We fit together that way. The sex part of our life is also a matter of minute adjustment and accommodation. Our habits are so familiar; they're like the interiors of uncurtained houses at night, a reassuring wedge of known lamplight, a corner of a familiar ceiling cornice, a wall of books, the top of a wing chair, always there, the same arrangements. "How odd," I said to him after some particularly aggressive lovemaking (the middle of November, the night of the season's first real snow storm).

"Odd?"

"That we go on doing this."

"I know."

"The same way we keep up the garden."

"And pay the bills."

"Can you forget, Tom? Tell me. Are you ever able to forget about her?"

A pause, then, "I don't think so. Not completely. Never. Do you?" (I do love him. When I ask him a question, he asks back.)

"No."

We must have drifted off to sleep after that conversation. (So there it is: we have regular sex and we are able, mostly, to sleep. It's almost negligent of us, two heartbroken parents; yet to all appearances, we are able to carry on with our lives.)

A hundred elements of today's culture outrage me, particularly the easy unthinkingness of people's claim to "spirituality," but I remain forever grateful for the good scrambled liberated days Tom and I came out of, the seventies. "To be young was very heaven," sang old Wordsworth, and we had that heaven, a taste of it anyway, the *veryness* of it. We had sex the first night we met, Tom and I, two students sitting side by side at a human rights rally in Nathan Phillips Square in downtown Toronto. We fell to talking, then walking around the downtown streets, then back to Tom's apartment on Davenport, the brown couch he had with the awful-smelling corduroy cushions, each one centred with a big hard brown button. I didn't phone home. I didn't phone the dorm. This was during a time when I seemed to have very little in the way of a real life, and now here I was, lying beside a man I'd just met. Two strangers held together in a save-the-earth era. Tom's hand had been under my sweater all the way from downtown Toronto. I was on the pill, there was nothing to discuss, nothing could have stopped us, it was like flying. I remember, afterwards, studying his face, trying to see what passion had accomplished, and grieving for just a moment that there wouldn't, couldn't, be another event quite equal to this, not if I lived to be a hundred.

Our lives don't really "befall" us; we tend to rouse ourselves to invention, to accommodation. It was spring. I was "in love." But I continued with my studies—I was doing Old Frankish now—and in the midst of strange vowels and blurred consonants, I turned a large portion of my life over to this person, this Tom Winters. The sound of the sixties had been "doo-wop." But the seventies said home, make a new home, create a home of your own, dress yourself in warm earth colours, get back to the earth, dig yourself into your life. People were starting to have babies again.

At various times I've talked to each of my daughters about birth control. Norah at seventeen placed her hand on my wrist and said with a smile: I already know. Chris laughed and said mysteriously: Okay, okay, I get it. Natalie—this was only a year ago when she was fourteen—said, tucking in her chin: Not to wo-r-ry, I'll look after that when the time comes.

But I must start thinking seriously about Alicia and Roman's sex life. I have to be braver about it this time round. An awful maidenly daintiness runs through the pages of *My Thyme Is Up,* a prudery that has nothing to do with sex in the twenty-first century. They *slept* together, Roman and Alicia. They melted in each other's arms, buttery and sweet. An ethereal transaction was attempted as they bedded down, yes, on their very first date. There was no fumbling with condoms, his or hers, no guilt, no actuarial accountings, no position three, four, or five bolstered up by beams and rope, just two human bodies humming up and down the musical scale of skin, bone, creases, shadows, cleanly, singingly, besottedly droll. But the real running syrups and juice of sex were absent. You could tell that none of this cost anything. You could hardly hear Alicia and Roman breathing. Their kisses tasted scrubbed, like fresh soap and water. Accessible. Decent! Dressed up for ecstasy, but not able to go there. The amperage was there, and Alicia and Roman were willing. Perhaps they lacked the self-forgetfulness that good sex requires, the wanting and then the retreat from want.

Other writers know how to do vivid sex scenes. They've got the chronology down, first the languorous removal of clothing, some slow dancing maybe to an old Sinatra record, then the nibbling, the rubbing, the sucking, the smelling, the tasting, the barking commands and screaming surrender, yes, yes, and then, finally, "he enters her." *Well, come right in, my fine fellow, and make yourself at home.*

I have three daughters; naturally I shrink from the thought of embarrassing them with what I publish. People in Orangetown will stare at Tom if I screw up my nerve and get into whips and leather and suchlike; his patients, out of suspicion, may drift off to other practitioners. I certainly would. Moreover, I don't know all that much about kinks and jinks. My imagination tends not to drift in that direction.

Oh, loosen up, Ms. Winters.

Sex talk is so eroded, that's the problem. We've all learned it at the movies, and the movies made it up. *Do anything to me. Take me. Overwhelm me. I'm coming. How was it for—?*

I can't, I can't. I grow rich with disgust, not with sex but with the vocabulary of sex. Besides, light comic fiction does not invite a step-by-step nipple-penis-vulva-clitoris-anus exposition. Alicia is a sensuous woman who understands her body but she does not dwell on the subject of her pubic hair. Pubic hair is out of place in this genre. Roman is allowed to be something of an athlete in bed; a man who plays the trombone, after all, knows about thrusting and triple tonguing and embouchure. Both Alicia and Roman want, both of them desire. Ridiculous word, *desire*. *Tu désires quelque chose?* Delete.

But they want tenderness as much as they want passion, they crave the feathered touch of softness, sweetness. They yearn—and this is what I can't get my word processor to accept—to be fond of each other, to be charitable, to be mild and merciful. To be barefootedly beautiful in each other's eyes.

And now, a November day, flattened by wind and worry, the trees throwing their bare branches about outside my window, I shut down my computer for the day, unwilling at this hour—five o'clock, already dark—to award them what they haven't the wit to define.

Thereupon

At the beginning of every month, now, I sit down at Tom's desk and write out a cheque to the Promise Hostel in Toronto. I allow myself to weep a few moderate tears while I fold the cheque and place it in an envelope, seal it, and write out the address on Bathurst Street. Still weeping as I affix a stamp, still weeping as I walk down the road to the mailbox. The tears are in appreciation of the extreme goodness of the Anglican congregation in Toronto, who some years ago turned a neighbourhood school into a refuge for homeless people. Where did such goodness come from? I know there must have been endless committee meetings, a call for volunteers, the striking of an official board, fundraising suppers, confrontations with the city council and with the local residents—all of that inevitable paperwork and bureaucracy that goes with public-spirited projects; but where did the goodness begin, the germ of goodness, the primal thought to offer food and shelter to strangers?

Following Christ's example, the Anglican community might say, though I doubt it, not in these ecumenical times. Social responsibility is more likely, but even this is to delicately bracket what is, in reality, a powerful tide of virtue flowing from the veins of men and women who will not be much rewarded or even recognized for their efforts. Frances Quinn, the director, is paid, but the dormitories at the Promise Hostel are swept and swabbed by people who come and go from their offices, their professional business addresses, from million-dollar houses in Forest Hill or Rosedale or the Annex. The same people, these chanters of church litanies, also do laundry, wash windows, clean up messes of urine and vomit, and make hundreds of chicken pot pies in the immense basement kitchen.

As soon as we discovered where Norah spent her nights we went to see the place, Tom and I, along with Chris and Natalie. We phoned ahead. It was a Saturday afternoon early last May. The rain had been pouring for a week, and when we arrived downtown, two men were squatting on the second-floor roof, patching a hole. Inside, Frances Quinn was busy on the telephone, but she waved at a volunteer, a man in his fifties we guessed, to tour us around. He showed us, without the least display of hushed piety, a small chapel on the ground floor and a dormitory for twenty women, a lineup of camp beds, neatly made up, a wall of lockers, and a communal bathroom. Norah lives here, I said to myself, she sleeps in this room. A clean towel was folded over the end of each bed. The room was spotless, but dust motes nevertheless swam in the beams of light from the windows, the kind of dust that is impossible to banish. The bare wooden floor creaked underfoot. Forty men sleep in a similar dormitory upstairs. In the basement was the dining hall and kitchen, where four women were gathered around an industrial wood-and-steel table collaborating on a list of some kind. They looked hearty, cheerful, plain, full of ease, and each wore a black barbecue apron upon which was printed the word PROMISE. Food donations are delivered at the rear entrance, one of them told us; today they had received a case of canned tomatoes, always welcome, and there were plenty of donations from downtown hotels and restaurants, though these tended to be last minute and required creativity on the part of the volunteer cooks who would be taking over the kitchen at four o'clock. The smell of potatoes and mould lingered in the corners of the room, but every surface was scrubbed clean. Dish detergent, or something stronger, spiked the air. The women talked about how they spent lots of time figuring out ways to freshen up day-old bread—they had a number of tricks—and for some reason this mention of freshening up bread sent them off into gales of private laughter. They pointed to the huge, recently acquired television screen in the dining hall, the gift of a major real estate dealer in the city. At six o'clock the hostel doors are opened for the evening; five o'clock in the winter months. Lights out at eleven, and everyone was expected to be out on the street by eight-thirty after a hot breakfast. No alcohol or drugs were allowed, but of course there were those who broke the rules. Upstairs a woman was playing the piano and singing brightly: "Art thou weary, art thou languid?" She repeated these first two lines several times, practising, stopping herself, starting again. At this point Christine slipped her hand into mine, as though she were a small girl.

After the tour we walked back to where we had parked the car and got in. It was still raining. The girls, in the back seat, were silent. I couldn't bear to turn my head and look at them. Tom sat behind the steering wheel with his seat belt on, but he didn't start the car right away. We sat and watched the rain streaming down the windshield. We looked at the long, narrow street of houses with their tiny front yards and their blue recycling boxes. The city trees were just leafing out, that pale hazy green I love so much. I put my fingertips lightly on Tom's knee. He moved suddenly, covering his face with his hands. Natalie in the back seat began to blub, and then we all did.

Despite

I continue, despite everything, to work away at the novel. There are always decisions to make. Does Alicia have a dog or cat or nothing? I decide on a cat called Chestnut. An old cat with one blind eye. Alicia is not a serious ailurophile, however; she neglects Chestnut, and Chestnut knows it.

Mr. Scribano's secretary phoned and told me in a tone of high seriousness how much they all were looking forward to seeing my manuscript and how much Mr. Scribano had been counting on it to sparkle up next year's list. They would like to be able to mention it in the spring catalogue, just the title and a brief description. A teaser, she called it. There was no reason to fear that Mr. Scribano's death would jeopardize such an old and well-established firm. A new editor was about to be appointed. She promised to keep me up to date.

We also continue to listen to the news. Tom and I have views about the news, which we express, even though we know how inconsequential the unfolding of political events is. People enter and exit the world; that's the real news. The rest is a residue, a crust left behind in the creases of the eye or mouth. The American election results have confounded everyone. In that great noisome nation the presidential decision has actually come down to two hundred people in the state of Florida. Two hundred people; they could all be crammed into the Orangetown Public Library, rubbing shoulders. How can that be? What about the proud old American constitution with its much-heralded system of checks and balances? Janet Reno appears on television and says something about how every vote really does count and this proves that democracy works. But wait a minute. It isn't working, Ms. Reno. It's something to talk about, all the chatter of chads and dimples. Natalie looks up chad in the dictionary, and yes, it really is there, it's been there all along. Good Scrabble word, Chris announces.

They are both studying for exams. Just because their older sister is living the life of a derelict doesn't mean there will be no exams. French, history, math, language arts. This is monstrous: that exams are being scheduled, that George W. Bush exists, that Mr. Scribano fell downstairs, that people are booking flights for their Christmas holidays, that Danielle Westerman accuses me of insufficient sorrow, that I am calmly wiping down the kitchen counters after a dinner of shepherd's pie and spinach salad, while at the same time plotting what Alicia will say to Roman about the need to cancel the wedding, and observing that outside it is snowing and the drifts are building thickly sculpted walls against the north side of our house, and Tom is settling down in his favourite chair with a new book on trilobites that arrived in today's mail. The wind is blowing and blowing. I am still I, though it's harder and harder to pronounce that simple pronoun and maintain composure.

Throughout

Early on we thought Norah's problem was a boyfriend problem. And Ben Abbot really is a boy, with a boy's face and gangling frame; it was this that Norah loved in the beginning, I suspect, the thoroughly innocent leanness of his shoulders, neck, the ribs bursting out above his jeans, barely covered by flesh. If he had an aura, it would be coloured by the state of beatitude. By thirty he will have acquired a supple, sexual bulk, but now he is quickness and nerve and seems always willing to be disturbed by his own body, taking its awkwardness as part of the gift of youth. I've never yet seen him sit back in a chair, relaxed. He perches, his eyes watchful, his mouth just a little open, a boy's observant, greedy mouth.

We live in the age of the long childhood, and no one expects heroism from a twenty-three-year-old kid who's still a student, who still gets monthly cheques from his parents in Sudbury, still lives in an untidy student apartment. His marks in philosophy are top notch. Harder work lies ahead, but he seems blinded by the darkness that work really represents, and ready to delay it as long as possible with thoughts of a doctorate, then perhaps a post-doc.

He and Norah met at a friend's party soon after she turned eighteen, and he was drawn to her at once. Norah was smart and pretty and appealing. You took one look at her and you knew she was one of the lucky people. This is how lucky people live—part of loving families, favoured by quality education, grateful rather than spoiled, able to set their references outside themselves somehow so that they escape neurosis, fixing on books or horses or basketball or piano or even cooking. Lucky people are not obliged to cultivate shrewdness. Good sense and balance belong to them naturally. When at last they encounter the sexual life, they accept it like a graft to their body, understanding at once that it is an offering and one of the greatest gifts they will be given.

Ben and Norah saw each other two or three times and then there was no separating them.

After Norah disappeared, in those frightening days in April after we found out she'd taken up daily residence at Bathurst and Bloor, I went to see Ben. Tom and I were distraught with worry, and Ben seemed the most logical person to approach. I didn't phone ahead; I simply drove into Toronto, parked the car in a side street, and rang the buzzer of his basement apartment.

Why would a young man of twenty-three be at home in the middle of the afternoon, three o'clock? Who knows why, but he was. He came to the door looking tousled, as though he'd been sleeping. We didn't shake hands or embrace. We just looked into each other's faces. Then he stepped aside awkwardly, gesturing to me, come in, come in.

A haze hung in the air, and only a little natural light entered from the tiny street-level windows. The room was timeless; it could have been a student apartment from my own generation, a place of ripped vinyl, worn chenille, posters taped to the walls, stacks of books and papers, rising stours of dust. He sank into the sagging old Salvation Army couch, rested his elbows on his knees, bringing the tips of his fingers together, those blunt, trimmed fingers that had struck me, on first meeting, as curiously carnal.

I caught myself at the edge of disapproval with Ben, wanting to pick apart his finer feelings, and then I thought: He's young and he's tasted disappointment; he has a girlfriend whom he may or may not love, and she has left him to live on the street. They've invested more than a year of feeling in each other—of absorption, of fantasy. This is stuff for crabbed old age, not for a young man with a young man's yearning for satisfaction and a belief that he'll get what he deserves. He's approached love with a young man's wonder and gratitude, only to find its abrupt withdrawal.

"She changed," he said. "Over a few weeks. Late January, February, March. She was short-tempered. Then she'd go quiet. Her professor, Dr. Hamilton, she hated him for some reason. I asked her what the guy had done, if he'd come on to her or something, and she was furious that I'd think of a thing like that, that that was what would occur to me, something sexual. She started giving me these, you know, these long, hard looks. Scrutinizing looks. Like she'd just suddenly realized what a dickhead I was or something. Then she left. One afternoon last week. I thought she was just going to Honest Ed's, but she never came back. Most of her stuff is still here. She'd stopped going to lectures by March, she just hung around the apartment reading or staring off into space. I would have phoned you after she left, but I thought she'd gone home, that she was with you. She was thinking about goodness and evil, about harm to the earth, that kind of thing. And then, it was just a couple of days ago, this girl I know said she saw Norah panhandling at Bathurst and Bloor, and I couldn't believe it. I went and looked, and there she was with that sign, sitting on the sidewalk. I walked up to her and said, 'What are you doing, Norah, what is this all about?'"

I watched him lean back into the torn couch cushions, and he started to sob unrestrainedly. He howled so long and so eloquently that I will never forget it. Tears streamed down his face and he made no effort to brush them away. His hands were spread out uselessly on his denim thighs. I wanted to reach out and stroke his hand, but I couldn't, I didn't. I knew it wasn't his fault, this poor young kid, but I felt myself harden. I felt the force of blame gathering. I just sat there and watched him cry. I felt my hopes flatten out and crush me with their weight. Now I knew it was true. There wasn't going to be anything I could do to save Norah from herself.

Following

How old is Alicia, the heroine of my novel? This matter is critical. She lives in the large city of Wychwood. She is an editor for a fashion magazine. She is engaged to be married to Roman, aged thirty-eight, and the wedding is just weeks away. This is her second marriage, and she has lived for short periods of time with two other men. I want her to remain grave and intelligent, yet still young enough to stir ardour. She is pert rather than perky, a wide-awake woman who already understands that the universe is supremely insufficient. She was thirty-four in the first novel two years ago, and so now I have assigned her the age of thirty-six. Forty lies ahead, and she is well aware of forty—but not frightened by it. She spends perhaps too much money on top-quality skin products, even though she knows what scams the cosmetic industry brews up. There is something hermetic about her disposition, but she doesn't really know this, not yet.

Does she speak her own story? In other words, is this to be a first-person narrative? Yes. For one thing, *My Thyme Is Up* employed the first person, and a sequel must be consistent in such matters. Her voice is ironic and quizzing, loose-jointed but pulsingly intimate. She is not in the least ashamed that she is detached from large slices of popular culture. She might say "shit," if she stumbled and scraped her knee, but she would never, under any circumstances, describe some person or some essence as being "shitty." That's where her delicacy shows itself, in her vocabulary. Certain people might call this prissiness. She is mildly musical, plays the piano a little and once was reasonably accomplished on the flute. Her degree is in journalism, from Columbia. An A-minus average. (She could have done better if she'd loved men less.) She wears shawl-like garments, loose loping jackets, long dipping skirts, heavy silk, slim silver jewellery, clever earrings.

She cannot be stunningly beautiful and possessed of a perfect figure, and this was made clear in the first novel. The genre of "light" fiction rules out bodily perfection. We are not allowed to garland our men and women with exceptional good looks. Romance novels, on the other hand, are able to fill their pages with dozens of strikingly beautiful women, and literary novels can permit a single heroine a rare beauty, one only. Light fiction, being closer to real life, knows better. Some imperfection must intervene, and usually this is in the nature of a slightly too long nose or a smaller than average chin. It is not necessary to award such disadvantages as giant hips or mannish shoulders and certainly not one eye larger than the other, although breasts may be on the small size or else more generous than normal. A passing prettiness is what I claim for Alicia, conveyed without a lot of heavy detail.

Does she believe in God? No, despite her Presbyterian upbringing. God and his Son are metaphors, representing perhaps creation and renewal; this certainty arrived like a bullet-shaped slug of pewter when she was about twenty, sitting in a church pew with her parents, reciting the Nicene Creed. She almost never speaks of it, it is so unimportant in her life, the question of belief or disbelief—and she and Roman have not really touched on the subject. There is a great deal they have not touched on, and this is beginning to worry her slightly.

Does she want children of her own? Yes, desperately. But vaguely. Does she see herself unbuttoning her blouse and offering her breast to a baby's gaping mouth? Well, no, she hasn't got that far in her thinking. A little girl would be lovely. Or a little boy. It didn't matter a great deal. She supposes she would go on working for the magazine after a short time spent at home, six months or so. She has just begun a new monthly series on accessories and is now researching the history of women's handbags. It is fascinating, really. It all began with the chatelaine of the medieval castle, the roving household manager needing something in which to carry her keys and her domestic accounts. It's true you often see the Virgin Mary in paintings with a little sack purse on the floor next to her chair, but this is most likely an anachronism, as Alicia informed Roman yesterday while they were having dinner at Maurice's, steak and frites and a good bottle of red wine.

"A what?" he said blankly. He hadn't been listening to her. She gave him a long, severe look.

"Never mind," she said crossly. Then she reached out and stroked his hand. Roman works as a symphony trombonist (note to myself: find out more about trombones); I was rather opaque about Roman's vocation first time round, he sometimes complains that Alicia's world of writing is narrow and inbred, forgetting that he and his fellow musicians form an exceedingly tight, self-referencing subgroup.

I too am aware of being in incestuous waters, a woman writer who is writing about a woman writer who is writing. I know perfectly well that I ought to be writing about dentists and bus drivers and manicurists and those folks who design the drainage beds for eight-lane highways. But no, I am focusing on the stirrings of the writerly impulse, or the "long littleness," to use Frances Cornford's phrase, of a life spent affixing small words to large, empty pages. We may pretend otherwise, but to many writers this is the richest territory we can imagine. There are novelists who go to the trouble of cloaking their heroes in loose crossover garments, turning them into painters or architects, but no one's fooled. This matters, the remaking of an untenable world through the nib of a pen; it matters so much I can't stop doing it.

Hardly

Not that I write with a pen. Nor do I know anyone else who does these days. But a little puff of romanticism still attaches to the idea of pen and ink, and testifies, falsely, to the writer's essential independence and freedom. No one is quite ready to give up pen and paper's metaphoric weight. I was thinking these thoughts when the kitchen telephone rang early on a November morning.

"I'd like to speak to Mrs. Reta Winters, please," said a man's resonant voice.

"This is Reta Winters speaking." I was holding the phone in my left hand and unloading the dishwasher with my right.

"Have I caught you at an awkward moment?" the voice asked. "You're not in the middle of breakfast?"

"No," I said and stopped bashing the china about. "This is a good time."

"I just phoned to introduce myself," said the deep baritone voice with its range of lighter musical notes. "My name is Arthur Springer from Scribano & Lawrence, and I have the great honour, Mrs. Winters, of being your new editor."

"Oh," I said, genuinely pleased; such professional civility was impressive. "Well, how nice of you to phone and introduce yourself, Mr. Springer."

"I hope you'll call me Arthur once we get to know each other."

"Well, then you must call me—"

"Reta. It would be a pleasure, Reta. I'm so pleased you feel that way. That will get us off to a good start. I want to say right off that I know I can't begin to replace the inestimable Mr. Scribano."

"Such a tragedy—"

"I can tell you, Reta, that our Mr. Scribano was delighted that you were working on a second novel, a sequel to *My Thyme Is Up*. He told me as much just a few days before his fall."

"Did he really? He was always very kind and encouraging—"

"I had nothing but respect for him as a person and as an editor. I've been with the firm since the beginning of last year and have had the good fortune to learn a good deal from him. Though, of course, we represent different generations and have our separate approaches. My own approach is very much dialogic. My training was at Yale, originally. Then Berkeley."

"Well, yes—"

"Now, can you give me an idea, Reta, of when you will next be in New York."

"Well actually—"

"I think it's essential that we sit down and go over the manuscript together. I'm a bit of a point-by-point man when it comes to editing, and, unlike many of my contemporaries, I lack faith in e-mail communications or even the telephone."

"But there is no manuscript, in a sense." I resumed my task of unloading the dishwasher, but very quietly now, lifting the plates out one by one, stacking them softly on the shelf. "That is, the manuscript is coming along, but very slowly."

"In percentage terms?"

"Sorry, I don't quite—"

"Are you at the halfway point, Reta, or three-quarters? Or?"

"Oh. Well, I'm not quite sure. But in any case, I'm afraid I have no plans to be in New York, not in the near future."

"Fine, fine. Just send me what you've got so far."

"But I don't think I can do that. You see, what's down on paper, or on disk really, is still very much in the, you know, the tenuous mode—"

"Oh, I assure you, Reta, that I appreciate the fact that a draft is a draft is a draft. That is one of the first things a fiction editor must understand."

"I don't see how I can—"

"Look, Reta, I'm going to give you our UPS number. Have you got a pencil handy? All you have to do is print out the pages and bundle them up. I'll phone and make the arrangements for a pick-up. What about later this afternoon? We're hoping for a fall publication, which means moving along very rapidly. You'll find I'm an appreciative editor. I like to bring out the best in a writer. Have you read *Darling Buds*? That was one of my writers."

"*Darling Buds*?"

"I'll courier you a copy right away."

"Oh, that would be—"

"There is just one thing I want to say, Reta, before we say goodbye. I love Alicia. Your Alicia. I want you to know that my devotion to her is enormous. I am greatly attracted to her reflective nature. I've read *My Thyme Is Up* several times now, and each time I love her more. There's a golden quality about her. As though she were a gold autumn leaf among others less gold. I've thought and thought about what it is that draws me to your Alicia. It's not her sensuality, not that she is lacking in that department, not in the least. The way she has of sitting still in a chair. Just sitting. Her generosity, that's part of it. Her tolerance too. But what really makes me want to take her in my arms is her goodness."

"I'm sorry. I didn't quite hear what you said, Mr. Springer, Arthur. Did you say—?"

"Her goodness. Her profound human goodness."

"Oh. Goodness."

"Yes, goodness."

"That's what I thought you said."

Since

"Arrange to have her kidnapped," people said when Norah turned up at Bathurst and Bloor, "and then have her professionally deprogrammed."

Sally said: "Have the police pick her up for questioning. They've seen lots of these cases and know how to handle them."

Other friends—Lynn, Annette—said: "Use a little force. If you and Tom force her into the car and drive her straight home, the shock will bring her to her senses. That's what she needs to break the spell, a shock." I did actually try this one day; I parked, illegally, on Bathurst, as close to her as I could get, got out of the car, and grabbed her by the hand. She screamed horribly and pulled back from me. I felt her glove coming off. It was as though she were an incendiary object, a hot coal. People started to gather, and I got back into the car quickly—forgive me, Norah, forgive me—and drove away.

Frances Quinn from the Promise Hostel said to us: "She is in good health at the moment. She seems sane, but rather determined. I've offered her counselling, of course, but she appears to be sure she knows what she's doing. She's not yet twenty. Time's on her side. I've seen stubborn cases before, and in the end they usually yield."

One friend—or acquaintance, rather—said to me: "You're all worked up about nothing. This isn't such a big deal, a kid taking a season out on the street. It happens."

Dr. David McClure, the psychiatrist we consulted, urged non-interference. "Her actions indicate that she is giving herself something. A gift of freedom, you might say, the right to be a truant in her own life. You may not think so, but she has made practical arrangements to stay alive. Vagrancy can be thoughtful or careless, and she has chosen the former. But then she is intelligent. Intelligence will see her through this crisis. Crisis, I say, but that isn't really the word I should have used. It is more in the nature of a behavioural interlude in which she is either escaping something unbearable or embracing the ineffable."

"Which do you think it is?"

"Ah, that is unanswerable."

Our daughter Chris said: "What happened? What terrible thing happened to her? There has to be a *thing*."

Natalie said: "I don't believe it, I'll never believe it, she'd never do this if she were in her right mind."

Lois, my mother-in-law, said: "I can't bear this. Not Norah, not Norah."

Willow Halliday said: "I've always heard that people begging on the street are frauds. That they make big bucks, a couple of hundred dollars a day. Some of them have cell phones, I've seen that myself in Toronto."

Have I articulated how difficult I find Willow Halliday, the mother of one of Norah's friends? Willow is a superb cook and she has said to me a dozen times—I exaggerate, but only a little— that she reads cookbooks the way other people read novels. "But wouldn't you be less of a bore if you read novels?" I long to say, but of course I don't.

Tracy Halliday, a horsey, popular girl, has been a friend of Norah's since childhood. Tracy and another friend made the trek down to Bathurst and Bloor, where they presented Norah with an enormous jar of marbles. (Natalie and Chris were there and later reported the incident to Tom and me.) Tracy knelt down and shouted into Norah's ear, explaining that each marble represents a Saturday, and that if Norah lives to be eighty, she will enjoy an astounding 4,160 such days. Of course, at nearly twenty, she has used up some of the Saturday mornings, but still has more than

3,600 left. If she takes one marble out each week, she will see her supply slowly diminish and will come to value time and her own life.

When I try to imagine Tracy looking at Norah, I understand that she sees no one. For a minute I was Norah. Norah the anchorite, Norah the outcast. I trembled with the thought of what Tracy might think of me.

The real Norah failed to respond, she sat all day with the jar of marbles beside her, and left them there when she returned to the hostel that night. In the morning, apparently, they were gone. I'm not sure what I think of this exercise. Someone told me the marble idea was floating around on the Internet. People wander into the Internet seeking diversion and instead they get a pelting of hard fact and gusty inspiration about the wonderfulness of life. Is this marble-counting exercise a recipe for savouring time or is it a cutting reminder that time cannot, however much we wish it, repeat itself?

I can go for months without seeing Emma Allen, who is a journalist in St. John's, Newfoundland, but just five minutes in her presence persuades me that she is the one person in the world I can tell everything. "Norah is alive," Emma said to me when she was passing through last week—my dear Emma, whose son died of a heroin overdose at age twenty-two. "Her limbs are intact. She hasn't mutilated herself or even shaved off her hair. She isn't drunk, she probably isn't on drugs. She's not shouting obscenities or spitting on strangers. You, her parents, know precisely where she is and something of her routines. That's the thing to remember, that you're still connected to her in time and space."

Professor Hamilton, who taught the Flaubert course in which Norah had been enrolled, said: "She was an excellent student, until she stopped coming to class. This was not long before exams. March twenty-eighth, she was at the March twenty-eighth lecture, I'm almost sure. But you know, many students fall away once the good weather begins. She was always alert and inquiring. Well, yes, we did have one or two altercations, you know how things go these days. Could Flaubert possibly imagine himself into a woman's life? The class divided on that issue, it happens every year. Norah saw Madame Bovary as a woman blandly idealized by Flaubert, and then reduced to a puff of romanticism, and capable of nothing else but kneading her own soft heart. Your daughter's view, and it is a perfectly viable view, was that Madame Bovary was forced to surrender her place as the moral centre of the novel. Others, needless to say, disagreed."

Tom doesn't say so, but he sometimes intimates that Norah is manipulating us. Either that or punishing us for some reason. I resist this interpretation. Tom goes every Friday morning to see her on the way to his trilobite research meeting—he is the only "lay" member of this small group—at the University of Toronto. He's given up talking to her. Now he just sits with her for half an hour, on a folding chair he takes along for that purpose, and slips her money in an envelope. Cash, not a cheque. Norah lives outside the realm of cheques and banks and signatures, even though there's a bank on the corner where she sits and another across the street. Is it when he's counting out the twenties that Tom thinks: manipulation?

An old school friend, Gemma Walsh, an active member of the United Church, has written to tell me that Norah's name has been added to an all-Ontario prayer list. I send her back my sincere thanks, which I sincerely mean. I didn't know I had this depth of sincerity in my soul. I thought sincerity had gone from our generation, driven out by post-sixties disillusionment and the marketplace.

Marietta Glass, Colin Glass's estranged wife, writes from Calgary, quoting Julian of Norwich: "All shall be well, and all shall be well, and all manner of things shall be well." Meaning all is well for the moment and for the moment that follows and the moment after the moment.

Danielle Westerman, with her adamantine certainty, has not swerved from her view that Norah has simply grown into the knowledge of her powerlessness and doesn't know what to do with it. "Subversion of society is possible for a mere few; *inversion* is more commonly the tactic for the powerless, a retreat from society that borders on the catatonic" (*Alive*, 1987, p. 304). I wasn't inclined to believe this statement when I first translated it, but now I believe it absolutely. Danielle's hypothesis has moved into my body and occupies more and more space.

Only

December 2, 2000

Dear Dennis Ford-Helpern:

I have recently finished your book, *The Goodness Gap,* and felt an impulse to put down my impressions. It's taken me a long time to read this book and digest it. (I've had to renew it twice at the public library.)

I was stunned, to say the least, by your theory of goodness being a kind of problem solving. As I interpret your text and epilogue, you see moral dilemmas sprouting like tables and chairs on the sidewalk, growing ever more quickly, nourished by advances in technology and by the decay of the ecosystem. Solutions to serious moral questions inevitably lag behind the problems that arise, hence the "gap." Your fourteen chapters sketch out examples of successful or unsuccessful problem solving. Closing the gap is dependent on quick resolution, sideways thinking, general creativity. All the problem solvers in your examples are men, all fourteen. I consulted the index and found that women are scarcely cited at all. This seems a moral dilemma in itself, don't you think?

Listen to me, how I natter on, just like—just like a woman, the way I fluff up my fantasies of persecution. It happens that I am a woman and the mother of a nineteen-year-old daughter, twenty in May, who is deeply troubled. She is alienated from our family and from society. We don't know the cause of Norah's malaise, but I am more and more persuaded that she is reacting—morally, responsibly, the only way she can—to a withholding universe. What she sees is an endless series of obstacles, an alignment of locked doors. Yet, goodness is exactly what she is seeking, the nature of goodness, how we learn to be good and what that means.

I don't think you intend to be discouraging in your book. I think you have merely overlooked those who are routinely over-looked, that is to say half the world's population. By the way, you may not be able to catch my tone in this letter, but I am trying to put forward my objection gently. I'm not screaming as you may think. I'm not even whining, and certainly not stamping my little lady-size foot. Whispering is more like it. The last thing I want is to be possessed by a sense of injury so exquisitely refined that I register outrage on a daily basis. Anger is not humanizing. It's a rehearsal for the performance that never arrives. Try to imagine my particular realm of feeling at this time of trouble and my belief that there is a circuitry linking your philosophical approach and my daughter's resignation from life, her consignment to dysfunction. Probably you will dismiss this as a crank letter from one of those women who go around begging to be offended, but you must understand that I am trying to protect Norah, and her two younger sisters, Christine and Natalie, who want only to be allowed to be fully human. And you should know, as I set down these words, that I am shaking like a tree of nerves.

Yours,
Rita Orange d'Ville

Unless

"'Virtue is performance,'" I said to Danielle Westerman on Wednesday when we had lunch in her sunroom. "A form of acting. Someone said something like that, but I can't remember who."

"Yeats, I think," she said dreamily, stretching in her chair.

"Yes, Yeats."

She is a woman with twenty-seven honorary degrees and she's given the world a shelf of books. She's given her thoughts, her diagram for a new, better, just world.

A high school in Ontario is named after her, and in France, in the small city of Mâcon, there is a Danielle Westerman Square, a surprisingly beautiful public space with linden trees and cobbled paths, where, when Tom and I walked there early last March, we seemed to move through the drifts of perpetual springtime, as though the people passing us, families, old people, had never known a time of fixed gloom or shame, that they had never been without the filtering, healing buzz of warm sunshine.

In her last years Danielle has become cranky, even with me, her translator. She suspects I've abandoned the "discourse," as she always calls it, for the unworthiness of novel writing. She has a way of lowering her jaw when she skirts this topic, and her eyes seem freshened with disappointment. She is such a persuasive force that I often find myself agreeing with her; what really is the point of novel writing when the unjust world howls and writhes?

Novels help us turn down the volume of our own interior "discourse," but unless they can provide an alternative, hopeful course, they're just so much narrative crumble. Unless, unless.

Unless is the worry word of the English language. It flies like a moth around the ear, you hardly hear it, and yet everything depends on its breathy presence. Unless—that's the little subjunctive mineral you carry along in your pocket crease. It's always there, or else not there. (If you add a capital *s* to *unless,* you get *Sunless,* or *Sans Soleil,* a very odd Chris Marker film.)

Unless you're lucky, unless you're healthy, fertile, unless you're loved and fed, unless you're clear about your sexual direction, unless you're offered what others are offered, you go down in the darkness, down to despair. *Unless* provides you with a trapdoor, a tunnel into the light, the reverse side of not enough. *Unless* keeps you from drowning in the presiding arrangements. Ironically, *unless,* the lever that finally shifts reality into a new perspective, cannot be expressed in French. *À moins que* doesn't have quite the heft; *sauf* is crude. *Unless* is a miracle of language and perception, Danielle Westerman says in her most recent essay, "The Shadow on the Mind." It makes us anxious, makes us cunning. Cunning like the wolves that crop up in the most thrilling fairy tales. But it gives us hope.

At eighty-five, she's not quite lost her superstitious hold on the belief in bad luck and good luck. She's had enough of both bad and good, so that even when occupied with changing the world, she comes on like an old-style Presbyterian, accepting her mixed lot. Her new book is selling briskly everywhere, praised for its originality and sinewy analysis. No author tour, hardly any advertising, but such a response. We talk about the reviews today over our smoked salmon and devilled eggs. Oh, what a thick, rich pile of reviews, one of them referring to the "incantatory" flow of the prose—I like that—and another claiming Danielle as a National Treasure—an epithet that makes her squirm slightly but to me signals her earned authority. After a while we get on to the subject of how we carry a double history in our heads, what is and what could be, and how we must try to keep them from inflating or deflating each other.

She has deleted the early roots from her life, or pretends to have done so. Papa worked for the post office in Mâcon, Maman in a bar in La Roche-Vineuse. Their *appartement* in this village was three rooms in a house on rue des Allemagnes. She refuses to speak of those days (though she did not hesitate to recommend La Roche as a tourist destination). She stored up her energy of repression in her early years and decided to spend it somewhere else. There must have been a day, a moment, when this decision was made. "They're dead," she says, meaning either her parents or the early years. And she adds: "To me they're dead." Her memoirs begin when she is eighteen, in Paris. She had passed her baccalaureate, boarded a train, and enrolled at the Sorbonne. So much for childhood. Miraculously, she has got away with this sketch of a life, so far at least.

"How do you bear it?" I ask her today. I've already told her about the New York editor who has bullied me into sending my half-finished manuscript to him. I've told her about seeing Norah early this morning, how instead of sitting on the pavement she was on her feet, pacing between the subway exit and the bus stop, back and forth, back and forth, her hands jammed into her jacket pockets, her neck bent against the cold, her sign, GOODNESS, hanging crookedly on a string around her neck. I told her about how, last Saturday, Natalie and Chris had decided not to go into Toronto to be with their sister; it was too cold, they said, a little too casually, and there was a volleyball tournament in Orange-town. And finally I've told her about the bitter disappointment I experienced reading *The Goodness Gap* and the letter I dashed off to its unreconstructed author.

"And did you mail this letter?"

"Well, no."

"Ah!"

I explain to her that I sometimes don't believe what I write. I can't rely on my own sallies and locutions, my takes on the imme-diate and devastating circumstances. Often, the next day, looking at what I've written, I'm left shaking my head: Who is the self-pitying harridan who has put down such words, who is the person writing pitiful letters to strangers? Last week, at a party, I was introduced to Alexander (Sandy) Valkner, to whom I had "written" a scolding letter, and found him to be humble, courteous, and kind.

So who is this madwoman, constructing a tottering fantasy of female exclusion and pinning it on her daughter? Often—I don't tell Danielle this—I don't bother to put the words down at all—I *think* my letters line by line, compose them in my head as I dust under the beds. That's enough to keep me sane. Yet I need to know I'm not alone in what I apprehend, this awful incompleteness that has been alive inside me all this time but whose name I don't dare say. I'm not ready to expose myself.

Does Danielle really get it? I thought she did, but now I'm not sure.

She shrugs her beautiful shrug. Thin shoulders, rather narrow, a blue wool knitted vest that should be replaced. A silver bangle on a wrist that looks like it's made of old wax, three silver rings, loose on her bony hands. Her beautifully kept nails are long and crimson. How does she bear it? All the words she's written, all the years buried inside her. What does her shelf of books amount to, what force have these books had on the world?

How do you bear it? I wait for an answer, but none is forthcoming. Tell me, tell me, give me an answer. Give me an idea that's as full of elegance and usefulness as the apple orchard behind my house, something from which I can take a little courage. She shrugs again. For a split second I interpret this as a shrug of surrender. But no. To my surprise, she breaks suddenly into a bright smile, her false teeth gleaming like tiles. And then, slowly, making a graceful arc in the air, she salutes me with her glass of tea.

Toward

On a December morning I went walking hand in hand with Tom in the Orangetown cemetery. God knows what we were looking for; it didn't matter, we were here, together, walking and talking. The cold weather had broken, and the tops of the old limestone monuments, sun-plucked in their neat rows, were shiny with melting snow. We wore light jackets and rubber boots. The alignments of stone whisper: quiet, please. This is something we often do on a Sunday afternoon, not out of morbidity but just wanting a quiet place. We're almost always the only ones here. Years ago, people visited cemeteries regularly, tending graves and supplying them with memorial flowers, uttering words of greeting to those who lay beneath the ground, just as though they believed the dead were really present, just inches away, and eager for a little human conversation. The Orangetown cemetery, cooled by stone on the hottest day, is famous for the quality of its lawn care and the eccentricity of its engravings. Here is an inventory of relics and fashion and a sentimental embrace of death, invoking what may well be the richest moments in a lifetime, the shrine of tears and aching history. People are astonished to find a piece of granite that has been carved into a life-size kicking infant, lying on his back and smiling and gurgling up at the clouds. "Our Little Jack," the inscription reads, "Gone to Eternal Happiness." The sight of this granite baby has always moved my daughters to tears. They always insisted, when they were younger and walking with me in the graveyard, on visiting little Jack, relishing their own tears as they stroked his curly stone head. The tragedy of it. A beloved child, snatched from his parents' arms. Here's where memory broke and shattered and was replaced by a frozen cherub, pawing the air with everlasting delight.

On another of the stones, ugly, vast, and arresting, is carved "Mary Leland, 1863–1921." Underneath are the simple words, "She Took Good Care of Her Chickens."

This inscription is baffling, which is why people are drawn to it. The stonemason must have meant children, not chickens. That's what some people think, that the chisel slipped slightly, imprinting a false message. But maybe there were no children for Mary Leland; maybe she really had nothing but poultry to serve and to advertise her charity. Or maybe a husband, embittered by his wife's neglect, was mocking her in her grave. Lately, I've been trying to focus my thoughts on the immensity rather than the particular. This requires an act of will. I steer my thoughts away from Mary Leland's chickens and, instead, focus on the rows of humped remains and tipped granite stones, three acres in all. So many people have died.

There are people who make a life out of dislocation. Tenancy is all they demand in their refusal to merge with particular neighbourhoods or rooms. But Tom is different. He burrows into the idea of home. I knew this from the beginning, from the first time we met, though I wasn't able, then, to articulate the thought.

It is not true that people in long marriages dissolve into each other, becoming one being. I touch Tom's elbow, the sleeve of his tan jacket; he places his long arms around me and his hands cup my breasts in the friendliest possible way. We are two people in a snapshot, but with a little cropping we could each exist on our own. But that's not what we want. Hold the frame still, contain us, the two of us together, that's what we ask for. This is all it takes to keep the world from exploding. There's that tan jacket of his, a windbreaker with its zipper and smooth microfibres, nothing to call attention to itself, the most generic of garments. On the other hand, there are men, the composed, noisy men from Bay

Street, who choose bright colours, teal or tangerine, for weekend wear, or else the skins of animals, goats, sheep, and so forth. They are men spangled with epaulettes, toggles, tabs, and insignias, the breezy rapists from the Nautica ads, cool and criminal in their poplins, shellacked with light, but they know they're in costume, that they've made an effort that other men, men like Tom, aren't forced to make.

My husband has only one childhood complaint: that his mother was a lousy housekeeper. Once a year (maybe) she got around to scrubbing the soap dish in the bathroom. He remembers how the melting block of Palmolive sweated with its own bubbled dirt, an object of such disgust that he refused to touch it. No one, however, noticed his avoidance of soap. This went on for years. No one thought it mattered, that every day his eyes met with soupy slop. He told me this in our early days together, wanting me to understand his fastidiousness about our bathroom arrangements and worrying that I might think he was one of those comically neurotic men you read about in novels. Unless you had a mother like that, you wouldn't understand. And unless you had been given an alternative glimpse of orderliness, you wouldn't mind. You needed to know about that silken bar sitting freshly in its little porcelain dish, that such an item was a possibility. Anyone's childhood can be an act of disablement if rehearsed and replayed and squinted at in a certain light, but Tom for some reason has fully recovered from his fear of dirty soap dishes, and nowadays his mother has grown obsessive about household cleanliness and even uses that blue antiseptic water in her toilet.

We were talking about his mother as we made our way between gravestones. Lois Winters, née Maxwell, a widow for twelve years now. She worships her son, Tom, her only child, and adores her three granddaughters. She likes me well enough, I think, but there are great windy gaps between us. She has my books, for instance, all of them inscribed, stacked on her glass-topped coffee table, but she has never read a single one of them. This is something a writer can sense immediately. A wall of numb radar rears up and reveals itself when she hears one of my books mentioned. I understand this refusal of hers perfectly, and the reason for it. It has nothing to do with rejection and everything to do with me being the mother of her grandchildren and her son's spouse. This arrangement cannot be challenged by my hobbies, my pastimes, my professional life, my passion.

She has changed since Norah went on the street, as though her brain has lingered too long, like a lettuce leaf in oil and vinegar, a slow deterioration. Since she has dinner with us every night—she brings the dessert, something sweet and homemade—we've been able to observe her gradual day-by-day withdrawal. There was a time, nevertheless, when she took a lively part in the conversation, asking the girls how they were liking their teachers, how the swim team was doing. Always a nettlesome woman, she had political opinions, rather conservative, it's true, but opinions nonetheless, and she listened to the radio, kept up with public affairs.

"Where is Norah?" she kept asking. "When is Norah coming home?" Finally Tom told her, making a careful incremental story of it; Norah had dropped out of university, she had parted from her boyfriend, she was pursuing a path to spiritual goodness, which the family couldn't quite understand, she was detaching herself from the rest of us, sleeping in a hostel, and yes, begging money at the corner of Bathurst and Bloor in downtown Toronto —but everyone held out hopes that she would return to being the Norah we knew and loved, that she would recover from whatever delusion had seized her, that we were doing everything we could for her and that she, as Norah's grandmother, was not to worry.

Well, of course she is worried about her oldest granddaughter, her best-loved granddaughter, if the truth were declared, her darling Norah. She grew steadily more passive at the dinner table, then silent. In recent weeks, her growing silence has become an uncanny reflection of Norah's silence, her posture is as defeated as Norah's. I wonder sometimes if we have all—Tom,

Natalie, Chris, Lois—become actors in Norah's shadow play, if in these last few months we've turned wary, guarded, angered, waiting to be given back what we once had, each of us frozen to the bone and consigned to a place where nothing ever changes. Even Pet has slowed down, his dog-smile retriever's face draped in acquiescence.

But that's not true for life outside our house. I look around and I see all kinds of changes, some of them astonishing. For one thing, our friends Colin and Marietta Glass are back together again; the last thing we expected. She's said goodbye to her lover in Alberta. The Glasses have forgiven each other for God only knows what transgressions and smoothed out their differences. It is astonishing, such an emotional reversal. Colin is tender and loving in her presence—I must admit, it's a joy to see him helping her into her chair at the table—and she, in return, awards him a gaze as soft and uninjured as a young girl's.

And Chrétien is back in power with a huge majority, though the American election results continue to be stalled. Margaret Atwood *did* win the Booker Prize. We *are* going to have a white Christmas, it is guaranteed. Norah has replaced her bedraggled sign with a new one, freshly inked—even this is cheering.

And Cheryl Patterson, the librarian in Orangetown, has married her Bombay dentist, Sam Sondhi. His divorce came through more quickly than expected, and a civil service was held a week ago Saturday, after which we had a reception in our house, a sandwich and champagne lunch for thirty of Cheryl's friends and our friends too, all in a celebratory mood. Who doesn't love a wedding! Richer or poorer, better or worse. Tom had fires lit in the living room and the den, and of course there was the Christmas tree in the hall, put up a few days early this year to accommodate Cheryl and Sam's wedding. The whole house boomed with overflowing spirits. In my long tawny velvet skirt, I passed slices of fruitcake on a silver tray, a tray I only get down from the top cupboard at Christmastime. There was a tiny silver Christmas ornament poked into my chignon, *une épingle à cheveux*, a gift from Tom some years ago. I was smiling, smiling, as I made my rounds, yes, isn't it a miracle they found each other, two divorced people, in a place like Orangetown, Ontario, in the great glistening continent of North America. I was smiling and saying: Please, try this fruitcake, my mother-in-law made it, it's marvellous, an old family recipe. And there was Tom, opening the wide front door to welcome yet another party of guests. He glanced in my direction and smiled broadly. Love of my life. On the buffet table is a salmon, pink and skinned. At certain moments, for no reason—the smell of apple wood burning in the fireplace—I become convinced that everything is going to be all right.

And then suddenly I will be thrown out of the circle of safety, aching all over with pain and feeling a fracture in my cone of consciousness, which is inhabited, every curve of it, by the knowledge (that pale sustenance) that Norah, in the cold and snow of downtown Toronto, has gone as far away as she could go. As was possible to go.

Stop it. Return to the lamplit murmur of now, this minute. Have some fruitcake. There's coffee in the dining room. I hear the voice in my head saying: careful, be careful.

We only appear to be rooted in time. Everywhere, if you listen closely, the spitting fuse of the future is crackling. Despite my mood of anxiousness, my novel, *Thyme in Bloom,* is almost completed. Alicia and Roman have been deconstructing their relationship with articulate arguments and with bad behaviour on both sides. Now and then they eat, drink, and make love, but mostly they systematically destroy what they once had between them, grinding down the core of love with their philosophical arguments so that nothing is left but burnt rice—this from a scene in which they, touchingly, desperately, try to cook a Greek meal in Roman's apartment. Alicia grows sleek, lubricious, and almost beautiful in her independence. We see a steady accretion in her observations, while Roman reveals an irksome antic side, those striped yellow socks, for instance. His strong chin becomes even stronger, and his sexual appetite more voracious. When he practises on his very expensive trombone, he punches great jagged holes in the air. He thinks aloud, and often, about his relations in Albania with whom he has lost touch, grieving for them, everything they've been through; yet what can he do? He went to Tirana in 1986 and tried to make contact, but was discouraged. He almost landed in jail, he was threatened, spat upon, but he loved the goddamn place.

There are two, maybe three chapters to go in *Thyme in Bloom.* Then the denouement, which will contain a twist that is certain to challenge any reader's good will, but I'm determined to go through with it. I'm working toward that moment, bristling with invention. How can this be? How can a woman who has lost her daughter and is suffering acute separation anxiety be capable of writing a comic fantasy?

Although it must be said that Mr. Springer, my new editor, does not agree with me about *Thyme in Bloom* being a comic fantasy. *Au contraire.*

Whatever

The sunshine at midmorning was flowing into the kitchen, and the telephone was ringing.

"Hello? May I speak with Ms. Reta Winters, please."

"This is Reta Winters."

"Oh, Reta, I am so sorry. I failed to recognize your voice."

"I have a bit of a cold—"

"It's Arthur calling. Arthur Springer."

"Arthur."

"From New York. From Scribano and—"

"Oh, of course, how are—?"

"I hope you had a happy Christmas. You and your family."

"Well, yes, yes, we did. We are. And did you—?"

"I do apologize for phoning you at home."

"At home? That's quite all right. In fact, this is where I—"

"And I apologize even further for phoning during Christmas week. This is the one time in the year when we should put all business aside and make merriment our first concern."

"Well, yes—"

"As a matter of fact, Scribano & Lawrence is officially closed until the new year, as per tradition, but I am so excited about your manuscript that I wanted to make immediate contact and I thought to myself that you might have the goodness to forgive me for breaking into the holiday so rudely, and no doubt I've phoned at an ungodly hour."

"Oh, no, we're actually in the same time zone as—"

"*Thyme in Bloom*! Where can I begin!"

"Well, I—"

"I finished reading the partial draft last night. I hardly slept. Alicia and Roman were so much in my mind, visceral beings, pressing against my consciousness, all they endured, their personal courage, their sense of their very selves as their insight grew and grew, their interior vision, piercing like a laser, you can imagine my— How I grieved when—and yet marvelled at— I woke up thinking, this is what life is, no one ever promised we wouldn't suffer as we make our way, our expectations are doomed to disappointment—"

"But, Arthur—"

"And Alicia—her persevering goodness. I told you that last time we spoke, didn't I?"

"Yes, you did. I was so pleased. I'm trying to work out what goodness is, in fact, its essence, and—"

"Such goodness of soul, of heart. It's integral, you don't even have to remark on it or put little quotes around it. You can see why I had to call you right away. Even if it was Christmas week, even if—"

"But, Arthur—"

"And Roman. That man. Roman, Roman."

"Yes?"

"Indescribable. The one word a writer must never use, but for us editors, well, we can only think: what an indescribable character! His complexity, I mean."

"Really?"

"Indescribable! I can't imagine how we're going to present him in the flap copy, but we'll work on it."

"You do know, Mr. Springer, Arthur, this isn't the complete manuscript. I've still got at least three chapters to finish and even what you saw is just a draft—"

"I do, I do, Reta, I remember our conversation. I know that what I've just read is a draft and a partial draft at that. But, and this is what's so wonderfully uncanny, I know where you're going with this. Now, don't, please, misinterpret my words. What I mean is, I know and I don't know. You haven't given anything away, you've been astonishingly stern and strict with the reader, letting him or her do no more than sniff and conjecture. But the form, and I am speaking of the form in its universal aesthetic sense, is so solidly there, and so is the sense that the form will complete itself in the only way it can."

"I'm so glad you feel that way—"

"I'm actually phoning you from the office. Mr. Scribano would do somersaults in his grave if he knew the Christmas holiday had been abused, but I had to come in and look up the reviews for *My Thyme Is Up*. I suppose I could have looked them up on the Internet, but I wanted to feel the weight of them in my hand. And to listen, actually listen, to what the reviewers said at the time. I am quite sure, Reta, that you have read some of them yourself."

"All of them, I think."

"Excellent, excellent. I have never found myself in accord with those writers who refuse to read their own reviews. And heed their reviews. It seems to me a more than arrogant position to take. Even though facing the critics is sometimes painful, it is only good sense to know whether or not you have actually connected with the reader. And at what level. And this is what I am anxious to talk to you about, Reta. The level, the tone, the intention of the book."

"Well, my—"

"And so I've read all the reviews now for your first novel. *New York Times*, *Washington Post*, et cetera. You had excellent coverage for a first novel, I feel. Truly, I mean it, excellent coverage."

"Yes, I was surprised at all—"

"I have them here spread out on my desk, and I've been sitting here for an hour underlining and circling, and here is the question I have for you, Reta. How did you feel about the book's reception?"

"I was pleased. Astonished, really."

"Good. You feel, then, that the book's intention was understood by the critical reader?"

"I . . . I think so. Yes."

"What, then, is your intention with this second novel, *Thyme in Bloom?*"

"You mean, what am I aiming for?"

"Exactly."

"Well, it's a sequel. So I suppose my intention, as you call it, is much the same. The same people, the same setting in Wychwood, the continuing problem of—"

"The problem is, Reta, you are writing, now, a pilgrimage. I have always been deeply drawn to the idea of pilgrimage. Always. You have written—and I have not forgotten it is a draft— you have produced a novel about human yearning. Do you know how rare that is? Your previous novel was—and I hope you will forgive me for putting it this way—it was a light romantic comedy about quite ordinary people."

"I remember one of the reviewers called me a bard of the banal. And this was in an otherwise quite nice review. We really laughed about that."

"Yes, yes, true. You do see, don't you, Reta, that there is a problem about presenting your new novel as a sequel."

"But it *is* a sequel. There's Alicia and Roman and their marriage plans and—"

"Anyway, I'm phoning to see when you can get to New York. Next week if possible."

"Oh! I can't possibly do that, go to New York."

"It's terribly important that we talk now, the two of us. Before you finish your draft, before you go any further."

"I'm afraid I can't leave home at the moment, Arthur. There are family considerations that—"

"I do remember Mr. Scribano saying there were problems, a worrying daughter, but surely you could get away for a day or two."

"No. It's not possible."

"Then I'll come to you! To Orangetown. Is this place near Montreal? I know Montreal very, very well."

"It's near Toronto."

"Ah. Toronto, yes. I can easily manage Toronto. I'll get a cab from there to your place of residence."

"You might want to rent a car."

"It will take us at least two days, Reta, to go through the manuscript. Is there a hotel in the village of Orangetown?"

"There's the Orangetown Inn. It's quite—"

"I'm looking at my calendar, I've got it right in front of me. Will January second be all right?"

"Let's see, is that a Monday? I've got the days all mixed up, you know what Christmas week is like. If it's a Tuesday or Wednesday I can't possibly—"

"January second. I'll get the earliest plane available. The Orangetown Inn. Don't worry, I'll phone right away and book for two nights, the second and the third. Keep them clear. There's so much to talk about."

"Are you sure we need—?"

"This is actually an excellent idea, getting away from New York into the countryside, much more profitable in every way. Tranquility, tran-quil-i-ty. And if I may say so, meeting like this is a splendid way to launch the new year. Happy New Year, Reta."

"Happy New Year. To you. Arthur? Hello? Are you there?"

Any

December 31, 2000

Dear Emily Helt:

For obvious reasons I am not a regular reader of the *Chicago Tribune,* but my New York editor (Scribano & Lawrence) has sent me a book review he picked up on the Internet, your long critique of Susan Bright's *An Imperfect Affair,* a novel which I confess I have not read. He was delighted to see that in your introduction you had mentioned me by name, believing, I suppose, that all publicity is good publicity. One does hear that quite often, and perhaps it's true.

Women writers, you say, are the miniaturists of fiction, the embroiderers of fine "feeling." Rather than taking a broad canvas of society as Don DeLillo does, or Philip Roth, who interprets relationships through the "lens of sexual yearning," women writers such as—and here you list a number of female names including my own—find universal verities in "small individual lives." This, you go on to say, is a "tricky proposition," which only occasionally works.

I surrender to your judgment about my own novel, *My Thyme Is Up.* It was a quick write and a quick read, with no broad canvas in sight and only a gesture toward erotic desire. Okay, okay. I am not offended in the least. I try to be objective about *particular* disregard; it is only *casual* disregard that is making me—shall I say it?—that is making me crazy, though no one, not even my family and close friends, suspects. Way back in high school we learned that the major themes of literature were birth, love, understanding, work, loneliness, connection, and death. We believed that the readers of novels were themselves "small individual lives," and so were the writers. They did not suffer, as you intimate, from a lack of range in their subject matter. These lives apprehended the wide world in which they swam, and from their writers' chairs they thrummed to the tune of sexual longing, but their gaze was primarily on the locked-up consciousness of their individual, human, creaturely being and how each separate person makes sense of all that is benevolent or malicious. There weren't any rules about good and evil, and no Big Rule. It just seems that our species is happier when we are good. This is observable, though difficult to document.

It happens that I am the mother of a nineteen-year-old daughter who has been driven from the world by the suggestion that she is doomed to miniaturism. Her strategy is self-sacrifice. I know what that feels like. She can have "goodness but not greatness," to quote the well-known Dr. Danielle Westerman. It is, as you say, a "tricky proposition." And she has been tricked.

Yours,
Xeta d'Orange

Whether

Danielle Westerman has absorbed, to the greatest degree possible for her, to the greatest degree *bearable* for her, the paradox of subjugation. She's probably come to the place where she knows this is as good as it's ever going to be. She hasn't the strength for yet another bout of resistance, but she's not going to surrender either. She refuses, for instance, to embrace the goddesses of old. There were never any such goddesses, she says: only appeasement, divagation, crumbs.

"What a terrible life she's had!" Sally said.

"No," I insisted, "she's had a remarkably satisfying life."

"It's not as though she hates men," Lynn put in.

"Far from it."

"Which wouldn't surprise anyone," Annette said. "If she did hate men, I mean."

"It's only," I said, hesitating, not wanting to speak for Danielle, "that she probably hoped for the big step forward. Not all these little legislative steps that hardly add up."

Annette and Lynn nodded at this, but Sally looked baffled. "My God," she said. "Just having a washer and dryer is progress. Just having running water. You've been to Africa. You've seen women who do nothing all day but carry jugs of water."

Sally doesn't get it. I'm not sure Lynn does either. Annette does, I think. Maybe because she's black as well as female.

Annette nods slowly. "I know."

"The misery!"

It is Tuesday morning, January 2 in the year 2001. I have

phoned Mr. Springer's office in New York and left a surprisingly assertive message, saying that I would not be available until the fifth of January, a Friday. Tuesdays I have coffee with my friends in the Orange Blossom Tea Room and Wednesdays I drive to Toronto; I didn't bother to explain the particulars to Adrienne, the secretary, but she phoned me straight back to say that Arthur had acquiesced. He could not manage the fifth but would definitely arrive on Friday the nineteenth, and that he would turn up on my doorstep at three in the afternoon and was looking forward to a country weekend.

"A country weekend?" Lynn Kelly said in her musing way. "What do you suppose he has in mind? Horses and things?"

"I suppose I could have a dinner party," I said. "But I really can't be bothered."

"A rustic dinner party?"

"A potluck thing?"

"You could take him to the Saturday-morning market. It's got much better lately. There's a woman who makes beads out of dried rose petals—"

"Yes! And they're supposed to have everlasting fragrance. She has some way of compacting them."

"That's what the original rosaries were made of—"

"Really! I never put that together."

"And there's that man who makes those outrageous twig chairs that—"

"That you can't actually sit down on."

"They're sculpture, in his view, not furniture. And there's someone new, he's got hair down to his waist, who takes chunks of wood and installs little secret drawers in them, and inside the drawers are other little drawers."

"What do you think he'll be like?" Sally asks. "Your Arthur Springer with his—"

"I don't know," I confess. "But I'm terribly afraid he's going to be—I can't pin it down exactly, but—"

"New Agey?"

"New Yorky."

"Cool type? Ivy covered?"

I shake my head. "I'm afraid he's going to be smarmy."

"Oh, my God."

"Don't let him get away with it."

"Just smarm him back."

"Pompously mandarin, like those—"

"I'll have to ask him to stay to dinner, and I have a feeling Tom's going to be driven up the wall. The girls too. They're formidable. They have this new word: kronk. It means shit or something like that. Kronk you, they say to each other. They call Tom the Kronkmeister, and he loves it. He does a little salute and clicks his heels. Natalie does these wicked imitations of—"

"Leave it to a teenager to see through genuine smarm—"

"Especially New York smarm. Or kronk, for that matter. When we were there—"

"I've talked to him on the phone twice now, and I couldn't help noticing that he always interrupts me just when I'm getting to the point of—"

"We're always interrupting each other. Have you noticed how we, the four of us—"

"That's different. It's all right to interrupt each other when there's no power structure to—"

"Really? Do you really believe that—?"

"It's how the conversation goes, how it gets made, brick by brick, but with these little chipped-in bits of—"

"But you and Arthur What's-his-name are definitely in a power arrangement, Reta."

"This man's your publisher."

"No, he's her editor, not her publisher."

"But he can decide what is going to be published, what is acceptable to the—"

"He can definitely influence Reta's novel."

"If you let him."

"At least you'll be on home turf. They always say with football that the home field has a definite—"

"You know, Reta, the very fact that he was 'unable' to come on the fifth as you suggested and changed to the nineteenth—"

"Definitely signals a power play."

"Absolutely."

"The final say."

"I've done it myself."

"How is it coming, Reta? The novel?"

"Slowly. I've slowed down a bit."

"The pressure from New York can't help. And so soon after Christmas when it's all we can do to gear up again."

"You're right. Just the thought of him makes me terribly self-conscious. The more he praises, the more doubtful I become."

This is true. I haven't looked at the manuscript for a couple of days. Before hearing from Arthur Springer it had been my darling baby, my greatest distraction. The only efficient way I had to palliate my worry about Norah was to melt into an alternative reality, to hie myself downtown to Wychwood City with its financial district and concert hall and statues and street corners and its luminous puzzles of space. And now I'm frightened by it, afraid to click on the icon for *Thyme in Bloom*. Instead I've been brushing up on trombones, astonished to find a sizable webliography on the subject. Trombones look idiotically simple, but in fact they're the subject of legend and romance, even greatness. Another distraction. I think about these brass instruments the way I look into the dregs of a coffee cup, idly, tipping it so that the circle at the bottom of the cup widens to an oval lake. There is so much to know.

Meanwhile, the novel is frozen by its own core of procrastination. Alicia is *still* trying to decide what she can do to save herself. She doesn't want to hurt Roman, her dear Roman with his thick rumpled head of hair and musky scent, like a wedge of cheese crusted over. But she must tell him soon what he long ago should have understood. Her mother will wail, her father will grouch, and Roman's family will think ill of her, everyone will be embarrassed. But she must secure her own survival. Yet that sounds selfish. She wants out of the engagement but she also wants to live with a good conscience. Surely there is some kind of ethical judgment she can draw on. Everywhere on this earth there exist lovers who dissolve their commitments; it's scarcely a crime. Alicia knows she and Roman will survive, but she—*she* will be the destroyer, the breaker of promises, hard-hearted, unkind, bringing corrosion and damage to an existence that has been underpinned with natural goodness. Love, marriage, children, a nest in which to nestle. The comfort of it, the natural curvature to which we cling.

Whenever Alicia thinks of idealized goodness, the image of granite comes to mind, polished surfaces, impermeable stone. But stone can be crushed, rather easily, in fact. Alicia has visited the quarry down near Straw Hill. She's seen the giant machines at work. Goodness is not guaranteed. A life of principle requires practice, and although a lot of contractual morality has been worked out, people continue to make mistakes. Then goodness becomes simply a matter of what we wanted to do all along. Whatever is convenient. Face it, goodness has no force; none. Decadence and transgression and overturned promises do occur, all the time, in fact. She's tried to describe her feelings to Roman, but he is occupied with other issues.

He wants to honeymoon in Albania, for one thing; he is being most insistent. He's bought a map. He's e-mailed his relations in Tirana and discovered that even in this poorest corner of Europe the e-mail network is potent. Alicia finds this honeymoon idea hard to entertain, never mind the marriage itself. Albania sounds like punishment to her. Nevertheless, Roman is wearing her down. They never seem to get around to having a real discussion about their future together. Roman doesn't yet understand that the marriage is not going to take place. His nerves are too tender to register the fact. Or else they're too coarse.

Furthermore, he has fallen out with the bassoonist in the Wychwood Symphony. The bassoonist's chair is just in front of Roman's, and she—Sylvia Woodall—complains that the bell of Roman's trombone is smack in her ear. She also complains that she gets wet when he moistens his slide with his little spray bottle of water, and her hair, which is naturally curly, goes into a witch's frizz and makes her lose her composure and her sense of where she is in the music. She wants him to move his chair back an inch or two, and Roman refuses. There's no room, he maintains. What can he do? Well, Sylvia Woodall says, then you can at least redirect the angle of the spray. I can't, says Roman, who might easily be accused of possessing an over-groomed sense of entitlement: it's impossible.

The two lovers, Alicia and Roman, are getting nowhere, and the wedding date is approaching. And I, the director of this comic romance, have reached an end to my thinking. A narrative apogee is called for at this time, and it slyly evades me. I keep stopping and trying to tease out from the lovers' quarrels those small illuminations that fit like a plug into a socket, but all I get is anger. I'm beset by a serious post-Christmas *énervement*. Is there any task as joyless as undecorating a tree? Yes and no. I always wait till the girls go back to school and Tom back to the clinic; they can't be trusted with the tedium of unhooking fragile ornaments, wrapping them in tissue paper, and putting them back in their designated cartons, and then easing the tree onto its side and dragging it out the big front door, then sweeping up mountains of needles and picking them one by one out of the baseboards. A whole morning of methodical and discouraging labour.

But there; it's done; I'm glad to have it gone. I welcome this reclaimed space. Now I can think.

I'm trying to reconstruct my phone conversation with Arthur Springer, but only a few particles survive. He said something about a pilgrimage, which makes no sense at all. I imagine now that a twinkling menace overhung the words he uttered. But then the kitchen was particularly noisy the morning he phoned.

Natalie and Chris, on Christmas break, had risen late and were making pancakes at the stove, trying to form their initials in pancake batter. They had the radio turned up, a particularly loud rock station. The dishwasher was running. Tom was clumping down the stairs. My heart was beating. It's a wonder I heard anything at all.

Ever

Natalie and Chris have resumed their Saturday visits to Bathurst and Bloor, and just before Christmas they took Norah an immense Christmas bundle, lovely things, all of them beautifully wrapped, a soft blue tracksuit with thermal lining, perfumed soap, a brush and comb, a stocking full of fruit and chocolate. Our collective guess is that she gave all these things away, immediately, to strangers, but we can accept that, we *have* to accept it since we can't stop thinking about it.

What I'd like is a lobotomy, a clean job, the top of my head neatly sawn off and designated contents removed. I'd get rid of that week last spring when we didn't know where Norah was. I'd extract the blood pouring out of Natalie's forehead that time years ago when her high chair tipped over in the garden and hit the fence. All body wounds, in fact, would go, including the scabs I saw on Norah's wrists last week, that half inch between her mittens and her coat sleeve, a ring of red sores. I'd take out the whole soundtrack of *My Fair Lady* and the memory of my mother painting china after she had to be put in the care facility because she couldn't cope, couldn't even remember her own name after my father died. Also that time I started menstruating on the train to Ottawa; naturally I was wearing my new white pantsuit. And that bout of cystitis Chris had when we were in France, when for five whole minutes I couldn't remember the word for bladder (*vessie,* noun, feminine). And that fight Tom and I got into on the third anniversary of our meeting in Nathan Phillips Square, over what I can't remember, when each of us said too much and too cruelly. Neither of us would dare go back to that moment when we came close to tearing each other apart, so that for days afterwards we trembled and whispered and hung on to each other all night long.

Tom was puzzled when I described the red scabbiness of Norah's wrists. Chilblains, he guessed, that odd, almost Dickensian ailment brought on by exposure to fierce weather.

"You don't think she could have taken a razor and—"

"No." Shaking his head. "You said it was more like a rash."

He had a look himself on Friday when he was in Toronto and now he isn't sure—but he had hesitated about getting too close to her as she paced back and forth on her corner. He didn't want her to think he was *peering*. Severe eczema occurred to him, and he left a jar of cortisone cream next to the square of cardboard she occupies, and, from Honest Ed's, a huge pair of sheepskin gloves that will come up to her elbows if she has the sense to put them on.

What a guessing game we play with this child of ours. She has not had such intense parenting since she was an infant, but this time round all our efforts are based on conjecture.

There are dance anthropologists—Annette Harris told me about this phenomenon—who attempt to reconstruct the lost ballets of Nijinsky, relying on scraps of music, reviews, the temper of the times at the beginning of the twentieth century, and half a dozen rough choreographic notes scribbled in the margin of a diary. This has to be heartbreaking work, doomed to failure, yet the exercise is very like what Tom and I do when we confer about Norah: her health, her sanity, the rash on her wrists, her nutrition, the glaze coating her dull eyes, what her sisters report, and what it is that passes through her brain as she walks to her corner every morning and then back to the shelter at night. And why?

Tom has come to believe she is suffering post-traumatic shock. The problem, he says, is identifying the trauma and making it visible. A brutal visibility, but authentication can transform the event from an ever-repeating reality to mere memory, which the brain can accommodate. He has all but deserted his trilobites for his current research on stress and trauma. He sits hunched over his computer in the evenings, deep into the Internet, webbing off darkly into trauma therapy, trauma stress, trauma case histories. In our bedroom we have a stack of books and journals on the subject.

Well, he is a doctor. The idea of diagnosis and healing comes naturally to him, a rhythmic arc of cause and effect that has its own built-in satisfactions, and how enviable, to me, this state of mind is. So simple, so clean. I wish now that I had made Roman a doctor rather than a trombonist, but it's too late. I can't see him without that flash of brass in his arms and his mouth pumping away, and besides, he was a trombonist in the previous novel and I can't arbitrarily send him off for four years of medical school, never mind pre-med and a disposition that begins at birth.

I passionately believe a novelist must give her characters work to do. Fictional men and women tend, in my view, to collapse unless they're observed doing their work, *engaged* with their work, the architect seen in a state of concentration at the drafting table, the dancer thinking each step as it's performed, the computer programmer tracing a path between information and access. Emma Allen believes that the great joy of detective fiction is watching the working hero being busy every minute with work; work in crime novels is always in view, work is the whole point.

I've read novels about professors who never step into the classroom. They're always on sabbatical or off to a conference in Hawaii. And artist-heroes who never pick up a paintbrush, they're so busy at the local café, so occupied with their love life or their envy or their grief. Does the brilliant young botanist with the golden back-swept hair, one wisp loose at her neck, wander up a grassy hillside and fill her pockets with rare species? No, we see her only after work or on weekends when she goes to parties and meets young novelistic lawyers who have no cases to work on, no files, no offices, no courtrooms in which to demonstrate their skills. That husky young construction worker does all his sexual coupling between shifts, and with a blonde-headed graduate of Mount Holyoke as his partner—what about that? Just once I'd like to see him with the pneumatic drill hammering against his body, shaking him stupid. But what if the novelist is a Yale grad, and his father before him? What would he know about how that drill kicks and jumps and transfers its nerves into the bones and belly of a human being? We might see the poor guy reach out for humanistic understanding, discovering Shakespeare-in-the-Park or French cinema, something like that, but chances are against seeing him *work*.

I love work. When I meet people I always want to ask them what they do, but Lynn Kelly tells me this is no longer an allowable conversational probe. There are too many people who are unemployed or else ashamed of what they do, assembly work in condom factories, for example, or exterminating cockroaches. Work can be ugly. Work is a sensitive issue. The last time I asked a woman what she "did"—this was at a Christmas party a couple of weeks ago—she gave me a look and said, "I don't do anything." Then she intensified her glare and said, "And I don't do courses either." (When the time comes for my lobotomy this is one of several social incidents I plan to remove.)

But why did I make Roman a trombonist in the first place if I knew nothing about trombones? Because I was sitting in my little box room, stuck on a paragraph in an early chapter, and idly springing a French paper clip back and forth in my fingers. When we were in France—admittedly this is an affectation—I brought back a large box of paper clips, which are pointed at one end instead of rounded. They look different from our North American paper clips, they look chic, they look French. And they're known to the French, who love to press endearments on objects, as *trombones*. This was how Roman acquired his vocation in the world of brass, through an accident of association, because I, the stalled writer of a first novel, happened one afternoon to be twisting *un petit trombone* in my hands and thinking about giving my male character some real work to do.

Horst Raasch, Roman's hero and teacher, claimed that the trombone should strive for a sound not unlike the cello, coming out in long slow heartbeats. Raasch taught him to attack the tone softly but clearly, keeping the tone stands steady. "Tonal beauty" was the ultimate goal. Roman began serious study at fourteen with a Kruspe Modell Weschke—which his family could scarcely afford; his grandfather saved coins in a pickle jar in order to purchase this instrument. The Sachse Concerto was chosen—Roman can't remember why—for his mid-term exam, and he succeeded brilliantly. He loved the idea of being brilliant, and began to practise more and more so that he could be brilliant all the time. He learned, eventually, to perform with exactitude, the eighths, triplets, sixteenth, and thirty-second notes. He developed an excellent high register. On off-hours he stumbled into jazz: "Sleepy Lagoon," "Stardust," "I'm Getting Sentimental over You," but he had to hide that side of himself from purists. He was good, more than good, as his appointment to the Wychwood Symphony confirms.

The trombone is a difficult instrument to master, since the tolerance between the inner and outer slides is so precise that lubrication is needed. At one time Pond's cold cream was the chosen lube, but recently there have been tailored-to-the-need products such as silicone drops, applied weekly and augmented by a creamy soapy liquid. Most trombonists also need an occasional squirt of water from an atomizer, keeping the mechanism moist and slippery. The F-attachment has, needless to say, made an immense difference to symphony trombonists, not least because it adds a few notes to the bottom range—and Roman loves the bottom range. He knows how fortunate he is to be employed by an eminent orchestra, but his feet are itchy these days, and his "differences" with Sylvia Woodall, the bassoonist, are coming to a head; he loathes the woman. In addition, he feels a longing to visit Albania, the land of his forefathers.

As a novelist, I am somewhat surprised by the complexity of Roman's vocation and have to ask myself, every day, how I got into such complexity.

Alicia I put to work at an unnamed fashion magazine, and this, too, I regret. My idea of magazine ambiance comes from TV or films. I have no idea what the fashion-magazine workplace looks like or how magazine people interact. I like to think that Alicia sees through the fraud of fashion or that she raises fashion to the level of style and style to the level of imprimatur, all of it stacked neatly under the elegant and sensible rubric of *being*. I pretend, when she writes about gloves or handbags or shoes, that she is looking at the history or the *philosophie* of these objects. She is amused by them, but respectful; otherwise she would, out of disgust, enrol at Wychwood University and do a doctorate in, say, Chinese women's poetry in the second half of the eighteenth century. But a work shift of that order is cataclysmic, and I doubt my ability to make the change plausible to readers who are quite happy to linger in the sleek, perfumed boardroom and corridors of X Magazine. Something would have to trigger the impulse, something *traumatic* to make loyal, hardworking, serious, sincere Alicia abandon the fashion world for academe. And then she would have to write a thesis, and I would become a woman writing about a woman writing about women writing, and that would lead straight to an echo chamber of infinite regress in company with the little Dutch girl, the girl on the bathroom cleanser, the vision multiplied, but in receding perspective. No.

The problem is, I'm not sure I believe in the thunderclap of trauma. A stubborn screen of common sense keeps getting in my way and cancelling the filigree of fine-spun theory. Isn't our species smarter than that? Somewhere, wired into our brains, there must exist a little bean-shaped nerve cluster that registers the relative *proportion* of events and separates the exceptional experience that we can shrug off simply because it *is* exceptional from the slow, steady accumulation of incremental knowledge, which is what really delivers us to the brink, one small injury bleeding into another until the whole system tips over.

I don't actually say this aloud to Tom as he delves into the subject of trauma, hoping to rescue or at least understand Norah by tracking down that "thing" that leapt out at her last spring and knocked her out of her life. I don't want to discourage his pursuit, which, even if it leads nowhere, at least affords him a distraction. As long as he finds parallel examples, he can believe. He is certain his own mother, for instance, has been traumatized by Norah's stance. He suspects Danielle Westerman suffers from some long ago childhood trauma, that she, at eighty-five, still reverberates with an unrecognized shame or loss or sorrow of a highly specific sort.

Because Tom is a man, because I love him dearly, I haven't told him what I believe: that the world is split in two, between those who are handed power at birth, at gestation, encoded with a seemingly random chromosome determinate that says yes for ever and ever, and those like Norah, like Danielle Westerman, like my mother, like my mother-in-law, like me, like all of us who fall into the uncoded female otherness in which the power to assert ourselves and claim our lives has been displaced by a compulsion to shut down our bodies and seal our mouths and be as nothing against the fireworks and streaking stars and blinding light of the Big Bang. That's the problem.

This cry is overstated; I'm an editor, after all, and recognize purple ink when I see it. The sentiment is excessive, blowsy, loose, womanish. But I am willing to blurt it all out, if only to myself. Blurting is a form of bravery. I'm just catching on to that fact. Arriving late, as always.

Whence

January 10, 2001

Dear Peter ("Pepe") Harding:

So! You've died. I read your obituary this morning in the *Globe and Mail*, while sitting in a sunny corner of my living room; you don't even want to know what it's like outside today; it's so bad the weather report on the radio broke into poetry and called what we're experiencing "bitter cold," which sounds like a phrase from an ancient Anglo-Saxon epic. There's a bitter wind, too, meaner than a junkyard dog, as the old song has it.

Years ago I belonged to a small writing group, and the leader of our group, a woman called Gwen Reidman, advised us to read obituaries because they carry, like genes packed tight in their separate chromosomes, tiny kernels of narrative. These little yelps of activity—Gwen always referred to them as putty—are so personal and authentic and odd that they are able to reinforce the thin tissue of predictable fiction and bend it into unlikely shapes. I recently read an obit, for instance, of an elderly deceased woman who had been the 1937 lacrosse champion of Manitoba. Think of it: this was a woman who carried her triumph through the years of World War II, through the riotous sixties, through the long leadership era of Pierre Elliott Trudeau and Ronald Reagan and Margaret Thatcher, all the way into the late nineties, when her grandchildren acquired—I am guessing—a computer with access to the Internet, where they found, after some minutes of searching, a number of Web pages devoted to the nearly extinct game of lacrosse—and a mention of a name, their grandmother's name, it was astonishing!—that name was still blinking out there in the detritus of time, a champion's name, a victor.

I was sorry to read that you have struggled so long with your cancer, but "bravely," as the report says, all the way to the end. What an interesting life you've led. I'm sure you didn't dream growing up on a hardscrabble Saskatchewan farm that you would be awarded the Douglas McGregor Scholarship and end up in Toronto, a beloved teacher at the very private and elite Upper Canada College, and that you would always give your "utmost" to your students, so that when you retired in 1975 they got together and held a roast at Hart House, an event of such warmth and tribute that it is still talked about today. Kaye, your wife, will miss you, as will your children, Gayle and Ian, and your three grandchildren, and your old colleagues who visited you in hospital, sitting upright in those stiff, steel hospital chairs.

You were comforted in your last days, the obituary notice concludes, by that pile of books on your bedside table. You would not be parted from them. Mark Twain, Jack London, Sinclair Lewis, Fitzgerald, Hemingway, Faulkner, Joyce, Beckett, T. S. Eliot, Leonard Cohen—their texts constituted for you an "entire universe." Another "entire universe" reached you through the earphones provided by the hospice and for which your family gives thanks: Bach, Beethoven, and Mozart; they sang you off to your death.

I am going through some bleak days, Mr. Harding, Pepe. (Difficult teenagers and so on, which you will know something about from your teaching years and from your own family.) I, too, am hungry for the comfort of the "entire universe," but I don't know how to assemble it and neither does the oldest of my children, a daughter. I sense something incomplete about the whole arrangement, like a bronze casting that's split open in the foundry, an artifact destined by some invisible flaw to break apart. Also, I'm frightened that I'm missing something, that Norah is missing something.

Goodbye, rest in peace. Go well, as they say in Swaziland, where my friend Sally Bachelli spent a year teaching village women to make dresses for themselves. Four-hour dresses, they were called; that's how long it took to make a dress without a sewing machine, Sally's own design.

I grieve for you too.
Rita Hayworth
Orange Blossom City

Forthwith

"Reta!"

"Arthur."

"I hope I'm not too terribly late. Traffic was a nightmare, and then the taxi got lost, thinking it was Orangeville I wanted, not Orangetown. It seems there's a great difference."

"About fifteen miles, it's awfully confusing, but do come in out of the cold. Here, let me take your coat. I thought you'd be older somehow."

"Thirty-nine. And you're forty-four—I looked it up in the clipping file."

"Almost contemporaries. But not quite."

"What a heavenly house. Wood smoke, I can smell wood smoke. Ah, and there is the fire, the source of that heavenly aroma."

"I thought we could sit—"

"There's nothing like a wood fire. Crackling away. In New York only the fortunate few have access to— And the price of firewood! Ten dollars for four little sticks, of course that's for very, very good firewood, hickory—What a splendid room this is, Reta—these lovely windows— Good God, it's already getting dark—not even four-thirty—of course, you're much further north—that would make the difference."

"Would you like some coffee? I've just—"

"Coffee, hmm."

"Or, since you've just got out of a cold taxi—maybe—it's early, but maybe you'd like a glass of red wine."

"I wouldn't want you to open a bottle just for me."

"I'm sure we have one open. I'll just—"

"So this is where you work."

"Well, not in this actual room. This is the living room. I have a little spot on the third floor that I—"

"Oh my!"

"I hope you're not allergic to dogs."

"No, I was just—just taken by surprise."

"He's entirely harmless, aren't you, Pet—with an extremely obedient nature, though it took forever to get him housetrained. That's what we call him. Pet."

"And your family? They're here at the moment."

"The girls will be home in an hour or so. They've got swimming after school today. And my husband, Tom, he'll be coming soon. We're hoping you can stay to dinner, just a simple—"

"I'd be delighted. Honoured to be welcomed so warmly. I don't want to be a nuisance but—this view with the fading light, that hint of rose in the air behind the trees, it must be a source of calm and, well—I do hate the word *inspiration,* it's grown to be such a cliché, but in this case I feel I can believe in such a thing, that living here, in such peace, these oaks and maples, the pace of each day quietly asserting itself—ah, thank you so much—the seasons rolling along— Hmm—a lovely light red, it's never too early in the afternoon for a red like this. Let me propose a toast to the new manuscript—to Alicia and Roman!—and now, tell me, how is it coming?"

"I printed it out this morning. This is it, or rather, most of it."

"Let me see. Hmm. The heft itself is most impressive—three hundred pages—oh my, Reta, you've added quite a bit since I read it in December. *Quite* a bit."

"I still have a hundred things to do. Some patching and poking. And the final chapter."

"Ah yes, the final chapter. The all-important final chapter."

"The most difficult chapter in a way."

"I absolutely agree. It's critical. What is a novelist to do?

Provide closure for the reader? Or open the narrative to the ether?"

"You mean—"

"I think of the final chapter as the kiln. You've made the pot, Reta, the clay is still malleable, but the ending will harden your words into something enduring and beautiful. Or else beautiful and ethereal."

"What an interesting thought. I was just thinking the other day about the way a bronze casting sometimes breaks unexpectedly in the forge. And now you mention pots in the kiln—"

"I meant it as a metaphor."

"So did I."

"I knew we were kindred spirits, Reta. Though I should tell you I am in favour, in your particular case, of not offering closure. There is a danger, you see, that you might trivialize Roman's search for identity, which is ongoing, a forever kind of thing."

"Can I give you a little more wine?"

"With pleasure. Lovely and dry, this red, just the thing for our first face-to-face meeting. The sort of meeting that could be difficult."

"I do want you to know, Mr. Springer, that I am completely open to editing suggestions."

"Arthur, please. That's wonderful to know, that you don't object to the editorial hand. I understand Mr. Scribano did not really edit *My Thyme Is Up*. He was the editor, of course, nominally, but he did very little, my sources tell me, in the way of reshaping the work."

"He did ask me to break one very long paragraph into two, and I thought that was an excellent suggestion. I was happy to—"

"I believe I told you on the phone that I like to have a much more hands-on approach with my authors. For their sake. And for Scribano & Lawrence. What we both want, editor as well as writer, is the very best book possible, wouldn't you agree, Reta? Have you read *Darling Buds*? For me that book, which I am proud to have worked on, is an example of a comic novel that never for a moment loses its investment of concern with its central image."

"Which is—?"

"Which is the pursuit of identity. I-den-ti-ty."

"Identity can be—"

"Identity is the dominant mystery of our lives, the numinous matter of self, and it can't help but surrender to its own ironic destiny. Which is this: the self can never be known. This is the calamity of our lives, simply that, which is why *Darling Buds* is such a profound statement of being. As a book it is *un succès d'estime,* I admit. That's a French expression. It means it—"

"Yes, I know."

"Not a bestseller, true. A nation of TV gluttons doesn't want to take art seriously, not while fast-food fare is available. But I am serious, Reta. I want you to know that *I,* your editor, care deeply about literature and its paramount statement. And I believe you do, too. In fact, I know you do."

"Perhaps you will let me refill that glass."

"A splendid wine. You see—let me explain—I'll lay it out for you. Scribano & Lawrence—and I am happy to make this statement—we don't need to publish megabuck books."

"But surely you have to keep an eye on a book's marketability and the readers who—"

"We happen to be in a very nice position at the moment. You've heard of John Lord Morgan? And Wilfred Laranzo?"

"Vaguely, but I haven't actually—"

"They're both ours. Morgan writes courtroom drama. Laranzo does interplanetary fantasy. We're glad to have them on our list. They make huge bucks, bucks enough to keep the rest of our writers viable. Our serious literary writers. Our gilt-edged writers."

"You're saying that—"

"I'm saying, Reta, that we're in the market for quality fiction."

"As opposed to—"

"As opposed to popular fiction."

"Oh."

"We want to publish your manuscript. We stand ready to do that. I don't want to confuse you on that point—"

"But—"

"But you must realize that *Thyme in Bloom* could be one of those signal books of our time. The possibility is there. Your manuscript could become a monument. Everything is in place, and with a mere two or three shifts of perspective you could move from a popular novel to a work of art."

"Gilt-edged."

"Right. I knew you'd key right in. You're an intelligent woman, after all, and this manuscript is so close to greatness that it would be a tragedy not to turn it around. We have that chance, Reta. That's why I've come all the way up here to the north. To tell you that your new novel is not in the same company as your first book. *My Thyme Is Up* was a completely other enterprise."

"It did win the Offenden Prize."

"Exactly."

"But the new book is a sequel to that book."

"That's the first thing we can turn around. Maybe I will have a little more wine. Hmm, beautiful. Did you know that a sequel, on average, only makes two-thirds the money that the original has earned?"

"But I thought you said money wasn't an issue—"

"It's not. And you did very well with your first novel. Not millions, to be sure, but what we call a very decent run. And the paperback did fairly well too. But your current work is of a different magnitude altogether. This manuscript, these pages before us, are about the central moral position of the contemporary world. I think it is exceptionally important that we not present this with the title you have suggested, *Thyme in Bloom*. Personally, I prefer *Bloom* on its own."

"Just—*Bloom*?"

"What a word that is. Suggestive but not literal. And you can see how it gestures toward the Bloom of *Ulysses*, Leopold Bloom, that great Everyman."

"But my name is associated with—"

"Associated with light fiction. This is why, in my thinking over the last two weeks, I've come to favour a pseudonym. The problem is to find the right one. Now what was your name before you married, Reta? And do you have a middle name?"

"Reta Ruth Summers."

"Wonderful, I love Summers. It fits perfectly with *Bloom,* doesn't it? Bloomsday, et cetera. The month of June. There's a kind of preternatural blood hyphen there, if we can just pin it down. We, Scribano & Lawrence, could present you as R. R. Summers. I like it. It sounds solid. Yet fresh. A new writer, a new discovery: R. R. Summers."

"Using initials, though, might make it sound like, you know, that I'm a male writer."

"Does it matter? You're dealing with universal themes. You've gone beyond the gendered world."

"But this book—well, Alicia is thinking quite hard about gender, at least in her own rather spacey way."

"Spacey, hmm. That's true, that's absolutely true, but even at this stage we can put a kind of torque on the book and move it toward the universal. I have a number of ideas that I want to put before you, Reta. The first is—"

"You make it sound as though we'll be rewriting the whole book."

"Just tweaking, that's all. Everything is here, Reta. Everything is beautifully here."

"I had thought—I've been thinking that the book was—almost done. I was going to write the concluding scene after—"

"Don't, please don't. Don't touch it. Not until we've discussed a few editorial ideas. I beg of you. We can make this one of the great books of the new century."

"But I was trying to—"

"You were trying to write a light comic novel. But you've done something quite other. You've made a literary statement, something for future generations of readers, and it would be a *catastrophe* if you now—"

"What would we have to do?"

"I've made a list of things. Here we go. First, there's the matter of Roman. His role needs enlarging. His interiority. His desire to make a pilgrimage to the land of his fathers. I see this as quite central to the novel."

"But Alicia is really the focus—I thought you—well, you said you admired her for her goodness. You said that on the phone, remember?"

"Goodness but not greatness. Who said that?"

"Danielle Westerman."

"Really? I haven't read the old girl, but I know Mr. Scribano gave her a helping hand at one time."

"She's eighty-five. She's a very well recognized writer. She really is extremely—"

"And I wondered if you would mind terribly making Roman a violinist rather than a trombonist. A violin sounds more serious, as an instrument, I mean, and I don't think a small thing like that would involve a compromise of your original—"

"Oh, I don't think I could do that—"

"You're thinking that he was a trombonist in the first book and so he must remain a trombonist. But if we get ourselves out of the sequel state of thinking, Reta, he can be anything. He could even be the conductor of the orchestra. Or a composer/performer."

"And Wychwood City—"

"Could easily be re-sited in New York. Or Boston. Chicago? Well, maybe Chicago. Even Toronto, though that would limit its readership—"

"Oh, I don't think so, not anymore."

"He suddenly, in mid-life, wants more. He yearns for more."

"Who?"

"Roman."

"Oh."

"I do think we might try to underplay some of the farcical scenes, though they are quite well done. As the no-longer-quotable Woody Allen once put it, the writers of comedy are always asked to sit at the children's table."

"But I can't see Roman as a serious—"

"His parents were immigrants. They sacrificed their language, their cultural roots. Think of that. He somehow got educated, became a musician. He is wonderfully attractive to women, that hair of his, that very physical body, and his ever active brain. His first marriage was a washout, and then he met Alicia, who works in, of all things, the world of fashion. Everything he despises. The marriage must not happen."

"I absolutely agree with that, the marriage must not happen, but—"

"I am so glad you are in accord with me there."

"But, really, it is Alicia who sees that—"

"She cannot understand his need to reconnect with his family, his heritage. His real love, of course, is Sylvia Woodall, Sylvia the bassoon player. I recognized what you were up to there, the minute she walked onto the page. Sylvia and her outrageous spirit. She responds to Roman's need. That need drills straight through the man's soul. I am talking about Roman being the moral centre of this book, and Alicia, for all her charms, is not capable of that role, surely you can see that. She writes fashion articles. She talks to her cat. She does yoga. She makes rice casseroles."

"It's because she's a woman."

"That's not an issue at all. Surely you—"

"But it is the issue."

"She is unable to make a claim to— She is undisciplined in her— She can't focus the way Roman— She changes her mind about— She lacks— A reader, the serious reader that I have in mind, would never accept her as the decisive fulcrum of a serious work of art that acts as a critique of our society while, at the same time, unrolling itself like a carpet of inevitability, narrativistically speaking."

"Because she's a woman."

"Not at all, not at all."

"Because she's a woman."

As

"Because she's a woman," I said, and at that moment three things happened more or less simultaneously. Arthur Springer lifted his arm in polite protest, and in so doing, knocked over the bottle on the coffee table, drenching the morning newspaper with red wine—an almost holy spreading stain, though luckily there wasn't much left—and scaring Pet out of his skin, so that he skittered backwards and sideways on the hardwood floor, landing in a corner behind the little glass table, where he lay, panting and shuddering with his face buried in his paws.

At that moment Natalie and Chris came in through the front door. They were loud and noisy, more big-footed than usual it seemed to me, scrambling out of their boots and throwing their books onto the hall floor. "Kronk City," I heard Chris shouting, and then the two of them were laughing themselves sick over something to do with our neighbour, Willow Halliday, who had kindly driven them home when they'd missed the school bus and when Tom failed to show up.

I was about to introduce them to Arthur Springer when I was distracted by the ringing of the telephone. I left Arthur to mop up the spilled wine with his handkerchief—a white linen handkerchief, I noticed out of the corner of my consciousness, you don't see people with real handkerchiefs very often. Pet followed, right at my heels, into the kitchen, and pressed his quaking side against my leg.

It was Tom on the phone. "Where are you?" I said.

"There's nothing to worry about, everything's fine." He said this so quickly that I knew something was terribly wrong.

"But—?" I sank into a chair.

"But it's Norah, she has pneumonia, she's going to be fine, she's sleeping right now, but—"

"Where is she?" I couldn't get my breath out.

"In Toronto General. They're taking excellent care of her and she's responding beautifully."

"I'll come right away." I was thinking fast. "It'll take me an hour."

"I'll be waiting in her room. It's 434, the West Wing. Unfortunately, there were no single rooms available—"

That doesn't matter, that doesn't matter.

"Drive carefully," he said sharply.

"Put your coats back on," I said to the girls, speaking with the same sharpness. "Norah's in the hospital with pneumonia. Your father's with her right now."

To Arthur Springer I said—I'm not quite sure what I said. Something about an emergency. I would have to leave at once. (Already I had my coat on and was scrambling for my boots.) I uttered something hurried and hostessy into his ear, something like: stay as long as you like, make yourself at home, there's food in the fridge, pasta, that white bowl with the plastic wrap on it, it just needs heating up, there's more wine in the cupboard, plenty of firewood, I have no idea when we'll be back.

I wasn't worried about him, not one bit. We were on the road in no time, Christine in the back seat, Natalie sitting beside me, up front. We drove as fast as I dared on the dark icy road, first into Orangetown and out the other end, then onto the highway with its uneven glare, heading south. The pink haze that was the city of Toronto lay before us in the distance. The traffic was going to be heavy at this hour. We were mostly silent, the three of us. We never thought about Mr. Springer, we never considered his comfort or convenience for one minute. We forgot Mr. Springer completely; we forgot my mother-in-law too, and only found out later what became of them.

He did make himself at home. He did open another bottle of wine. I keep the corkscrew in an unlikely spot in the dining room, behind a beautiful piece of local pottery, but he found it nevertheless. Then he must have looked around for the television. It was six o'clock, time for the *Lehrer NewsHour*. There! He found the TV, in the den. And there was the remote, where it almost always is—on the little side table. He probably settled down in the big corduroy wing chair with his glass of wine and thought: My God. Why am I here? How on earth did I get to this place?

Very gradually he became aware of someone knocking persistently at the back door. He wasn't familiar with the house, and so it took him a little while to figure out where the knocking was coming from. Pet, no doubt, was still huddled in the kitchen, recovering from the clunk of the wine bottle and the sense of there being a stranger in the house.

It was Lois, with a dish of bread pudding in her hands, one of her rectangular Pyrex casseroles from fifty years ago.

She pushed her way into the warm house, explaining who she was, that she had awaited the usual signal that dinner was ready, the closing of the red curtains, and then she grew worried and thought she'd come over to investigate. She could see the flicker of the TV, so she knew someone was at home. She'd phoned, but there was no answer. She knew, of course, that a guest was expected to dinner, that's why she'd made a larger than usual dessert. She hoped he liked bread pudding.

Mr. Springer explained that he had had the volume turned up rather loudly. He also explained who he was and why he was in the house and where the rest of us had gone. He was all apologies. He hadn't heard the phone ringing. He was so sorry. But, he exclaimed, it was an unexpected pleasure to meet Reta's mother.

Mother-in-law, she corrected him. Reta was married to her son, Tom. Well, sort of married.

Oh.

Norah and pneumonia, she mused aloud. Well! Pneumonia was once a serious illness, but now it was more a matter of antibiotics and people up and about in no time. Still, it was gravely worrying.

Mr. Springer was sure Norah would be fine.

Lois mumbled something about Norah not being fine, that she hadn't been fine for some time, this first and dearest granddaughter. Then she caught sight of Pet. The poor creature. Had he been fed?

Mr. Springer was so sorry, he hadn't thought about the dog, he didn't exactly know what to do. He wasn't very good with animals, they seem frightened of him, and he had, quite frankly, forgotten the dog was in the house.

Like all goldens, Pet is greedy. He consumes supper with great joy and afterwards presents a mighty belch. I'll just get him looked after, Lois said, hanging up her coat and taking charge. Pet was used to being fed at around six-thirty, then he liked to be let out for a bit, he never strayed off the property, he had a keen sense of where he belonged.

Which is more than most of us have, Mr. Springer responded. He said this philosophically.

Yes, Lois agreed. Yes, indeed. Then she suggested that they go ahead and have a bite to eat. There was no telling how long Reta and the girls would be gone.

Mr. Springer remembered something about pasta in the fridge. He hadn't taken in the details. Everything had happened in such a rush.

Lois busied herself with warming up the pasta in the microwave and she urged Mr. Springer to go back to the TV. She would have the meal ready in two shakes.

He hoped he could help her. He had been watching the news and there was nothing interesting at all. Now and then, not often, there comes a day when nothing seems to happen.

Yes. Lois certainly agreed with him on that topic.

It's like God's decided to give us a day off, Mr. Springer said, or something to that effect.

Lois, taking in his smooth, strong face, explained how she could always tell from the first news item. If it was about new safety standards for hockey helmets, that was an indication that nothing terrible had happened. No bombs or murders or riots or fires.

I love those blank days, said Mr. Springer.

So do I.

They're so rare.

Lois suggested they set the table in the kitchen, since there were only two of them.

An excellent idea. Mr. Springer insisted on helping. If Lois would just show him where the knives and forks were kept—

She dimmed the lights slightly. She explained, as she served out the pasta onto two heated plates—she was a genius at heating plates—that Reta had prepared her usual artichoke dish with black olives and chunks of tomato and asiago cheese. Reta always made the artichoke dish when she wasn't sure if people were going to be vegetarians or not. It was safe. Unless they happened to be those people who don't eat cheese, vegans they were called, but there weren't too many of them, thank heaven.

Mr. Springer poured himself another glass of wine, but first he poured one for Lois, asking her with a lift of an eyebrow if she would care for a bit. She nodded, and then the two of them sat down, at the same instant, as though a gong had sounded.

And now, said Mr. Springer, leaning over his steaming plate of pasta: Tell me all about yourself, Lois.

Beginning With

So, she told him, beginning with a play she saw several years ago, she couldn't remember the name of it or even whether she enjoyed it or not. Directly in front of her in the audience sat a young couple. The woman was exceptionally slender and beautiful, with a low voice and a smiling way of inclining her head toward her young man. He could scarcely take his eyes off her. He held her hand in his throughout the play. He kneaded it hungrily. Several times, while the actors shouted and dashed around the stage, he brought her hand to his lips and held it there. Lois had never seen such tenderness between a man and a woman. She scarcely slept that night, and several times she brought her curled hand up to her own mouth and pressed her lips against it. She was about forty years old at that time, a wife, the mother of a son.

Twelve years ago she was widowed, but she never uses that word. Instead she says, "My husband died in 1988. I've been alone since then." She knew exactly how pathetic that sounded.

On winter days she often found herself in her kitchen looking out the window at the largest of the old and leafless oaks. But not quite leafless. One brown leaf, only one, remained. The wind blew and blew, but that particular little leaf refused to let go its grasp. There were two ways you could think about this leaf. Either it was exceptionally healthy and strong, or else it was somehow deformed and unable to engage the mechanism that allowed it to fall to the earth where all the normal leaves lay buried in snow. The unfallen leaf was an anomaly; something ailed it. Just as Pet was almost a golden retriever but not quite, standing two inches shorter than the regulation male dog, when only a single inch was the permitted tolerance for the breed, not that Lois cared one fig about that.

She hoped Mr. Springer liked a good bread pudding. She had a list of one hundred desserts, alphabetized in a recipe box, beginning with almond apples, moving to date pudding, on to nut brittle mousse (frozen) and ending with Zweiback pastry cheesecake; she rotated this list around the year. It is no longer easy to find Zweiback biscuits, but graham crackers can be substituted. Needless to say, seasonal ingredients mean that the desserts themselves are not served alphabetically. She once overheard her granddaughter Christine making fun of her dessert list. She can understand this in a way, but she still thought it was rather mean.

She was twenty-four hours in labour when Tom was born. When she first started having pains she insisted that her husband drive her to the hospital straight away. "Ten minutes apart?" the receptionist said coolly. "Didn't they tell you not to come till the pains were at five minutes?" At that point a woman could be heard screaming from another floor. "Is that woman having a baby?" Lois asked the receptionist, who rolled her eyes and said, "That's an Italian woman having a baby."

Her first granddaughter was named Norah Charlotte Winters, a beautiful baby. The Charlotte was after a friend of Reta's who died very young in a car accident. Lois never met this Charlotte person. She herself was in a car accident once, a fender bender really, but a terrible shock. So much so that she gave up driving.

A woman named Crystal McGinn once lived next door with her very large family, four children at least, teenagers, boisterous youngsters. Once Crystal invited Lois over for a cup of coffee and she had asked where Lois had gone to university. Not *if* she'd gone to university, but where. Mrs. McGinn had gone to Queen's and studied economics. Lois did not tell Mrs. McGinn that she herself had attended secretarial college for six months in Toronto, and then married her husband, a young doctor, and moved to Orangetown. She felt strongly that Crystal McGinn had over-stepped with her question about *which* university. They hadn't seen much of each other after that, nothing more than an occasional wave. She regrets this now. She realizes that Mrs. McGinn's question was not cruelly intended, only a little tactless.

Especially considering that Lois was the doctor's wife. There was a certain prestige in that role, at least in the early days. It became her habit to remind herself of that fact, standing in front of the hall mirror, sucking in her stomach and saying musically: I am the wife of a physician.

She won a prize at the Orangetown Fair once for her German honey cake. When she registered for the competition she was advised to call it Swiss honey cake. She complied. But what did it matter?—she won anyway. She was given a blue ribbon, which her husband accidentally threw away when he was cleaning out the attic, years later. He felt terrible about that.

She loves Oprah. She arranges her day around Oprah. She has found a new self-courage recently, as a result of watching Oprah.

Her granddaughter Norah, her favourite—an endearing sweet-ness at the girl's core—has been going through a hard time. She herself understands about times of difficulty. When she was in her early fifties she stopped baking and went to bed for two weeks. Her husband wanted to take her to the Mayo Clinic; that was all he talked about, the Mayo Clinic. Then she got up one day and cleaned the bathroom as it had never before been cleaned. That plunge into hygiene seemed to set things right. She was better able to cope after that.

Except lately. She can't talk anymore. She doesn't trust herself. Toads will come out of her open mouth. She'll hurt people's feelings. She has an opinion about what happened to Norah, and she doesn't want anyone else to know. They'd think she was crazy. Women were supposed to be strong, but they weren't really, they weren't allowed to be. They were hopelessly encumbered with fibres and membranes and pads of malleable tissue; women were easily injured; critical injuries, that's what came to you if you opened your mouth.

On the other hand, she knew Norah would be all right in the end. It was a matter of time, though the pneumonia was worrying. She did wish Reta would telephone. She was so glad, though, to have good company on a winter's night. Bread pudding with lemon sauce. A cup of tea. She had been bending his ear off. This was so unlike her. She didn't know how she got started.

On the whole she believed things worked out for the best. Didn't Mr. Springer agree?

Already

"They're burns," Tom said, gesturing toward Norah's hands and wrists. Norah was asleep, with an oxygen tube connected to her nose, Snow White in her glass case, and the girls and I are gathered around the bed like curious dwarves. The skin of her face was white and puffy. Someone had brushed out her hair so that it fell cleanly on the pillowcase and on the shoulders of her blue hospital gown, tied in a bow at the back of her neck. My darling Norah. To be sitting on a moulded plastic chair so close to her like this was heaven, never mind that her lungs were still partly filled with fluid.

She has been sleeping ever since we arrived. The pneumonia was still present but under control—that was a huge relief—but I was alarmed by her reddened, scarred hands lying exposed on the white cotton blanket. I felt like a voyeur, a transgressor in this room, and that any minute my daughter would open her eyes and accuse me. Of what, though?

"A combination of severe second-degree burns," Tom continued in a voice I distantly recognized, its ups and downs carefully modulated—and his tone carrying me back to a walk we had once taken in the woods behind our house, the shrubs in full summer leaf, the crumbling earth giving way underfoot, when he told me that my mother's cancer had advanced, that it had metastasized to her lungs, and the remaining time would be short, just a week or so.

"You can see she has experienced infection on the backs of both hands," he said calmly. "There's a fair amount of scarring, and some of it might have been avoided if she'd been properly cared for."

When did the burns occur? Why hadn't we seen the condition of her hands before? Some of these questions came from Dr. DeVita, who was attending her, and some from Frances Quinn from the Promise Hostel, who had recognized late yesterday evening that Norah had been coughing for several days and probably needed to be looked at. Both Tom and I remembered glimpsing what we thought had been a rash or else chilblains.

"She always had gloves on," Natalie reminded us. "Even last summer when it was boiling hot, in the middle of July even, she wore these old floppy gardening gloves."

"Yes," Chris said. "We thought it was weird."

"That's right," I said. The garden gloves—she was wearing them the first day we found her last April at Bathurst and Bloor. The eleventh of April, a Tuesday, a day I would never forget. I had supposed she wore them to protect her hands from the rough pavement. What silent pain she must have suffered.

She slept in those gloves, Frances Quinn had told Tom earlier in the day. Every night at the hostel. The staff thought it was odd, but then so many of the hostel clients exhibited eccentricities.

What about when she ate in the dining hall?

She took off her gloves when she ate.

And what was the state of her hands?

Red. What looked like a rash. Well, it's really the destruction of body tissue, a step in the healing process. Someone, one of the volunteers, remembers her hands were bandaged when she first arrived, the first couple of weeks.

And when exactly would that have been?

It's all in her file. She came to Promise for the first time on the twelfth of April—but Tom and I already knew that. Ordinarily people were allowed to stay for just three months, that's the rule, but Norah was so quiet, so accommodating. It just got overlooked, her long stay. No one raised an objection.

"I would say those burns are at least six months old," said Dr. DeVita, from the burn unit.

Six months. That would take us back to early summer. Or even spring.

"I wonder if Ben Abbot knows anything about a fire," I said. I had difficulty invoking the name of Norah's old boyfriend. It stuck in my throat. It was easier not to think of him.

"I've already phoned him," Tom said. "Early this afternoon. He doesn't have the least idea how she might have burnt herself. He was very sure of that. I had to believe him."

"Is she still in pain? Her hands, I mean."

"Probably not. But these burns haven't been looked after. You can see where the granulation has taken hold."

It was close to midnight. The room felt full of hard surfaces, shadows arching up into the corners of the ceiling, just one tiny light burning over Norah's bed, and in another bed, behind a cloth screen, a stranger tossing and moaning between her sheets, having nightmares, muttering in some language I couldn't identify.

It occurred to me, then, to phone my mother-in-law and tell her we would not be home tonight. Norah was doing well, but we would be staying in the hospital. A family room had been found for us at the end of the corridor, and the girls were about to go to sleep.

Lois sounded exceptionally cheerful for some reason, even though I'd wakened her from a deep sleep. "Don't worry about Pet," she told me, "I fed him and let him out for a run." I promised to phone her in the morning. After I hung up I remembered I hadn't asked about Arthur Springer. I had forgotten his existence.

"You should go to sleep too," Tom said to me. He touched the side of my face lightly with his hand.

"No, I can't. I'll just sit here. In case she wakes up."

He left me there. He had a couple of phone calls to make, and he was talking about checking something on the Internet.

A nurse arrived every hour or so to take Norah's pulse. She

came and went silently, gliding on her rubber-soled shoes. Fine, fine, she nodded at me. She's doing fine.

I might have dozed a little in my chair, but I doubt it. Two o'clock, then three. Natalie and Chris were sound asleep in the family room, and so was Tom. I sat in my chair and kept my eyes on Norah's face. My thoughts drifted briefly to Alicia and Roman and their doomed wedding plans in Wychwood City. I realized I didn't care what happened to them. Their lives were ephemeral; they could be moved about like beads of mercury. I didn't need them anymore. They were undeserving of anyone's attention, least of all mine.

Just before three-thirty Norah opened her eyes.

I pressed my lips close to her cheek. "Norah," I said.

She smiled faintly in my direction, then reached over and covered my wrist with her roughened hand.

"Norah," I said again quickly. "You're awake."

Her mouth made the shape of a word: "Yes."

Hitherto

February 1, 2001

Dear Russell Sandor,

I have recently read your newest short story in one of the
monthly magazines we subscribe to, the story about the Czech
philosophy professor who moves to Los Angeles, and how raw
and thin and undigested he finds American culture, the hideous
fast food, the erosion of spoken English, and especially the
grotesque insult of passing by an L.A. medical supply shop and
seeing in the window, among the rest of the merchandise, a
mastectomy bra. There it was, undisguised. An assault to all that
he valued. Dangling there, a filthy object. It was identified by a
large sign, in case he didn't know what it was: MASTECTOMY
BRA. Placed there in order to outrage his fine sensibility, up front,
right in his face. He felt disgust, then nausea.

Get a grip, Mr. Sandor.

A mastectomy bra is a bra like any other. It is clean and well
sewn, usually in cotton. Your professor character has lived in
Europe, as you repeat several times, where women's bras hang
everywhere over the street on clotheslines; a woman's bra drying
in the Mediterranean breeze is close to being the Italian national
flag. The French flag. The Portuguese flag. A mastectomy bra
varies only in that it has two little pockets into which one can tuck
the appliance that replaces a real breast when it has been cut off,
usually because of breast cancer. Some women—Emma Allen, for
instance—have had a double mastectomy, and so both pockets are

padded out with prostheses made of moulded jelly stuff encased in a thin plastic skin. Emma has lost a husband (lightning), a son (suicide), and now the integrity of her body. She's earned her moral upholstery, as she calls it. I went with her when she purchased her new bras, one in black, one in ecru. The shop was a tiny place at the north edge of Toronto where you could also buy, if you were inclined, such things as fake chest hair for men.

The Czech professor in your story wonders why he gags at the straight-in-the-eye sight of a mastectomy bra. I suggest the obvious: that he hates women, and his hatred of women extends to anything that might touch the body of a woman—the chair she sits on, the clothes she wears—and particularly the matter of women's ink, self-pitying, humourless, demanding, claustrophobic, breathless.

I am shockingly offended, and yet your professor says he fears giving offence. I've written several letters this year to those who have outraged me in one way or another, but I have never mailed any of them or even signed them. This is because I don't want to be killed, as your professor almost kills his wife, holding a penknife over her sleeping body. But now I don't mind if you kill me. I have suffered a period of estrangement from my daughter— she is now at home, safe—and the period of our separation has been very like having a cold knife lodged in my chest.

It happened that her life coincided with a traumatic event; her father suspected this was the cause of her distress, and mostly he was right. It was a case of pinning things down, pairing the incident with a missing day in our daughter's life. A spring day like any other. Only it wasn't like any other. It was a moment in history; it was reported in the newspapers, though we didn't read closely about it for some reason; it was recorded on videotape, so that we have since seen the tragedy replayed and understand how its force usurped the life of a young woman and threw her into an ellipsis of mourning.

My own theory—before we knew of the horrifying event—was that Norah had become aware of an accretion of discouragement, that she had awakened in her twentieth year to her solitary state of non-belonging, understanding at last how little she would be allowed to say. There were signs; she was restless, turning inward, recoiling as we all do from what we *know,* discovering and then repudiating, but it is also probable that I was weighing her down with my own fears, my own growing perplexity concerning the world and its arrangements, that I had found myself, in the middle of my life, in the middle of the continent, on the side of the dis-favoured, and it may be that I am partly right and partly wrong. Or that Tom is partly right and partly wrong about his theory of post-traumatic shock. Or that Danielle knew from the beginning. We'll never know why. In any case, Norah took up the banner of goodness—goodness not greatness. Perhaps because there was no other way she could register her existence. In the obscuring dis-tance, melting into sunsets and handsome limestone buildings and asphalt streets and traffic lights, the tiny piping voice of goodness goes almost unheard, no matter how felt and composed it is. Norah had no other place to stand after the "event"; she was all perch, she and her silent tongue and burnt hands.

Goodness, that biddable creature, cannot be depended upon, not yet—I found that out. I have thrown myself into its sphere nevertheless. Goodness is respect that has been rarified and taken to a higher level. It has emptied itself of vengeance, which has no voice at all. I'm afraid I don't put that very clearly. I'm still sorting out the details. But I am trying to be one of the faithful, and so I will sign my name to this letter not truthfully, but exactly as it appears in the local telephone book.

Reta Winters
Six Corners Road, RR 4
Orangetown

Not Yet

A life is full of isolated events, but these events, if they are to form a coherent narrative, require odd pieces of language to cement them together, little chips of grammar (mostly adverbs or prepositions) that are hard to define, since they are abstractions of location or relative position, words like *therefore, else, other, also, thereof, theretofore, instead, otherwise, despite, already,* and *not yet.*

My old friend Gemma Walsh, who has just been appointed to a Chair in Theology (hello there, Chair) tells me that the Christian faith is balanced on the words *already* and *not yet.* Christ has *already* come, but he has *not yet* come. If you can bring the two opposing images together as you would on a stereoscopic viewer, and as traditional Christians bring together the Father, Son and Holy Ghost of the Trinity, then you will have understood something about the power and metaphysicality of these unsorted yet related words.

The conjugation and (sometimes) adverb *unless,* with its elegiac undertones, is a term used in logic, a word breathed by the hopeful or by writers of fiction wanting to prise open the crusted world and reveal another plane of being, which is similar in its geographical particulars and peopled by those who resemble ourselves. If the lung sacs of Norah's body hadn't filled with fluids, if a volunteer at the Promise Hostel hadn't reported a night of coughing to Frances Quinn, and if Frances hadn't called an ambulance, we would never have found Norah at the Toronto General.

By chance it was a Friday, the day Tom drives by the corner of

Bathurst and Bloor for a glimpse of her. She was not there. For the first time since April she was not there.

Unless, unless. He rang the bell at the hostel and was told she had gone into the hospital early in the morning, but, since Norah was of age, over eighteen that is, Frances Quinn was not at liberty to say which hospital. Tom decided to phone them all. Has a nineteen-year-old girl with a heavy rash on her wrists been admitted? Yes—lucky on the third call—she had been checked in that day.

Unless. Novelists are always being accused of indulging in the artifice of coincidence, and so I must ask myself whether it was a coincidence that Norah was standing on the corner where Honest Ed's is situated when a young Muslim woman (or so it would appear from her dress), in the month of April, in the year 2000, stepped forward on the pavement, poured gasoline over her veil and gown, and set herself alight. No, it is not really a coincidence, since Norah was living in a basement apartment close by, with her boyfriend, Ben Abbot. She had walked over to Honest Ed's to buy a plastic dish rack, which she was holding in her hand when the self-immolation began. (Why a plastic dish rack?—this flimsy object—its purchase can only have evolved from some fleeting scrap of domestic encouragement.) Without thinking, and before the news teams arrived, Norah had rushed forward to stifle the flames. The dish rack became a second fire, and it and the plastic bag in which it was carried burned themselves to Norah's flesh. She pulled back. Stop, she screamed, or something to that effect, and then her fingers sank into the woman's melting flesh—the woman was never identified—her arms, her lungs, and abdomen. These pieces gave way. The smoke, the smell, was terrible. Two firemen pulled Norah away, lifting her bodily in a single arc, then strapped her into a restraining device and drove her to Emergency, where she was given first aid. A few minutes later, though, she disappeared without giving her name.

If the firemen hadn't pulled her away in time, if Honest Ed's exterior security video hadn't captured and then saved the image of Norah, her back anyway, her thrashing arms, instantly recognizable to members of her family, beating at the flames; if they hadn't turned the video over to the police, unless, unless, all this would have been lost. But it's all right, Norah. We know now, Norah. You can put this behind you. You are allowed to forget. We'll remember it for you, a memory of a memory, we'll do this gladly.

Unless we ask questions.

If I hadn't asked Danielle Westerman point-blank last week what it was that interrupted her childhood. Was it her mother or her father? I put it baldly. Her mother, Danielle said. She was eighteen, but had lived in fear most of her life; her mother had tried to strangle her when she stayed out late one night. She left home immediately, the next day, with only a hundred francs in her pocket and a train ticket to Paris.

Why have you been so silent all these months? I asked my mother-in-law, Lois. Why didn't you tell us what was wrong?

Because no one asked me, she said.

But Arthur Springer did ask you?

Yes. He leaned across the kitchen table, his chair scraping on the floor, an oddly deliberate and intimate act, and said, "Tell me all about your life, Lois."

And you *did* tell him?

Yes, I'm afraid I did. The poor man. Everything I told you, I told him.

No one, not even Tom, has ever said to me: Tell me all about your life, Reta. No one has ever offered that impelling phrase to Annette or Sally or Lynn. They swear it.

I phoned Arthur Springer and asked him directly: How did it happen that he asked my mother-in-law such an odd and intimate question?

"Well," he said (abashed, I'm pleased to say). Hmm, he'd learned the technique recently at a publishing workshop on personal relationships that, hmm, Scribano & Lawrence had sent him to; this was after the author of *Darling Buds* went stomping off to

Knopf. Something tactless *he'd* apparently said, a rather large fuss over a very small nothing. But he was asked to sign up for an immersion weekend on power relationships. Vermont; an old hunting lodge; a half-dozen humbled professionals. The key, he learned from the workshop director, was simple. One had only to ask people—especially writers, but anyone will do—for a recital of their lives, and they fall right into it. It's a harmless strategy, and effective. He's only tried it out a few times, but always with enormous success.

"You didn't say it to me," I said. "You didn't ask me to tell you all about myself."

"Oh. Well, I could. Shall I?"

"No. It's too late."

"I'm so sorry, Reta. Really, I mean it. I do want to know all about the real Reta Winters. One day, when we have time."

Meanwhile—another one of those signal words—meanwhile, I have brought *Thyme in Bloom* to a whimsical conclusion—Alicia triumphs, but in her own slightly capricious way—and the book will be published in early fall. Everything is neatly wrapped up at the end, since tidy conclusions are a convention of comic fiction, as we all know. I have bundled up each of the loose narrative strands, but what does such fastidiousness mean? It doesn't mean that all will be well for ever and ever, amen; it means that for five minutes a balance has been achieved at the margin of the novel's thin textual plane; make that five seconds; make that the millionth part of a nanosecond. The uncertainty principle; did anyone ever believe otherwise?

Scribano & Lawrence expect a reasonable success. Mr. Springer withdrew his editorial reservations when *My Thyme Is Up* was analyzed exhaustively in an essay for *The Yale Review* by none other than Dr. Charles Casey, the octogenarian dean of humanities. The article, which came out in February, is a surprise reappraisal and appreciation, and the buzz has been picked up by the popular press, even *Entertainment Weekly*. The subversive insights of the novel had not been grasped, it seems, by its original reviewers two years ago. A correction is in order. What was simple is now seen as subtle. A brilliant tour de force, says Professor Casey, and this quote will, of course, appear on the cover of the sequel. The name Dr. Charles Casey will be printed in the same size type as the name Reta Winters, but I am trying not to think what that means. And I've noticed something else: Professor Casey's clever perspective has caused a part of my mind to fly up to the box-room skylight, from whence it looks down on me, mockingly.

Danielle Westerman has given up on me. She has decided to translate her own book, and the portions she has shown me are both accurate and charming—yes, charming, that concept I thought I had given up on—but now I see that charm can be a gesture toward the authentic when it allows itself to be caught in the wings of an updraft and when it pushes its way into a different kind of cultural weather. She translates about a page a day, which she faxes to me for tweaking; I send it back within the hour, thinking every time I push the start button: What an elegant machine this is, sitting in its own corner so wise and respectful and willing when compared to the ugliness of an e-mail. She is adding to her memoir, writing about her mother, admitting, finally, that a memoir must have a mother somewhere in its folds. The two identities she never reconciled—daughter, writer—are coming together. Translation is keeping her mind sharp, she says, like doing a crossword puzzle. A daily task to begin and complete. She's just turned eighty-six.

I am already thinking about the third book in the trilogy: *Autumn Thyme.* It will open to a wide range of formal expression. I want the book to have the low moaning tone of an orchestral trombone and then to move upward toward a transfiguration of some kind, the nature of which has yet to be worked out. I want it to be a book that's willing to live in one room if necessary. I want it to hold still like an oil painting, a painting titled: *Seated Woman. Woman at Rest.* Half my work will have been done for me, at least for those who have read the first two books. These readers will stand ready to accept the fact that my Alicia is intelligent and inventive and capable of moral resolution, the same qualities we presume, without demonstration, in a male hero. It will be a sadder book than the others, and shorter. The word *autumn* taps us on the head, whispering melancholy, brevity, which are tunes I know a little about. A certain amount of resignation, too, will attach itself to the pages of this third novel, a gift from Danielle Westerman, but also the heft of stamina. There you have it: stillness and power, sadness and resignation, contradictions and irrationality. Almost, you might say, the materials of a serious book.

Day by day Norah is recovering at home, awakening atom by atom, and shyly planning her way on a conjectural map. It is bliss to see, though Tom and I have not yet permitted ourselves wild rejoicing. We watch her closely, and pretend not to. She may do science next fall at McGill, or else linguistics. She is still considering this. Right now she is sleeping. They are all sleeping, even Pet, sprawled on the kitchen floor, warm in his beautiful coat of fur. It is after midnight, late in the month of March.

I would like to thank a number of others who in one way or another encouraged me in the writing of *Unless*: Sharon Allan, Marjorie Anderson, the late Joan Austen-Leigh, Joan Barfoot, Clare Boylan, Marg Edmond Brown, Joan Clark, Anne Collins, Cynthia Coop, Patrick Crowe, Maggie Dwyer, Darlene Hammell, Blanche Howard, Isabel Huggan, Carl Lenthe, Madeline Li, Elinor Lipman, Anna and Sylvie Matas, Margaret Shaw-Mackinnon, Don McCarthy, Peter Parker, Bella Pomer, Christopher Potter, Linda Rogers, Carole Sabiston, Floyd St. Clair, Eleanor Wachtel, Cindi Warner, Mindy Werner, the John Simon Guggenheim Foundation, and, as always, my family: John, Audrey, Anne, Catherine, Meg, Sara, and, especially, Don.